PLUM GONE

A SONOMA WINE COUNTRY COZY MYSTERY: NO. 2

AJ CARTON

For L&M

CONTENTS

1. Saturday Lunch – Disturbing the Peace   1
2. Saturday Afternoon – Second Thoughts   13
3. Saturday Night – Date Night   21
4. Sunday Morning – Plum Perfect   30
5. Sunday Night – The Devil's Business   42
6. Later Sunday Night – Jack Who?   51
7. Monday Morning – Under the Bus   57
8. Monday Afternoon – Plum Suckers' Revenge   67
9. Tuesday – Look Who's Coming to Lunch   77
10. Tuesday Afternoon – Ghost Writer   90
11. Wednesday – Conflict of Interest   105
12. Wednesday Afternoon – Hasta La Vista   117
13. Thursday Morning – Two for the Road   131
14. Thursday Afternoon – The Good Housekeeping Seal   138
15. Thursday Night – More Secrets   147
16. Friday Morning – Hard Times in Puebloduro   153
17. Friday Noon – A Girl Named Maria   163
18. Friday Afternoon – Breaking the Cowgirl Code   172
19. Saturday Morning – Just Friends   181
20. Saturday Afternoon – Whole Lotta Food   186
21. Saturday Night – In Your Facebook   192
22. Sunday Morning – Where Is Maria?   203
23. Sunday Evening – Guess Who's Coming   212
24. Monday Morning – Love Grows   217
25. Monday Afternoon – No Way Out   231
26. Tuesday Morning – Bo Shambles   235
27. Wednesday – Back at the Ranch   241
28. Thursday Morning – A Cooperative Effort   246
29. Friday – Plum Done   254
30. Saturday – Itchy Feet   261

About the Author   277
Fiction Disclaimer   279

SATURDAY LUNCH – DISTURBING THE PEACE

"This is serious, Jack!" Emma exclaimed. "It's the closest thing to an argument I've ever had with my son-in-law. But this time, Piers is totally out of line. I can't tell my boss to drop Gomez's unfair labor practices lawsuit just because he's suing one of Piers' richest clients."

"I dunno," Jack raised his shoulders in what Emma fondly called his 'Sicilian shrug'. Close as they were, Emma knew she and Jack Russo didn't see eye to eye when it came to lawsuits.

"I read about that case in the papers," he continued. "Against old Curt Randall from the club. Sounds kinda flimsy..."

The scream of a police siren drowned out the rest of Jack's sentence. It was so loud it sent a shiver down Emma's spine. She froze. Almost nothing ever happened in Blissburg, California to warrant such a deafening sound. There was something about the sleepy little prune farming community turned wine country hub that discouraged discord.

Stranger still, the police car emitting the earsplitting screech raced at unheard of speed right through the middle of town past the restaurant where Emma and Jack had just sat down at their usual table. Indeed, everyone at Blissburg's trendiest new lunch spot stopped eating to look up and wonder.

It was May in the Sonoma wine country. The worst of the rain, such as it was in the drought ridden county, was over. Not a cloud in the sky; the temperature in Blissburg was a mild seventy-five. Perfect for lunch al fresco at The Trough.

Emma always thought 'The Trough' was an unlikely name for Blissburg's refined culinary icon. Just as she always thought that she and Jack made an unlikely pair.

Jack, a short, stocky Sicilian immigrant bricklayer's son from a hardscrabble neighborhood in Providence, was a Harvard graduate, former Olympic ice hockey star and rich venture capitalist. But with his salt and pepper hair swept back off his forehead and his stoic bullish stare, he reminded Emma more of a cross between a gangster and a priest.

Emma, on the other hand, was the daughter of a civil rights lawyer whose mother emigrated from Bologna, Italy to San Francisco to sing Grand Opera and cook. Emma was tall, gray haired, blue-eyed and chalk skinned. As her Nonna had often reminded her, first the Celts and later the Austrians had left their genetic trace. Even wearing sandals, Emma towered two inches over Jack.

She could eat a plate of pasta off his head, her unforgiving forebears used to say.

Of course, Emma hardly ever wore sandals. She had no patience for pedicures. And while Jack dressed impeccably in mostly high-end Italian sportswear bought for him by his daughter, Emma had worn 'dressy' black sweat pants from the Cotton Shop for lunch that day, along with an Indian paisley tunic from a street fair. Like many whose roots lay buried in the fertile soil of the Emilia Romagna province of northern Italy, Emma was as thrifty as a New Englander at heart.

Yes despite all these differences, at least once a week Emma Corsi and Jack Russo could be found head to head at a shady table, deep in conversation about anything and everything that was on their minds – from the morning's NPR discussion of the Middle East to their grandchildren's latest accomplishments to that day's gripe about their sons-in-law.

Moreover, hard as it sometimes was for Emma to believe, in the nine months since they'd first met at an opera fundraiser – and Jack had literally saved Emma's life - she and Jack had become friends. Very close friends. But just friends. No romance. Jack, she knew, still grappled with the death of his wife of some forty years. Emma, a retired paralegal who volunteered at Blissburg's free legal clinic, had finally launched what promised to become a successful second career as a food writer. She was hesitant to tie herself down with a new and undoubtedly very demanding partner. They were friends and, Emma told herself, both of them wanted to keep it that way.

Nonetheless, much to her surprise, in these past nine months Emma had grown closer to Jack than to anyone she'd ever known. She told him things she'd never told Mary, her best friend since grade school. The woman whose death almost two years before had precipitated her move from her native San Francisco to Blissburg, the newly chic community an hour north of San Francisco where her daughter, Julie, son-in-law, Piers, and grandson, Harry, had previously relocated.

Of course, when Mary was alive, Emma wouldn't have changed her shower curtain without discussing it with Mary first.

But Jack was different. She and Jack talked about 'life.' And Emma told him *everything*. Even about the brick of quiet panic she woke up with on her chest some mornings all alone in bed. It wasn't really a brick. It just felt that way. And she told him about her divorce, her fear of becoming dependent, her fear of the other Big D, death. Along with all her other worries. Like that Harry was spoiled – *she* thought he needed a sibling. Or that Julie, her daughter, worked too hard. Or that her latest cookbook deal might fall apart.

Of course she and Jack talked about fun things too. Late at night on the telephone. Sometimes for hours. Books. Opera. Cooking. Movies. Art.

Now, staring across the table complaining about her son-in-law, Emma reminded herself for the umpteenth time that, considering their profound differences, it was amazing she and Jack always found so much to talk about.

The waiter had just arrived with their drinks when another siren broke the stillness and a second patrol car raced down Blissburg Avenue in front of the old plaza. Followed by a third.

Emma looked up from the piece of focaccia she'd just dipped into some peppery, grass green olive oil, and thought to herself that in almost a year living in Blissburg she could not remember hearing that many sirens.

Jack must have thought the same thing. "Used to hear that sound all night in the neighborhood where I grew up," he noted, undoubtedly relieved to change the subject from Emma's son-in-law who, after all, was Jack's lawyer too in the elite, rural community.

"Now I never hear it," he continued. "I dunno, don't ya sometimes think this place is just a little too," he hesitated.

Emma wondered if she'd ever met anyone who edited as much as Jack did between what he thought and what he said. Not that, by now, she hadn't heard the man blow off steam. And when he did, everything came flying out of his mouth with a crude eloquence Emma had come to admire.

"Unreal."

At least, Emma thought that's what Jack said. The word he uttered was all but drowned out by a fourth screaming siren and another Blissburg police car racing north on Main Street.

Jack squinted in the direction where the police cars were headed.

"Four cars. That's the whole fleet," he said.

The sound of more sirens erupted to the north on 101.

"Whatever's comin' down ain't good," he added.

Ten minutes later, however, the familiar quiet Blissburg buzz had resettled over The Trough – a gentle breeze rustled the poplar leaves, crickets chirped, birds twittered and muted voices floated over from the plaza in an expectant hum that reminded Emma of the San Francisco Opera House before the curtain went up.

"So, can we talk about my party now?" Jack asked. "Instead of complaining about my favorite lawyer, your son-in-law, Piers Larkin? Given the weather lately, I'm thinkin' we eat in the yard." Except Jack pronounced it 'yeahd'.

"Sounds perfect," Emma replied. Close though they were, Emma hadn't actually seen Jack's 'yeahd' yet. But she knew his address well enough to know that, thanks to his daughter, it probably resembled a private park landscaped by Capability Brown.

"I mean, I paid $5000 for it. We do the party my way not yours, right?"

Emma winced. "Not exactly," she replied. In the nine months she'd known him, the nine months since he'd bid on her 'dinner for six' auction item at the opera fundraiser, she'd also learned that once Jack Russo made up his mind, he didn't back down.

"See," she explained. She'd been hoping to avoid this discussion. "I donated the dinner so I have to prepare it. I'll be in the kitchen. I can't do that and be a guest at the same dinner. You can invite six people including yourself and besides me. You said you were inviting my daughter, Julie, Piers, and your daughter, Cara, and her husband Mike. So they could all meet..."

As she spoke, Emma inwardly cringed. Important as their small families were to them individually, Emma and Jack didn't hang out with each other's children. Emma liked it that way. She'd only met Jack's daughter, Cara, once, shopping with her father at one of Blissburg's elegant men's stores. She was buying her father half a dozen fancy Paul and Shark polo shirts.

Emma was trying to find a nice pair of socks for her fussy son-in-law for Christmas. At the time, Emma found Jack's daughter – a brusque, attractive fortyish Stanford researcher and physician - quite intimidating.

"That leaves one more place besides you. In fact," she added, taking the plunge, "why not invite someone who's *not* family? I can cook for our kids anytime."

Jack cast Emma a withering glance. "As I said before, I want the kids to meet. Cara is so busy she has no lady friends. Just colleagues at the lab. What's wrong with getting her and Julie together? They have a lot in common. Besides, it's too late to invite someone else. The party's on Saturday."

Emma nodded, guardedly. There was one more detail about the dinner that was awkward. She hadn't even mentioned it to Jack. The fact was, her ex husband, Andy Bodreau, had donated his services as sous-chef and heavy lifter for the party she donated to the Opera. That was before she'd even met Jack Russo – much less come to count him as her best buddy in her new wine country abode.

Now Andy was bored. Still under house arrest in Santa Rosa for a real estate deal with a client gone sour. He'd been pestering her about the dinner all spring, having convinced his probation officer to OK the outing *cum* ankle bracelet thingie.

Emma decided it was time to break the news.

"Actually, Jack," she said, "when I donated the dinner, Andy offered to help. So it's technically *his* dinner donation, too. I think it might be less awkward if you include another couple or two. Eight – nine people. Honestly, I don't care."

Emma watched the muscles in Jack's jaw tighten. With his right hand he set his glass of *Sancerre* back down on the table while the fingers of his left hand tapped heavily on the varnished pine.

"Now *that*," he finally said, "should have been disclosed before anyone bid on your party."

Emma glanced sideways at her friend. Close as they were, they'd agreed their 'relationship' was strictly arms length. Yet here he was bristling at the mention of her ex husband.

"Sorry," was all Emma managed to respond while the waiter served her pea shoot salad and Jack's lobster roll

"Not that I care what you do, Emma," Jack back peddled. "It's just...you know. I don't like the guy in my house. I'm your friend. I don't like the way he treated you. It's not like I'm interfering...."

Jack had folded his arms across his chest and squinted his eyes. Emma knew the ex Olympic hockey player well enough to know what was up. She'd uncovered a weak spot in his defense system. He was planning his next move.

Before he recouped, she cut in, "Look, Jack. You're right. That's awkward. So here's what I'll do. I just won't tell Andy about the dinner. Maybe he's forgotten about it," she lied. In fact Andy had emailed her the week before, having heard about the dinner from her son-in-law, Piers.

The trouble was, Andy liked Jack. From the moment they shook hands at the opera fundraiser where Jack and Emma first met. Now he was dying to reconnect with the successful VC and sports celebrity who nine months before made Blissburg front-page news by saving Emma's life.

Emma forced a smile. "No worries, Jack. I'll make sure Andy doesn't come. Let's decide on a dessert." In spite of herself, her voice sounded strained when she added, "This is going to be fun."

She took a bite of her salad. "These pea shoots are delicious," she said hoping to change the subject.

Jack's first bite of *his* lunch also appeared to distract him. Then Emma realized it hadn't.

"You know, Emma," he began after swallowing a mouthful of food, "lobster rolls always remind me of summer on Cape Cod..."

Emma settled back in her chair. Going back to his roots was a move straight out of Jack's playbook. Taking the offensive when he felt out of control. Turning the tables when he thought the game wasn't going his way. Like her five-year-old grandson Harry turning over the checker board when he thought he was going to lose.

"One of my uncles had a little trailer he parked in Yarmouth for the summer," Jack added, pronouncing it '*Yeahmuth*.' Over the past few months Emma'd also noted that Jack exaggerated his working class accent when he wanted to distance himself from her.

He tapped his nose with his forefinger. "I'm talkin' about the *real* Cape, not the snooty one. Route 28. Peewee golf. Salt water taffy. The Cape where real people like my family went for their two weeks off each year." He smiled, then added without skipping a beat. "It's where I took Fran for her first lobster roll."

Emma tried to quell her annoyance. Jack wasn't Sicilian for nothing. But really, bringing up Frannie as payback just wasn't fair. Jack's deservedly sainted dead wife vs. her ex, the philandering felon, was a face off she'd never win.

"Yeah. It must have been *so much fun,*" she answered, concentrating on finishing her salad.

But she needn't have bothered about Jack's verbal vendetta. Her phone beeped. She glanced beside her chair where her cell was visible in the bottom of her tote. It was her son-in-law, Piers. "Need 2 talk. Call. Now."

Jack must have noticed her purse light up, too. "What's that?"

"Piers," she replied. "That's odd. He never calls in the middle of the day. It's probably just the Gomez lawsuit I was telling you about. The one my boss filed against Piers' rich client. Still..." she hesitated and winced. "I hope everything's OK."

As usual, Jack read her mind. "Forget the lawsuit. It might be about Harry. Phone him. Now. I don't mind."

Emma's look signaled her gratitude. "I'll just be a minute," she said standing up, walking out to the sidewalk and across the street to the plaza to make the call.

EMMA SAT down on a newly painted bench shaded by a magnificent flowering pink magnolia tree. The benches in the plaza all bore dedications. Emma noted the inscription as she sat down. This one read: "John Robert O'Leary." She stared at the dates written underneath the name. And then at the memorial. "For Pops. Thanks for all the ice cream cones we shared here, and for the laughter and the smiles."

Emma's eyes teared up. From the dates underneath the memorial, she knew that Pops was only seventy-two when the Big D knocked on his door. She was sixty-five. She did the now automatic calculation in her head. When she was seventy-two, Harry would be twelve. *I better make the most of it*, she told herself. Whichever way you figured, there wasn't *that* much time.

She pulled her cell phone out of her purse and stared at it for a moment. She could feel Jack's eyes transmitting his concern from across the street. But she was in no hurry to make this call to her son-in-law. Appreciative as she was for Jack's solicitude whenever family was concerned, this time she was sure Piers was not calling about her grandson. Piers' curt text conveyed annoyance not angst over an injured or ailing child. Besides, if the message was about Harry, she knew he'd have called, not texted.

In fact, as Emma had explained to Jack, she was pretty sure she knew exactly why Piers was texting. She was also pretty sure she didn't want to talk about it. One of Piers' biggest clients, Curt Randall, an ornery old reclusive widower who'd lost his only son in the Viet Nam War, was selling a vast parcel of land between Blissburg and Cloverdale. Over five hundred acres of plum trees that once had been a mainstay of Blissburg's economy. Randall also owned thousands of acres of farmland down south, near Coachella. But this parcel was special. Randall claimed that his distant relative by marriage, the famed Santa Rosa horticulturalist, Luther Burbank, had planted the plum trees himself over a hundred years before.

Now, at the bitter old age of eighty-eight, Curt Randall, left by his son's untimely death without an heir, was finally selling the Sonoma property. All five hundred plus acres of it. To a Chinese investor who planned to convert the plum trees to vineyards – a new-to-California variety of grapes – for wine to be marketed in China. Piers was handling the deal.

The exact terms of the sale were secret. The Chinese demanded it and Piers intended to keep it that way. But the rumor around Blissburg was that, if the deal went through, by the following spring all the prune trees would be gone and the acres of rolling hills would be planted with a cheap new Chinese variety of grapes. Now even Sonoma wine would be "Made in China."

Needless to say, the sale was controversial. All the more reason for Piers to keep its provisions secret. Many of Blissburg's older natives – the few that were left – remembered when plums, or more accurately prunes, got the residents of Blissburg through hard times. Most of them working as prune pickers and packers shipping the famed Blissburg plums all over the world.

Emma's eyes drifted across the street to Jack then back to her phone. She reluctantly hit the call return button. Sure that her son-in-law's concern was about the Gomez lawsuit that Steve Zimmer, her boss at the free legal clinic, had filed on behalf of a Mexican worker at one of Randall's Coachella farms. The complaint accused her son-in-law's client of providing his employee with substandard housing and not enough water and shade in the blistering Coachella heat.

A week before, Piers had all but ordered Emma, privately, to ask Steve to drop the lawsuit. To settle it, quietly, before it jeopardized the plum ranch sale.

Emma, however, decided not to act on the request. For the very first time, she thought her son-in-law was out of line. Now she was sure Piers was texting to find out why Steve still hadn't dropped the lawsuit so he could close the plum ranch sale.

Emma listened to the phone ring. It was the direct line to Piers' office. And braced herself for her son-in-law's annoyance.

She heard the click of someone picking up the phone and putting her on speaker.

"Emma?" he began, Piers' caller ID having already identified the source of the call. "Bad news." He stated the two words slowly, giving equal weight to each. "Very bad news…"

Emma felt her heart plunge into her stomach. In the middle of the night, she'd imagined such a call – always about her grandson, Harry.

"Santiago Gomez…"

"What?" Emma couldn't understand what Piers was saying.

"Santiago Gomez," Piers repeated. "The Mexican farm worker. The guy your boss bullied into suing Curt Randall…"

Emma still couldn't answer. Her heart was thumping hard in her chest and she hadn't caught her breath. When would Julie and Piers learn that, for her, "very bad news" only meant one thing? Harm to them or to Harry.

The phone went silent while Emma slowly exhaled.

"Emma," Piers demanded. "Are you there?"

"OK," she finally said. "Yeah. Santiago Gomez. I was just talking about him. Listen, Piers," she rushed to add. "I haven't had time to talk to Steve about that lawsuit yet. In fact, I'm not sure I'm going to be able to…"

Piers cut her off. "I know you're not going to be able to talk to Steve about dropping the Gomez lawsuit," he said. "Gomez is dead. The police just called. They found his body. With a knife through his throat."

"Oh my goodness," Emma whispered. The blood was retreating from her ears in loud whoshes and her heart still beat staccato. *It's OK.* She tried to calm herself. *Everyone's OK.* Everyone meaning Harry, Julie and Piers.

Suddenly, Emma remembered the sirens. Barely an hour before. Sirens heading north out of town.

"Where?" she asked.

"That's the point," Piers replied. "Gomez's cousin found the body on Curt Randall's ranch this morning. A quarter of a mile from the road. The police have already identified the murder weapon hidden under a tarp in Curt's garage. Now," he continued, "thanks to Steve's self-serving lawsuit, the police believe Curt had a motive to kill Gomez. They're holding him for murder. Of course, Curt's madder than blazes. Not to mention that he's my client and he's innocent."

Piers paused, apparently waiting for Emma to sympathize with his outrage. When she didn't, he added, "Emma, a young Mexican is dead and a broken-spirited, eighty-eight-year-old innocent man has just been led away in handcuffs. Now don't you wish you'd convinced that fool boss of yours to stop making trouble and drop that trumped up lawsuit?"

2

SATURDAY AFTERNOON – SECOND THOUGHTS

By the time Emma returned to the restaurant, Jack had already heard about the murder. Bad news traveled fast in Blissburg.

Maureen Tompkins, the police chief's wife, was seated at their table, her spikey, red-haired head dipped in close to Jack's.

"Harry's fine," Emma replied to Jack's questioning look as she sat down next to Maureen. "Piers was calling about all those sirens we heard an hour ago."

Maureen nodded knowingly. "I just told Jack all about it." Suddenly her dark, penciled-in eyebrows shot up. "Of course! Piers is Curt Randall's lawyer." She studied Emma's face for a second. "You know that the old man's been arrested for murder?"

"Piers said they found the murder weapon hidden in Curt Randall's garage," Emma shrugged.

Maureen's eyes narrowed. "The Mexican's throat was slit. With a pruning knife. The kind they used in the old days. The Chief says it has a very distinctive elk horn hand…"

Maureen clapped her hand over her mouth. "You didn't hear that, right? About the murder weapon."

Emma and Jack shook their heads. Emma knew it wasn't the first time Maureen's big mouth had gotten the better of her. She wasn't knicknamed "Loose Lips" for nothing.

"I didn't hear a thing," said Emma.

"Hear what?" Jack said.

"Thank goodness for that!" Maureen exclaimed, patting her heart with her hand. "Top secret," she added. "The Chief would kill me if..." She took a deep breath and exhaled. Like someone who had just dodged a bullet. She stood up. "I gotta go."

Emma glanced at Jack and rolled her eyes. Then she frowned. "I can't believe it, Jack. The victim is Santiago Gomez. The Mexican worker who is – I should say was – suing Curt Randall for unfair labor practices. He's our client at the free legal clinic. Gomez's cousin found his body this morning at the ranch. Now they're holding Randall for murder."

"I just saw Curt," Jack replied.

In less than a year living in Blissburg, the East Coast transplant seemed to have met just about everyone within a thirty mile radius of the Blissburg plaza.

"Hard to believe he murdered someone," Jack added. "The guy's in his eighties and sick. Although," he raised his shoulders fatalistically again, "he made no secret of how steamed he was about that lawsuit. Just last week I heard him ranting at the Chatham Club. Said he'd like to get his hands on the Mexican - he used a different word - who filed it. Something about migrant worker housing...?"

"Seasonal worker," Emma interjected. "I think the proper term is 'seasonal.'"

Jack ignored the interruption. "Down in Coachella where he owns all that farmland. Substandard housing conditions. Not enough shade and water. Randall told the bartender he'd spent every summer as a teenager living in the *exact* same housing, working for his father under the *exact* same conditions – as did his son before he died. And all it did was 'build character'. I quote."

"Doesn't make it right," Emma scoffed.

Jack nodded. "But it does make it hard for a bitter, angry, heart-broken eighty-something-year-old to understand."

They had finished eating. Jack motioned for the waiter to bring the bill. He always paid for lunch.

"You heading for the clinic?" he asked.

Emma nodded. It was Saturday, one of the days she volunteered. The place would be buzzing with news of the murder.

She stood up and grabbed her purse. "Yeah, I'd better run. I'm late."

They kissed each other lightly on each cheek, Sicilian style.

"*Ciao bella*," he called after her. He was learning Italian and interjected such phrases whenever he could. "And you're right. I won't worry about the dinner. It's gonna be fine. Without the ex. And don't forget tomorrow night at Sergio's. We're picking out the wine."

Emma waved back. Grateful for the reminder. She'd almost forgotten about the wine.

HALF AN HOUR LATER BARBARA, the receptionist, nodded to Emma as she stepped through the sliding glass doors of the Blissburg Free Legal Services Clinic aka the BFLSC. The cement box of a building sat in an abandoned shopping center on the outskirts of town.

Barbara, a Blissburg native and divorced mother of five grown sons, was a rare free clinic lifer. One of two paid employees out of a transient staff of volunteers. The other paid staff was the clinic's resident attorney, Steve Zimmer, a classmate of Emma's son-in-law from the prestigious Cal Berkeley law school, and now Emma's boss.

"I'm warning you," Barbara jerked her thumb behind her. "Steve's bummed. You heard about Gomez?"

Emma nodded.

Barbara looked back down at the book she was reading. Emma noted the title, *Born to Sin*. On the book's paperback cover, a hunky cowboy clad only in a Stetson and blue jeans hauled in a shapely schoolmarm by a lasso attached around her waist. At least Emma thought it was a schoolmarm, complete with wire rimmed glasses and ruffled high necked blouse. Emma acknowledged that the cross dangling around the heroine's neck could also have signaled the preacher's daughter.

Barbara didn't look anything like the women on the covers of the western romance novels she read by the truckload. That day the overweight blond wore a V-necked see-through lace tunic over khaki shorts, along with bracelets and a necklace made out of bullet casings.

Emma walked past Barbara's desk and entered the warren of make shift cubicles constructed out of second hand plastic room dividers. She never got over what a far cry the legal clinic was from the downtown San Francisco law firm where she'd worked as a paralegal for so many years.

At the clinic she worked for free and loved her three-day-a-week, volunteer job. There was nothing abstract or impersonal about it. Unlike her old job. No corporate clients spewing endless downloads of documents to review, catalogue, summarize, locate - and re-create when a forgetful partner left his entire discovery binder on the Larkspur ferry.

How could that possibly have been my fault, Emma asked herself. Wondering for the hundredth time why the lawyer blamed *her* for all the hours it took her to make him another copy. The criticsm had even come up, *again*, in her exit review.

No. The clinic was different. Now work was about people, not paper. Real people with real problems. Like how to get green cards or health insurance. How to avoid eviction. Find a runaway child. Get a restraining order against an abusive spouse. Sue an employer for unfair...

Emma was about to enter her cubicle when she was reminded of

Gomez. *Poor Gomez*, she thought to herself. She'd never met the man. But she'd glanced at the complaint right before Steve filed it.

The claims Gomez made were unusual for Sonoma. A county reputed to be squeaky clean with regard to its seasonal workers. What local grower wanted tourists, out for a weekend of wine tasting, distracted by images of exploited farm workers?

"No seasonal workers here," she'd recently heard one prominent vintner remark to a tasting guest who'd just seen the movie about Cesar Chavez. "Just full time employees living in new housing we subsidize out of our profits."

Emma and Jack had been sipping wine at the Buchanon Vineyards tasting room when their friend, Barry Buchanon, made the comment. Emma was doing research for her new collaboration with Buchanon Vineyards, a cookbook titled, *What a Pair: Eating and Drinking Locally in Sonoma County.*

Later, privately, Emma had asked Jack if Barry's boast about seasonal workers was true.

Jack had nodded. "Sure. Here in Disneyland," he added. "The vineyards are stage sets. Entertainment. They have to be. But down south," he shrugged.

And sure enough, a brief glance at the Gomez complaint told a very different story. Of laborers at Randall Farms Enterprises earning less than minimum wage paid by the bag full of vegetables picked under the punishing Coachella sun without adequate water and shade. Of families warehoused cheek to jowl in squalid shacks untouched for half a century.

Emma stood in the doorway to her cubicle and thought about Piers' call. A month ago, when Steve first filed his lawsuit against Randall, her son-in-law went ballistic. He accused Steve of bullying Gomez into leaving a good job at the plum ranch to move south and work at Randall's vegetable farms. All so Steve could file an unfair employment practices lawsuit against Piers' rich client.

And maybe Piers was right. Emma knew such things were done

by lawyers, like Steve, who were on a personal mission to change the world.

In any case, she now found herself caught between two warring attorneys. They couldn't have been more different – her son-in-law, Piers the crisp corporate suit and Steve her long-haired legal activist boss.

More importantly, a poor young Mexican man was dead. But who'd have thought that frail eighty-eight-year-old Curt Randall was capable of murder?

Instead of sitting down at her desk to check her emails, Emma turned around, walked down the hall and entered Steve's office. He was on the phone.

That afternoon, he quickly excused himself from his call and smiled up at her from his desk. Unlike most lawyers Emma knew, the pale, pony-tailed thirty-something, dressed in a T-shirt and baggy shorts, really loved his job. Every poorly paid second of it.

"What can I do for you, Emma?" he said. Then a cloud crossed his face banishing the smile. "You heard, right? About Santiago?" He shook his head and shuddered.

Emma knew that unlike many of Steve's colleagues, Steve genuinely loved his downtrodden clients. They were his friends. "Steve, I'm so sorry. Poor man," she added. "What a shock! I never met him, but..." she shook her head. "Is there family?"

"A wife," Steve nodded. "Three kids. Two, five and eight." He rubbed his face in his hands. "He wanted to file that suit, you know. It was *his* idea, not mine." He looked up at Emma. "But I encouraged him. I have to live with that. I just never thought..." The young man hung his head.

"Steve, let it go," Emma cut in.

Nonetheless, her son-in-law's voice still rang in her ear. "Tell Steve at least to withdraw the suit till after the plum ranch is sold. Once that's done, Curt will settle Gomez's claims. Out of court. Privately. No litigation. He wants to sell the whole southern operation next year. He's an old man. His health is bad. His only child is dead and his wife is gone. Can't Steve let him die in peace?"

But after her conversation with Piers, Emma didn't "tell" Steve to drop the suit. She told herself it wasn't her place. Her son-in-law was out of line and Steve wouldn't have listened to her anyway. Now the poor Mexican was dead, and somehow she felt responsible.

"You thought you were doing the right thing, Steve," Emma continued as much for her own sake as his. "How could anybody know?" Then she added, "Shall I take the hearing off calendar? I mean, without a client...What do you want me to do?"

Steve glanced up quickly. His answer wasn't what Emma expected.

"Drop the lawsuit? Heck no!" he said. "We are filing a new lawsuit on behalf of Santiago's wife and children and all similarly situated employees of Randall Farm Enterprises. Santiago had already begun collecting signatures for a class action. That's why he was up here. Contacting folks, like his cousin who used to work for Randall in Coachella."

As he spoke, Steve's face assumed the determined look Emma had seen so many times before.

"In addition to the criminal charges, we're also going to file a civil action against Curt Randall, personally, for wrongful death," he added. "We're going to get Santiago's wife and children every penny they deserve on account of what that monster did. Strip him of his millions and make sure Yolanda Gomez never has to worry about money again."

Emma's heart sank. She was pretty sure Steve wasn't using the 'royal we' when he spoke. His "we" included *her*. What, she wondered, was she going to tell Piers?

Before she thought of an answer, Steve added, "I have some phone calls to make, Emma. Let's meet 10:00 Monday morning to plan our strategy."

Steve picked up the receiver, hit a button on his phone and said, "Barbara – get Yolanda Gomez on the line."

Emma glanced at Steve and cringed. If, as her son-in-law believed, old man Randall hadn't murdered Santiago Gomez, then someone had better find the real killer fast. Before Steve filed those lawsuits.

3

SATURDAY NIGHT – DATE NIGHT

S aturday night was Date Night. Not Emma and Jack's date night, Emma mused as she drove her silver Prius up the winding path to Piers and Julie's estate. Their home was located about a quarter of a mile off Silver Creek Road, the chic address heading east out of Blissburg dotted with dot com vineyards and mansions. Piers had bought the estate for himself and Julie with money from a trust fund he'd inherited from his grandfather. He maintained it with his lucrative wine country law practice.

No, Emma thought to herself as she parked in front of Piers' mini Versailles. *Saturday Date Night belongs to Julie and Piers.*

The young couple had bought their faux French chateau, complete with meadow, garden and swimming pool, five years before. When Harry was born and Piers and Julie fled San Francisco to open the boutique law office and raise their son in beautiful Sonoma County. A year later, Julie opened a PR firm specializing in wineries. Both their businesses were thriving. Though Emma thought they were too busy for everyone's good. Not that she'd ever say so to anyone but Jack.

Nonetheless, every Saturday night since she'd moved to Blissburg, she volunteered to babysit her grandson. She readily admitted that Date Night was no sacrifice at all. In fact, it was Emma's favorite night of the week.

Surprisingly, Emma discovered Jack felt that way, too. Shortly after moving to Blissburg, he'd also volunteered to babysit his grandsons on Saturday nights. He drove his navy blue Tesla along the scenic route from his home in Blissburg to his daughter's winery in Calistoga texting Emma before leaving home. Later, when the little ones were asleep, they rehashed their evenings over the phone - like teenagers.

PIERS GREETED Emma brusquely at the door even before she rang the bell. He'd obviously been waiting for her. "Julie's still in the shower. Can we talk a minute in the living room? Harry's in the middle of that jungle puzzle you bought him. By the way," a smile finally lit up his blue-eyed patrician face. Piers had always reminded Emma of someone in a Ralph Lauren ad. "He's done it about twenty times. It's rated for eight year olds and he's only five."

At the mention of his son, Piers' customary good nature finally broke through. Despite his sometimes quick temper, Emma's fair, All-American son-in-law possessed the openness and easy confidence of someone to whom everything had always come easily – success, friends, money.

It was an ease and openness that Emma knew her daughter lacked. For Julie, life was a battle she had to win, not a farm-to-table, gourmet picnic laid at her feet on a sunny day. And no wonder. Piers was the adorable and adored only son of millionaires whose forbearers made a fortune in a Midwestern grocery store chain. In parts of Nebraska, Piers' last name, Larkin, was a household word.

Julie, on the other hand, had been an ugly duckling through most of high school. An ugly duckling whose father, Emma often reminded herself, all but abandoned her at the age of six. Julie fought her way to the top of every class with hard work. All the way to Stanford, on a scholarship, where to everyone's surprise – including Emma's – she blossomed into a darkly beautiful swan. And, two weeks after Piers' law school graduation, married her Stanford schoolmate, Piers Larkin.

"Glad Harry liked the puzzle so much," Emma replied, following Piers into their decorator, antique-filled living room. She hoped Piers would hold on to his good mood if she kept the conversation focused on his son.

The ploy didn't work. By the time she'd sat down, Piers' sunny smile had soured into a scowl.

"I talked to Steve Zimmer this afternoon," he said. "After I talked to you, I called him about the Randall lawsuit. Our reply is due; and I figured – I hoped under the circumstances, that we could work something out short of litigation."

Emma cut in, "Steve has no control over the police taking Mr. Randall…"

Piers didn't let her finish. "Of course not, Emma. I know that. But the bottom line is that Randall didn't murder Gomez. He's out on bail and sooner or later the police will drop the charges. All I was asking was that Steve give us a chance to fix whatever complaints he has about my client's Coachella farming operation without litigation. Curt will cooperate. I've convinced him. He's too old and too sick to fight."

Emma opened her mouth to protest that she had no control over Steve, but Piers interrupted, pointing a finger at her as though in warning.

"As I told you before, Emma," he continued, "Steve is the one who dreamt this lawsuit up in the first place and convinced Gomez to change jobs so he could file it. It appears that Gomez was trying to get his cousin, a fellow named Jose Diaz, to join in. His cousin worked at Randall Enterprises as a fruit picker before going to work at the Sonoma ranch. But Diaz didn't want to join the lawsuit. The two had argued about it a couple of days before Gomez was murdered. According to Curt, they came to blows. On Curt's property. Curt suspects it was because Gomez was trying to blackmail his cousin into cooperating. Something about a smuggling ring bringing illegals over the border. Curt's foreman called the police. Steve knows it, too."

Emma sucked in her breath. "What are you saying, Piers? That you think Gomez's cousin killed him?"

"Not my words, Emma," Piers smirked. "But there's more. Gomez's cousin also told my client that Gomez had been sticking his nose in other places it didn't belong. Specifically, up the skirt of another worker's wife down in Coachella. That, according to Diaz, had been going on a while. The woman's husband found out and threatened to kill Gomez if he didn't back off."

Emma winced. "Doesn't prove anything, Piers," she said.

"My point," Piers continued, "is that Santiago Gomez was not well liked by a lot of people besides Curt Randall. I suspect the police will find, upon further investigation – and there will be further investigation, Emma – that Santiago Gomez wasn't welcome in a lot of places. That's for the police to investigate, of course. But Curt Randall has the resources to give them help."

Emma nodded. She suspected Piers had already lined up a whole team of San Francisco's top criminal defense attorneys and private investigators to assist the local police in their work.

"Moreover," Piers added, "I can almost guarantee that when the truth is known, far from picking old Curt Randall's pockets clean, the Gomez family will have had their name dragged through a lot of mud. Is that really what your boss, Steve Zimmer, wants for a grieving widow and her children? Instead of a private settlement of the employment grievances that I can convince the old man to deliver? If, I repeat, if Steve convinces us that any kind of bad labor practices ever existed at Randall's Coachella farm."

"What do you mean?" Emma started to inquire.

"This is what I mean," Piers continued. "You convince Steve not to file that wrongful death claim. And I'll finalize the plum ranch deal. After that closes with the Chinese, Randall is ready to pay off the Gomez family and sell the Coachella farms – as soon as I can switch the trust beneficiary for Randall's estate to that animal shelter he supports in Petaluma." Piers snorted. "It'll be the richest animal shelter in the world when the old man dies, but that is not my call."

"Animal shelter?" Emma had asked. "Doesn't Randall have relatives?"

"Just one nephew on his wife's side," Piers replied. "A fellow named Rob Peters. When *he* finds out Curt is changing his will, he'll go ballistic. Again, not my call."

"Piers, look," Emma began. As far as she could tell, Piers assumed she had more influence over Steve Zimmer than was the case. "I don't..."

But Piers interrupted her again. "Don't tell me you don't know what I'm talking about, Emma. When I talked to Steve yesterday about his plans, he told me he was filing a wrongful death claim for millions of dollars against Curt Randall on behalf of Gomez's widow and children. He also told me that you, Emma..."

Piers had raised his voice. Emma's agreeable, well-mannered son-in-law was actually shouting at her.

"...have known all about Steve's plans. In fact, he said that you and he are meeting Monday morning to 'discuss strategy.' His words not mine. Whose side are you on?"

Before Emma could offer a word of explanation, Harry burst into the room.

"Nonnie! Nonnie's here!" The little boy flung himself into his grandmother's arms. "Come see the puzzle. The jungle puzzle you gave me. It's all done. I did it for you."

Harry grabbed Emma's arm and dragged her out of the living room.

To her dismay, Piers called after her, "To be continued."

· · ·

A FEW MINUTES LATER, Emma's daughter, Julie, found Emma and Harry admiring his puzzle in the breakfast room. If she knew anything about the Gomez matter, Julie hid it. More likely, Emma told herself, Piers hadn't mentioned it to Julie.

Unlike Steve, her boss, Emma's son-in-law, Piers, was a mediator by nature. A peacemaker at heart. Always looking to resolve a conflict *before* anyone litigated. To unruffle feathers and think of a solution out of the box. Maybe, Emma thought, it was a life skill he learned early as the only child of two rich, headstrong, overeducated parents. It was probably why, now, he specialized in trusts and estates. Locking up family fortunes so heirs would not have to argue about them later.

"Please Mom, take some," Julie insisted a few minutes later, offering her mother a steaming plate of leftover *beouf Bourgignon* while they watched Harry devour a chicken quesadilla. He was already tall for his age, Emma noted, and growing like a reed.

"If I know you," Julie added, "all you've had since breakfast is a few spoonsful of yogurt."

Emma nodded. She couldn't help noticing Julie had gained a few pounds. Her face had filled out. Not that she didn't look adorable in her skintight jeans and Prada sweater.

Living in Sonoma County, food capital of Northern California or possibly the world, Julie had recently taken on cooking the way she took on everything – competitively. Determined to know it all and be the best. Where, Emma often wondered, had she gotten that trait? Certainly not from her mother who ran from competition like a house on fire. Or her father, Andy Bodreau, who refused to play by anyone else's rules.

"Rules, shmules," she remembered him saying early in their marriage when another couple tried to teach them to play bridge. "Rules are for dummies." *So much for the white-collar criminal with the ankle thingie*, Emma thought. *How did I miss those signals?*

Julie passed Emma a hand painted Deruta plate full of rich

brown cubes of beef simmered for hours in a thick vegetable gravy. "Try this. I'm done with the Contessa," Julie laughed, dipping the serving spoon into a navy blue ceramic stew pot and licking off some sauce. "I've decided to work my way through *Mastering the Art*."

"*Of French Cooking*," Emma added under her breath. Only her daughter would take on Julie Childs' tome in the 21st century. Most people Emma knew were content to watch the cooking diva's reruns on Netflix for a laugh and a good drool.

Emma stared at her plate and raised her eyebrows. "Looks like you actually did all seven steps this time," she noted. Even she, an accomplished cook and food writer, skipped the seventh step of Julia's *beouf Bourgignon*.

Julie nodded. "Do it right, or don't do it at all. Passed the whole thing through a sieve."

"Wow," Emma exclaimed after taking a bite. "This really *is* good. But you're wrong about skipping lunch. I had pea shoot salad at The Trough."

Emma didn't mention that she'd had lunch with Jack. Mentioning Jack's name still seemed to put her daughter on edge.

Julie rolled her eyes. "With Jack?" she grimaced. Despite Jack's having saved Emma's life – or maybe because of it – Julie always appeared to resent Jack's close relationship with her mother.

"Don't worry. We're just friends," Emma assured her daughter wondering why everyone seemed to assume there was more.

"Speaking of Jack," Julie added as though trying to sound off-hand. Harry had finished his quesadilla and returned to the living room to play with his dad. "Do we really have to go to that dinner party he's planned with his daughter next weekend? I mean, what's that about? The one time I met the woman – at Little Pete's Gourmet Grocery – she was buying healthy food for her dad. What? Does she run his life?"

Emma nodded. As far as she could tell, Jack's daughter *did* run his life.

"Anyway," Julie continued, "she looked like kind of a pill. Can't imagine this 'get together' is going to be fun. Besides, with you there, who's going to babysit Harry? He's not used to anyone else, Mom."

Emma nodded again. That was for sure.

"Look, honey," she said. "I don't really get the point of this dinner, either. But Jack did make a $5000 donation to City Opera to get my home cooked meal at the auction. It's kind of *his* call. I think the best thing is for us to go along with it. Though, I agree, Cara seems a bit overbearing." *Not to mention, intimidating*, Emma added to herself.

Julie wasn't convinced. "Piers isn't happy about it either. In fact, he's dreading the dinner. Jack's a client. Never mix business and ..." She didn't finish the sentence.

"I'll make it up to Piers," Emma cut in. "I'll babysit all day Sunday."

Julie shrugged, not appeased. Determined to rub it in. "A radiologist and a medical researcher? What will we talk about?"

"You're intelligent people. You'll manage," Emma replied, marveling that her daughter had already Googled the couple. Then, hoping to change the subject, she glanced pointedly at the clock above Julie's massive, navy blue, eight-burner stove. "Aren't you two going to be late?"

Julie looked at the clock too. "Holy cow! Piers," she shouted. "I'm ready. We need to go."

As USUAL, Emma stayed up playing with Harry well past his bedtime. They watched *Frozen* for the fifth time. Over the past year, she and Harry had developed a conspiracy. She let him stay up late as long as he went to bed ten minutes before the end of whatever movie his parents had gone to see. Emma checked the run times right after his parents left.

So Harry was in bed, eyes closed if not asleep, when his parents returned from the movie. Emma was in the living room watching *Saturday Night Live*.

Piers merely nodded at her and sat down to watch the end of the show.

"How was the movie?" she asked.

Julie, standing in the doorway to the living room, answered. "So, so. Thanks Mom. I'm bushed," she added before climbing the stairs to bed.

Piers got up from the couch to follow Emma to the front door. As he opened it to let Emma out, he whispered, "Sorry I came on so strong earlier this evening. But I'm right this time. Talk to Steve. Curt's an old man. His health is bad. He's bitter about his life. But he wouldn't hurt a flea. This litigation will kill him. We can work things out so everyone gets what they need. Without publicity. Without a fight. Steve's gotta understand. Do what you can, Emma. Please."

4

SUNDAY MORNING – PLUM PERFECT

On the drive back home, Jack called to compare babysitting notes. And gripe about the new *au pair*.

"She doesn't stimulate them," he complained. "She doesn't read. She eats and texts. The boys were watching videos when I arrived. Then the boyfriend rang the doorbell. Who knows what rock she found *him* under? Covered in tattoos."

Emma let the tattoo comment pass. Chances were he'd never see the tiny butterfly she'd acquired traveling with Andy in the south of Spain.

"She's nineteen, Jack, and until a month ago, probably never left her village in Poland," Emma exclaimed. "What do you expect? Mary Poppins?"

She could almost hear Jack shrug. "No. Maria Montessori. At least she's a *paisan*," he added with a laugh. "Look, what do you expect, Emma? They're my grandsons. I want the best for them and their mother is just too dang busy."

Emma then filled Jack in on her lecture from Piers. But instead of taking what Emma thought was her side, Jack agreed with Piers.

"I don't know," he answered after patiently listening to her replay Piers' tirade. "I say settle the grievances. Privately. Let the old man die in peace – or whatever there is left of peace for the old geezer. Face it, Emma, he never got over the death of his son. Probably poisoned his marriage too. Apparently all he's been living for is his dog and that animal shelter he gives the annual BowWow benefit for..."

"Yeah," Emma chimed in. "Looks like it's turned into more than an *annual* BowWow benefit." Then she added, unable to resist the joke, "Apparently the whole of Randall's fortune is going to the dogs."

"What do you mean?" Jack asked. "I thought Rob Peters was getting Randall's estate. The nephew. Word is he's already spent half the inheritance on a vineyard he's run into the ground."

"Wait a minute," Emma replied, suddenly realizing she'd said too much. "You'd never tell anyone I said that. I mean, you'd never repeat what Piers told me about Randall changing his will. It's utterly confidential, Jack. Do you actually know this guy?"

"Peters? Sure I know him," Jack answered. "He and I are on the Blissburg Historic Preservation Committee. He's not the sharpest knife in the drawer. But he's pro growth – pro development. Don't worry. I won't repeat a word. I'm just surprised, that's all. Seems like he's been waiting for old man Randall to die for years. If what you say is true, the poor joker's in for a big surprise."

"I'll say," Emma answered. "But please, remember. What I said about the will is confidential."

"My lips are sealed," Jack answered. "And by the way, I won't make it to tomorrow's Sunday Stroll. I'm taking the boys ice skating at the Snoopy rink tomorrow morning. Cara's back in Palo Alto. Some emergency at the lab. And my son-in-law's at a conference in Colorado. So guess who's chaperoning the *au pair*? I'll see you tomorrow night at Sergio's, though," he added. "Remember? We're picking the wine."

· · ·

THEY SAID goodbye just as Emma pulled into the driveway of her home. The two story wood frame house, that once belonged to a legendary California mountain man, sat under the shade of an enormous magnolia tree. It was surrounded by a garden behind the small Victorian cottage Julie used as the office for her PR firm. Julie and Piers had seen the property when they first moved north from San Francisco, hoping to convince Emma to move there, too. When Emma's best friend, Mary, died, they got their wish.

Now Emma rented the quaint yellow and white wood farmhouse from her daughter and son-in-law. Her daughter's tenant! It was the last thing an independent single mom had expected. But the home had two bedrooms, a living room, a beautiful wainscoted dining room, a huge new kitchen, a redwood deck and an enormous yard backing onto a wildlife preserve. A few weeks after Emma moved, she realized she had never been happier.

She'd left the outdoor lights on. Up a short flight of stairs to the wrap-around porch, she opened her front door. And sighed. Home. She was home. And everything was just the way she liked it. The living room with its comfortable overstuffed furniture covered in hand woven Mexican fabrics. The dining room big enough for her grandmother's walnut table and the painted cupboard she'd brought from her San Francisco condo.

Emma climbed the stairs to her cozy bedroom, went to bed and quickly fell asleep.

Three hours later, however, she was wide-awake. Her conversation with Piers played a loop in her head.

Why, in the middle of the night she wondered, did everything sound more ominous than it did by light of day? If Piers was right that Curt Randall had *not* killed Gomez, then a murderer was on the loose in Blissburg. And if not Randall, then who? A jealous husband? An angry heir?

Worst of all, in the middle of the night Emma wondered if she could have prevented the tragedy. If, perhaps, she could have convinced Steve to drop the lawsuit. And had she done so, whether Santiago Gomez would now be alive.

IT SEEMED to Emma that she had not slept a wink when her alarm sounded at exactly 8:00 a.m. It was time for the Blissburg Sunday Stroll, a weekly event Emma hadn't missed since the second weekend after she moved to Blissburg.

Emma had looked forward to this particular Sunday Stroll all week and was disappointed that Jack wouldn't be there. He often knew more about the history of his newly adopted home than the tour leader himself.

Then again, Emma reminded herself, *how could the ex Olympic hockey player resist a chance to take his grandsons to the "Snoopy" rink?* An ice hockey facility built by Snoopy's creator, himself. The same rink where Jack still played, once a week, in what he called the "old guys league."

Emma walked up Blissburg Avenue for a latte at Claud's. The truth was, she admitted to herself, her life and Jack's pulled them in different directions. It was hard to imagine how that might ever change.

By the time she arrived at the plaza, twelve or so of the usual suspects had already gathered at the Spanish style fountain that graced the center of the square. Most of the Strollers balanced coffee and still-warm sour cherry *galettes* from the Plaza Bakery in their hands.

The second she arrived, Tom Fitzpatrick waved at her. The eighty-something year old triple divorcé owned the Blissburg dump. He'd been trying to worm a dinner out of Emma since they'd met on a Sunday Stroll. Emma was starting to feel guilty about putting him off so long. But for some reason every word out of the old man's mouth jarred her.

She quickly turned to greet four members of the Walkie-Talkies, the local women's walking club. Dressed for the stroll in what Emma described as their uniform of black linen pants, long black T-shirts and pastel Wallaroo hats with brims so wide they reached half way to their elbows, the Walkie-Talkies reminded Emma of latter day nuns. An order dedicated to good gossip instead of good works.

"Hi honey. Where's Jack?" Trish, the ubiquitous Sotheby realtor shouted across the gurgling fountain.

Emma thought she detected an overly arched eyebrow as well. Or perhaps Trish had simply been careless with her makeup that morning. In any event, there was something that annoyed Emma about Trish's assumption that at 9:00 a.m. on a Sunday morning Emma would know exactly where Jack Russo was. And that if she didn't, something might be deliciously wrong.

Of course, Emma *did* know *exactly* where Jack was. That very minute he was stick handling, or whatever he called it, with his grandsons at the Santa Rosa rink. In fact, he'd called her from there not ten minutes before to boast that eight year old Joshie was a "natural," on the ice.

"I dunno," Emma replied to Trish, unwilling to fuel more Sunday morning gossip by a detailed description of the man's whereabouts. Half of Blissburg, including her own daughter, assumed that she and Jack were having an affair. *How wrong they are*, Emma mused. But since Jack was now her closest buddy, there was no one to whom she could protest her complete innocence with regard to *that*. No one who would believe her, that is.

When Trish registered Emma's response, her eyebrow really did shoot up at least half an inch. She glanced at her companions. Emma couldn't help noticing the sparkle of excitement in the woman's eye. And wondered how many dinner invitations Jack was about to receive when three of the Walkie-Talkies immediately excused themselves for a quick pee before heading into the van.

"Don't leave without us, Silas," the Walkie-Talkies' newest member, Jill, a transplant from Oakland who bought out Blossoms and Bulbs, called over her shoulder. Silas was the amateur local historian who'd organized that particular Sunday Stroll.

Meanwhile, Emma and the remaining Strollers boarded the minivan. It was Emma's first Sunday Stroll that was not conducted entirely on foot. Emma was pleasantly surprised when Silas Bugbee, their slight, bespectacled thirty-something leader, grabbed the seat next to hers.

Emma did not know Silas well. Carter Olsen, the director of the Blissburg Historical Society, usually led the Sunday Stroll. But Emma had encountered Silas during the renovations to her farmhouse in his professional capacity as city architect and head of the Blissburg permit board.

Since the day she first saw him, and he lovingly presented Piers with a copy of the original site map of the legendary California mountain man's farm, Silas Bugbee had reminded Emma of a nineteenth century New England zealot. *A Walden Pond groupie*, she had thought to herself.

Even his clothes signaled Thoreau wannabe – thin white billowy shirts tucked into slim, high-waisted beltless serge pants and high-topped leather shoes. The shoes didn't have buttons, but Emma swore they could have. And while Silas didn't really have a black silk ribbon tied around his neck in a loose bow, something about the lanyard he always wore on a shiny thick black ribbon reminded her of one. Where, Emma wondered, did one buy such clothes? Maybe there was a Louisa May Alcott website.

To make matters worse, Silas's thin freckled face half hidden behind a lank curtain of stringy yellow hair, radiated so much zealous excitement that the poor man always seemed on the verge of tears. Indeed, the morning Emma and Piers showed him their architect's plans, retaining the farmhouse kitchen's footprint and preserving the original stone hearth, Silas was so appreciative that tears did form at the corners of his eyes and his nose began to drip. Forcing him to remove a really badly stained white cloth handkerchief from his hip pocket to blow his nose and wipe the tears away in that order.

Now, sitting next to him in the van, Emma noted a hand-hammered silver wedding band on Silas's left ring finger and tried to imagine how Mrs. Bugbee might appear. Dressed, perhaps, in a long grey cotton dress, cinched in a tight v at the waist, with ham hock sleeves. *Like the kind those cult people wear in Utah*, Emma mused, imagining a pale blond woman with hair tucked under a white cotton bonnet. Then she remembered something. Was it Tom Fitzpatrick who mentioned that Tiffany had worked as a waitress at Hooters?

In any case, Silas was incredibly knowledgeable regarding Blissburg's social and architectural history. Emma was eager to discuss it with him on that day's short ride to the home of the famed local botanist, Luther Burbank.

Silas Bugbee, however, apparently had a different plan. As soon as the Walkie-Talkies returned from their pee 'n text and the van hit the road, he turned to her.

"Emma," he began, "today's lecture is going to be a wee bit of a challenge for me. I may need to turn to you for moral support."

Emma cocked her head. *Am I imagining it?* she wondered. *Or are tears already sprouting at the corners of his eyes?*

"How so?" was all she managed by way of reply.

"I know," Silas nodded, withdrawing what looked like the same stained handkerchief Emma had seen before and wiping his eyes, "I'm a professional. It's my job to remain impartial." He blew his nose and appeared to regain his composure. "It's about the plums. The plum *trees*," he added. "I'm sure you've heard. If the Chinese purchase goes through over at the Randall Ranch, why, by next year all those historic trees will be gone. All *gone*."

Another thin stream of water threatened to overflowed the rims of the young man's eyes. Emma had to turn away.

"*Will* the sale go through, Silas?" Emma asked staring out the window. "After that *murder* on Friday," she added with a shrug. "Well, I don't know. With old man Randall in jail, I mean, can he even sell the place?"

"He's out on bail," Silas reminded her, curtly. His clenched jaw signaled that as far as Silas Bugbee was concerned, old Randall could rot in jail for the rest of his life. "Technically, I've been told he *can* consummate the sale. I'm sure his *lawyer,*" Silas emphasized the word in a not nice way, "has figured that out. I believe the question is whether Huang Ho, the Chinese developer who is buying the ranch, will now try to renegotiate the sale."

"You mean because of the arrest?" Emma asked, glancing back at him.

Silas shook his head. "No. I've been providing the site maps for HoCo's due diligence. You see, there's a problem. Pollution has been detected in one of the water tanks. No one knows for sure how deep it goes. Into the wells? The water table? Of course, no one around here cares about historic trees. The question is whether the pollution of our water table might generate a little public outrage to block the sale."

Emma stared back at Silas in surprise. "You mean, cause Mr. Ho to back out?" Piers hadn't mentioned a thing about pollution of the Randall plum ranch water supply, but it certainly would explain his desire to close the deal quickly.

"Mr. *Huang*," Silas corrected her. "They do it backwards in China." He blushed and, for a second, Emma thought he was going to cry again. "I thought you might have heard something..."

A light suddenly went on in Emma's head. Silas had seen Piers' name on the purchase and sale documents and knew she was Curt Randall's lawyer's mother-in-law.

"HoCo won't back out," Silas continued, lowering his voice. "But surely the Chinese will ask to renegotiate the sale price. Randall's *lawyer* will probably push to close the sale quickly. Before anything worse comes to light and the locals finally wake up. But face it, HoCo won't do anything about pollution to our water table. The Chinese don't care about pollution. Just look at Beijing. Of course, as far as I'm concerned destroying those historic plum trees is criminal. You may remember that I tried, unsuccessfully, to organize a protest about *that*."

Silas glared at Emma when he spoke. As though she were personally to blame for his failure.

He rolled his eyes and gestured at the handful of people in the minivan, "But, of course, who cares about *history* these days." He smirked, "Maybe poisoning our water supply will awaken these idiots to what's happening to *our* land."

Emma looked away again. She well remembered Silas's attempts to rally support to save the plum trees. In fact, at the time, she'd felt guilty about not joining in the cause. Even more guilty because she knew the only reason she didn't call the number on the flier she found in her mailbox was because her son-in-law was involved in the deal. *Other people will help save the trees,* she'd assured herself. But no one had.

Silas touched her lightly on the arm. When Emma glanced back at him, something about the intensity of his stare almost frightened her.

"Is there anyone you could talk to, I mean directly?" he said. "Someone, perhaps, who's involved in the deal? Anything you could do, personally, to stop this...this slaughter of our trees?"

Emma felt her jaw clamp shut. "I can't," she whispered through clenched teeth, angry at being pulled further into the old man's conflict.

Silas shifted his gaze over her shoulder and out the window. The van had pulled off the highway and was headed into downtown Santa Rosa. A few minutes later, it came to a stop across the street from City Hall.

Silas rose from his seat and turned to address the occupants of the van. "All right everyone..." He glanced around the bus. "We have reached our morning's destination. The van will drop us at the main entrance to the Luther Burbank Home and Gardens. I will guide you on a tour of this extraordinary man's home. Do not wander. Please stay with me throughout our tour of this registered national, state and city historic landmark."

The van deposited its occupants at the front entrance of the white wood framed Victorian building. In many ways, Emma noted, the famed Luther Burbank's home resembled her own little Blissburg farmhouse. Half the house was one story, its entrance off of a long covered front porch. The other half was two stories high, with two large downstairs windows and a single window in the middle of the second story under the peak of the roof. Indeed, many old houses in Santa Rosa resembled the modest, welcoming little cottage – a far cry from Burbank's much larger brick Lancaster, Massachusetts birthplace pictured inside the Santa Rosa museum.

But that was Luther Burbank's style, Silas informed the Sunday Strollers as they stood listening to his informative lecture, staring about the horticulturalist's unpretentious living room. The inventor of the Russet potato, the freestone peach and the beloved Santa Rosa plum – to name just a few of the over 800 varieties of plants that the world famous horticulturist and botanist developed over his fifty-five year career – was, Silas explained, a kind and humble man. A man devoted to humanity and to nature in all its forms. His home, where he had hosted friends like the inventor Thomas Edison and the industrialist, Henry Ford, bore witness to his simple tastes.

As one friend and admirer, the Paramahansa Yogananda phrased it, in a quotation from his book, *Autobiography of a Yogi* that Emma found printed on a T-shirt in the Burbank Home and Garden gift shop:

"...he knew the worthlessness of luxury, the joy of few possessions."

Later, in the garden, while extolling the special qualities of the famed Santa Rosa plum, Silas Bugbee broke down one more time:

"You see," he explained, "the Santa Rosa plum was Mr. Burbank's crown jewel."

Silas had been speaking to the Strollers gathered in the middle of the lush Burbank gardens. As he spoke the words "crown jewel," like a magician pulling a rabbit out of a hat, the young man produced a perfect, golf ball sized plum out of the coarse leather saddlebag he always wore strapped across his chest. The effect was as dramatic as the gesture. Strollers gasped. He might as well have pulled out the Crown Jewels themselves.

"The full, sweet flavor," Silas explained, biting into the taut, perfectly colored skin, "is balanced by just a hint of tartness. Note how the rich, purple hue on the outside hides juicy yellow flesh blushing along its perimeter as though embarrassed by its own sensuality. Finally," he added inhaling deeply while sticky juice overflowed his glistening lips and dripped down his fingers, "experience the mouthiness, if you will. The compact size, pulsing with flavor."

As he spoke, Emma experienced what felt like a hot flash. Trish, standing next to her, inhaled sharply and opened her fan. Then, just as he finished speaking, Silas pulled more flawless purple Santa Rosa plums out of his satchel, and passed them around.

There was a brief pause in the lecture while the Strollers sucked on their plums.

"On a personal note," Silas continued, "unfortunately Luther Burbank, a transplant himself, from Massachusetts - the man who knew how to make anything and everything increase and multiply - "

At this point Silas did choke up and was unable to continue. He pulled out his hanky and wiped his eyes.

"Except," he finally resumed his lecture, "except for himself. Unfortunately, Luther Burbank died childless."

Silas' performance was so moving a few of the Walkie-Talkies embraced him in a group hug before breaking down in tears.

Silas waved them away so he could continue.

"This true servant of humanity," he concluded, "gave generously to local schools, worked tirelessly to provide better and more abundant nourishment to mankind, and eventually, without heirs of his own, gave all this," Silas gestured to the home and gardens, "to us. He died, here, on April 11, 1926 and is buried on these grounds near the greenhouse. We will now make our way to his last resting place. If you will please follow me."

"Wow," Emma remarked to Tom Fitzgerald as they walked to the famed horticulturalist's grave. "Somebody sure had his priorities straight. I think I'll bring my daughter here. And my grandson."

"Too bad a man like that never had children," Tom replied.

Emma was about to agree, but Silas had overheard Tom's remark. Before Emma could speak, the young man shook his head.

"No," he snapped. "You are wrong, Tom. If Luther Burbank had had children, he'd never have left all this to us." He gestured around the property again, the gardens blooming with roses, the hothouses filled with endlessly new varieties of life. "These *are* his children." He glared pointedly at Emma. "Too bad *our* children don't understand the priceless nature of his gifts."

5

SUNDAY NIGHT – THE DEVIL'S BUSINESS

Emma spent the rest of Sunday preparing for the wine tasting at Sergio's restaurant. Over the past year its owner, Sergio Santagrata had become her good friend. And Jack's new business partner. Jack had actually bailed Sergio out of serious financial difficulties shortly after saving Emma's life. Sergio was a fine chef, but he was a terrible businessman.

Emma had recently enlisted his help preparing her new cookbook in collaboration with Buchanon Vineyards: *What a Pair: Eating and Drinking Locally in Sonoma*. The cookbook consisted of thirty breakfast, lunch and dinner menus. Emma's job was to research and test each recipe described in the book using only locally grown ingredients.

She would serve one of the dinner menus for Jack and his guests at the dinner for six he purchased at the Opera in the Vineyards fundraiser the night they first met. The dinner she selected included one of her personal favorite recipes: spinach and ricotta gnocchi consisting of light fluffy balls of cooked chopped spinach, ricotta cheese, egg yolks and parmesan rolled in flour and boiled for a few seconds in water till they floated to the top. The trick with the *malfatti* (meaning "badly made" in Italian) was to make sure they didn't fall apart when they were boiled. There was no miracle cure if that happened - like adding ice cubes to a curdled *sauce Bernaise*. There was just a soggy mess.

Emma intended to serve the *malfatti* in a sauce made by sautéing a large clove of garlic and a few chopped basil leaves with fresh cherry tomatoes in a little olive oil, and letting it simmer until the tomatoes burst into a light sweet *sugo*. The trick with the sauce was not to burn it. And finding the right ratio of olive oil to tomato. The *malfatti* were light. Too much tomato drowned out their flavor. Too much oil...well, of course, that was *never* good.

Those were the two recipes she tested all Sunday afternoon, and intended to "pair" with just the right wines at Sergio's that night. Even for home-testing the recipes, she had bought almost all the ingredients locally. The ricotta from Sorellina's Creamery. The spinach from Tasso Farms. Of course, May was too early for local tomatoes. Many Sonoma gardeners didn't even plant their tomatoes until the end of May. Emma tested her recipe with greenhouse tomatoes. Good local tomatoes would not be available until late July at the very earliest. The best did not appear until September.

At quarter to five Emma had finished cleaning up her kitchen. She stored the sauce she made in a glass container and put it in the fridge. Then she climbed the stairs to her bedroom to dress for dinner. Jack would arrive in a few minutes. He hated to wait.

She was just buttoning up a vintage Marimekko tent dress in bold pink and red stripes when she saw Jack's Tesla pull into her driveway. She shoved her feet into her old, comfortable black loafers and grabbed her black cotton French painter's jacket out of the closet. The night promised to be mild. Her faux Goyard sac hung on a peg by the front door. She let herself out and locked up. Jack was getting out of the car.

They kissed each other lightly on each cheek before he opened the door for her. Jack's manners never ceased to amaze Emma. Though he wore his working class background on his sleeve, Jack's manners were strictly Emily Post. The original 1922 edition of the etiquette book. Emma suspected that somewhere along the line Jack had memorized it.

Emma settled back into the now familiar passenger seat of Jack's navy blue luxury car. The one the VC had invested in. Early. The only car that Jack once said he "truly desired." *He said it like he meant it*, Emma thought, staring at Jack's determined profile maneuvering the car around the old magnolia and down the driveway to the street. *Like a man still capable of desire.*

He wasn't a handsome man, she reminded herself. His face was too beat up for that. Too many broken noses, dislocated jawbones and black eyes playing hockey. But she had to admit the man was attractive. At least the women of Blissburg thought so. Maybe it was because all that damage somehow proved he was a survivor. *Women like survivors*, she mused.

As for what the men of Blissburg thought of Jack? Emma had learned that what you heard about Jack Russo depended on whom you spoke to. Those who'd *had* a run in with Jack offered grudging respect. Those who hadn't – or those like her son-in-law who worked for him – treated him gingerly, like an unexploded hand grenade.

One thing was certain, however. Men trusted Jack Russo. They trusted him to be an enormous pain until he got his way. Which he usually did.

"How was the Stroll?" Jack asked as Emma buckled her seatbelt. "What's new with Luther Burbank?"

"The Stroll was interesting," Emma answered. "And a little bit sad. It seems the man who knew how to make everything else increase and multiply never had any children of his own."

"So he left us Santa Rosa plums instead," Jack replied. "They were his children." He stopped talking for a few seconds before adding with a sigh, "And I'll bet those plums never broke his heart."

Emma waited for Jack to continue. When she determined that he would not, she decided there was no use prodding him. She changed the subject.

"How was hockey?" she asked. Talking about his grandsons always brought a smile to Jack's face.

"You know, Emma," he replied, his voice recapturing all the enthusiasm it had lacked a moment before. "I was just thinkin' about that driving over to your place tonight. Why the heck do I get such a kick out of being with those boys? There is very little, in fact, that I enjoy more than their company. I'm ashamed to say it, honestly, I don't remember having so much...fun...with my own..."

"Do you think it's because now you have boys?" Emma asked.

For a few moments Jack seemed lost in thought. Then he shook his head.

"No," he finally said, decisively.

He didn't look at Emma, which was unusual because he frequently took his eyes off the road to glance at her when he spoke.

"I really don't think it's that," he continued. "See Cara was always very athletic. She even joined an ice hockey team – I think she was around eleven. Looking back, I guess the poor kid was tryin' to get my attention. I traveled a lot," he shrugged. "Always chasing a deal."

"It's a pretty common story, Jack," Emma said.

"Yeah," he answered. "But that's water under the bridge, isn't it?" He shook his head, "Anyway, what I figured out is that grandchildren are different. I don't mean that cliché about how grandparents get to have fun and then drop the little buggers off with the parents when they're tired and cranky. I'm talkin' about how the whole thing is different."

He stopped for a moment as if to collect his thoughts. Then he continued. "At the rink today, Emma, it was like hockey practice when I was a kid. I never wanted to get off the ice. I looked at my grandsons skating around the rink – Josh skates backwards great, by the way. Mikey junior – not so good. I wasn't lookin' at my watch wondering when it would end. I wasn't checkin' email. I was there. I didn't want to be anywhere else. And the best part is, the kids knew it. That there was nowhere else their granddad would rather be than with them. Havin' fun."

Emma felt a surge of something when Jack stopped talking. It was warm, and crept over her in places she hadn't felt in years. She hoped it wasn't love. That would complicate things. She liked their friendship simple. The way it was.

She took a deep breath. "You know, Jack," she said. "I don't think I could have phrased it better, myself. That's exactly how I feel when I'm with Harry. That I don't want to be anywhere else."

And because that was true. Because Jack's treasuring his time alone with his grandsons gave Emma the freedom to treasure her time alone with Harry, any jealousy she might have felt about his comment vanished into thin air.

They had pulled up to the service entrance behind Sergio's restaurant. Since bailing Sergio out of his financial troubles and buying into the business, Jack had a parking space just to the left of the restaurant's back door. He turned off the ignition and got out of the car. By the time Emma had gathered up her purse and unbuckled her seatbelt, Jack was opening her door.

SUNDAY NIGHT at Sergio's was wine pairing night. Representatives of three or four of the many local vineyards prepared a tasting and then educated the customers on the optimal wine for each of their courses. That night, among others, Barry Buchanon from Buchanon Vineyards had brought along his master vintner, Giuseppe Pieri, an eighty year old Italian from Lucca in Tuscany. Despite almost fifty years living in Sonoma County, Peppino, as he was locally known, still spoke Italian like a Tuscan, pronouncing the soft "c" before a vowel like a "sh". So for *cento* or a hundred, he said "shento" instead of "chento"; "shinque" for "cinque" or "five".

Emma loved practicing her Italian with the tall, blue-eyed,

ruddy-faced man when she visited the Buchanon Vineyard to research her book. Even in his eighties, Peppino knew how to flirt.

"*Ciao, bella,*" he called to her from behind the restaurant's sleek mahogany and steel bar - interrupting an animated conversation in Italian with Sergio, the restaurant's owner and celebrity chef.

Emma waved back. Then Sergio broke away from the conversation to take Emma and Jack to what had become their usual table near the kitchen.

"*Ciao,* Em-ma," he greeted Emma with a cursory kiss on each cheek, pronouncing each of the m's in her name, Italian style. "*Come va,* Jack? What's up?" he added to Jack. Despite his friendly greeting, something in the young man's tone signaled to Emma that Sergio was annoyed.

"*Senti,* listen," he added, squatting down by their table as they took their seats. "Peppino will be over in a minute. I know you want to talk to him about some wines for your dinner, Jack. But I gotta warn you, the old man's making me trouble."

"Trouble?" Jack asked.

"He's steamed because the HoCo guys dropped by tonight for dinner. They're staying out at the Honorage Inn and Spa. This morning, Barry invited them up to Buchanon Vineyards to look around and Peppino lost his temper. You know. Same old thing about the Made in China wine. Now they turn up here as my customers and Peppino refuses to talk to them." Sergio pounded the table in frustration jiggling the forks and knives. "I told him, I can't do that. Somebody comes to my restaurant, I gotta serve them. And you know what he says?" Sergio looked at Jack.

Jack shrugged.

"He said, 'just like a Sicilian. You'd do business with the devil,'" Sergio replied.

Jack's eyebrows shot up. "What did *you* say?"

"Nothing," Sergio answered. "Next thing, you two walked in.

Besides," he added, "what could I say? I *would* do business with the devil – as long as he pays his bill."

"Forget about it," Jack said, eyeing the customers in the restaurant over Emma's shoulder. "So where are they?"

"Who?" Sergio asked.

"The Chinese," Jack replied, his eyes still scanning the room. Then he stopped and squinted at a table in the far corner of the crowded restaurant. "*Do* they pay their bill?"

"I'll say," Sergio laughed. "And they know a lot more about what they're eating than the dumb clucks from Marin who don't know a *Bolognese* sauce from tomato ketchup. But when they practice their Italian..." he shook his head. "It's murder. I gotta give them credit, though. They try. And the clothes?" Sergio kissed his fingertips. "Hand made suits – Kiton, Etro sportswear. I wish I could afford to dress like that. Look at them."

Emma turned, in spite of herself, to follow Sergio's and Jack's eyes to the table. Four Chinese men sat there conversing, obviously enjoying their meal. Even from a distance, they looked impressive in their beautifully tailored suits and designer ties. Emma guessed there was nothing "Made in China" about them except themselves.

"So, what did they order?" Emma asked.

"Potato *gnocchi* and the veal *Bolognese*," Sergio answered.

"What wine did they choose?" Jack added, "without the benefit of Peppino's expert advice, I mean."

Sergio waved his hand up and down, sideways. "They knew exactly what they wanted. And they chose well. A 2011 Soliste St. Andelain *Sauvignon Blanc* with the gnocchi. And a 2012 Two Shepards Saralee *Grenache Noir* with the veal. I might have chosen a different red; but..." he shrugged. "All this in Italian, mind you. Which was pretty good except for putting the accents on all the wrong syllables."

"They're dropping a bundle," Jack laughed. "You're right. Only a dumb Lucchese like Peppino Pieri would turn away business like that."

Emma winced. Peppino was waving, walking towards their table. Thank goodness the only thing wrong with the hearty old Tuscan was that he was hard of hearing.

Twenty minutes later, after Peppino offered them a dozen or so wines to taste, Jack selected a 2012 Preston GSM, a 2012 Macphail and a 2010 32 Winds Hirsch *Pinot Noir* for the dinner.

"I'll have it all delivered to your house tomorrow," Peppino promised, patting Jack on the back with a paternal smile.

But when the old man turned to bid Emma goodbye, she saw his eyes meet those of one of the Chinese men seated at the table behind her. Emma looked over her shoulder at him. The man waved, obviously motioning Peppino to his table. Instead of waving back, the winemaker scowled, turned on his heel and walked in the opposite direction.

Emma knew Jack saw the exchange as well.

"Great way to make enemies," she mused. "Barry won't be happy with that performance. I've heard from Piers that Barry has been trying to make nice with the Chinese."

"Enemies?" Jack shrugged in his fatalistic Sicilian way. "At Peppino's age, who cares?"

By then, they had finished dessert. *Zuppa Inglese*, an Italian riff on English pudding made with custard and home made ladyfingers. It tasted so much like Emma's grandmother's version of the dish, it brought tears to her eyes.

And Emma laughed so hard she almost *did* cry when the woman at the neighboring table complained that Sergio didn't list the ubiquitous *tiramisu* on his menu.

"What kind of Italian restaurant *is* this?" she pouted. "Imagine," she said addressing Jack, "no *tiramisu*."

As they got up to leave, Jack turned to Emma. "Do you mind stopping by my house before I take you home? I thought you could help me figure out, you know, how to plan this party. I took your advice and invited Bob Monroe and his wife. You know Bob? He runs Monroe Realty."

Emma nodded. She'd heard of him. "Good call," she added, somewhat relieved. Bob was young. His presence, and that of his wife, would ease the awkwardness between their daughters.

Jack nodded. "I thought Cara and Mike would enjoy them. My point is I've never given a party before. I mean, all by myself. I'm gonna need some help."

At that moment, Emma noted Jack did look helpless. There was something endearing about it.

"Sure, I'll stop by," she said. "If you don't mind my poking around a bit – like for glasses, dishes, cutlery, placemats. I can lend you stuff if you need it."

Jack nodded. "I feel better already. And the place might be a little messy tonight. Celina doesn't come on Sunday."

"You mean, she comes every other day?" Emma asked.

Jack raised his hands palms up and stuck out his chin. "Whaddaya think? I lost my wife. That's bad enough. Now you think I should pick up after myself, too?"

Moments later, as they headed north in his car, Jack turned to her. "That reminds me of something," he said.

"What?" Emma replied.

"Housekeepers," Jack answered. "It reminds me of something Celina told me yesterday. About the Gomez murder. Curt's housekeeper, Teresita, told Celina that Curt has an alibi. Seems she saw him, dead asleep in his armchair, all plugged into this oxygen tank the night Gomez died. Teresita claims the old man was still there, in the same position, fast asleep, when she returned the next morning. She swears the guy never moved."

6

LATER SUNDAY NIGHT – JACK WHO?

Jack's house was located at the border of Blissburg's city limits off chic Silver Creek Road. Further to the northeast lay the famed Alexander Valley, home of some of California's most famous and prestigious wineries.

Jack pulled his Tesla into a long paved driveway up a small incline. Emma noted that the house, wherever it was, sat hidden behind a growth of old oak trees. The main house, when it came into view turned out to be a two story white gingerbread Victorian surrounded by a wide porch that wrapped the perimeter like the flounce around a rich lady's skirt. A few yards away, Emma also noted an iconic old barn that appeared to have been turned into a guesthouse – probably for Cara and her boys. Emma had to admit the place was gorgeous, even if it didn't look the least bit like Jack.

He glanced at Emma when they got out of the car.

"Cara picked the house out for me. It's beautiful – but way more than I need." He scratched his head and gave her a sheepish grin. "Not that, right now, Emma, I have any idea *what* it is I need."

Emma stopped for a moment to survey the flower-filled front garden and the meadow between the house and the barn, all shaded by enormous oak trees and surrounded by vineyards.

"It's..." Emma shook her head, "...breathtaking."

Jack motioned with a nod of his head. "Come inside. You can take a look at the yard before it gets dark."

Climbing the few stairs to the front door of the Victorian jewel, Emma noticed the porch was decorated with chic white metal furniture cushioned in blue and white cotton canvas. None of it looked used.

Inside, things were much the same. To the right of the entrance Emma glimpsed an immaculate pearl gray living room dominated by a cool white marble mantle over a hearth that clearly had not been lit in years. To the left, a library filled with books. All the furniture in the library was white against a background of Wedgewood blue walls. *At least that room looks lived in*, Emma noted. Books and papers cluttered the tables and floor. Six remotes of all shapes and sizes littered the coffee table along with a plain white mug of coffee half full. And there were shoes. Shoes everywhere. Running shoes, loafers, even a pair of gray crocks stuck half way out from under a vast white canvas covered couch. Emma blushed. She felt like a voyeur.

"Let me show you the yard," Jack said leading her past a formal dining room with a glass and chrome table that would easily sit fourteen.

An enormous white marble kitchen spanned the back of the house. Jack motioned to her to follow him through double French doors opening onto a beautiful patio. The moon was just coming up – a cold white, almost full moon.

"Here," Jack said pointing to a large stone table. It sat a few feet from a forty-foot swimming pool surrounded by lawn, fruit trees and evergreens. "I thought we could eat outside. I've never had a party here before, but I think this would do."

"Jack," Emma sighed. "This will do perfectly. In fact," she added, "I can't think of a more beautiful spot."

It was almost dark by then, and getting cold.

Jack motioned to Emma to return inside. "See, Emma, Frannie could have thrown a party here in her sleep. Sometimes I think Cara really picked this place out for her mother, not me. It's just too bad she isn't here to enjoy it, huh?"

Tears welled up in Emma's eyes. She wanted to give the man a hug – but she knew that wasn't what he was after. And for some reason, knowing that made her sad.

"You want something to drink while you look around the kitchen?" Jack asked once they were back inside. He had taken off his sports coat, and helped her off with her jacket. "To make sure you have everything you need."

"Just water," Emma answered. "Tap water is fine."

"Please look around," he called over his shoulder as he reached into a cupboard for a tumbler. "I probably have everything you need, but how would I know?"

He handed her the glass of water, and then opened cabinets one after another. They were all stocked with plain white china – probably enough for twelve. Cups, saucers, plates of all sizes, bowls, mugs and glasses. Lots and lots of glasses.

Emma inventoried it all in her head, thinking through each course, from hors d'oeuvres to dessert, coffee and after dinner drinks, imagining exactly what they would need.

"Have you got table linens?" she asked.

Jack opened a cabinet of short, wide drawers. They were full of linens. Emma pulled out a set of eight paisley placemats and napkins.

"Use these," she said. "And tell Celina about the party in advance. So she can make sure everything is clean," she added unnecessarily. The place mats, she noted, still had the price tags on.

Next Emma pulled open the deep, sliding drawers under the kitchen counter looking for serving dishes, pots and pans. Beside the professional Viking range, she found a cupboard filled with All-Clad cookware. Every size and shape imaginable. All brand new.

After spending about twenty minutes looking around, she turned to Jack.

"Honestly, I think you are all set," she announced. "In fact, I don't think I've ever seen a better equipped kitchen. Except maybe my daughter's," she added with a laugh.

"Great. Shall I take you home?" Jack asked.

EMMA HAD TURNED to put her glass down by the sink when her eyes rested on the only personal clutter to be found in the entire, virtually unused room. It was a random collage of photographs stuck to the oversized stainless steel SubZero fridge. She set down her glass and walked up close to the refrigerator to look at the photographs while Jack went to get her coat.

One picture, Emma guessed, was obviously of Frannie, the multi-talented and beloved saint/wife. From the photograph, which appeared to have been taken when Jack's wife was in her fifties, she looked to have been a pretty brunette. Perhaps a little overweight, Emma noted. In the photograph, taken somewhere at a beach, she wore black slacks and a black cotton T-shirt that covered her hips, much like the uniform the Walkie-Talkies wore.

There were also photographs of two boys at various ages. These must be the grandkids, Emma surmised, recognizing them from photos Jack had shown her on his cell phone. And there was a wedding photo of Cara with a stiff, serious young man who she assumed must be the radiologist, Mike Perkins.

One photograph in particular, however, caught Emma's eye. It was of a little boy – obviously one of the grandchildren, Mikey or Josh. Emma guessed that in the photograph he must have been around three. He was an exceptionally bright-eyed little imp, laughing, full face into the camera. What struck Emma most of all, however, was that he was the spitting image of Jack.

When Jack handed Emma her jacket, she pointed to the photograph.

"Which one of the grandsons is that, Jack?" she asked. "He looks exactly like you."

Jack folded his arms across his chest and shook his head. Then that wistful look crossed his face again that she had noticed before. It was few seconds before he spoke.

"That's Johnny," he finally said. "That's my son. He died six months after that picture was taken. Of leukemia."

Emma felt her heart free-fall into her stomach. "Oh my..." she said. "Oh, Jack..."

She couldn't continue, afraid her voice would crack. Even though she realized that the little boy in the photograph had probably been dead now for over thirty years.

"I'm so sorry," she finally said.

Jack shrugged in his fatalistic way. "Funny thing, Emma," he said. "He's been gone now over thirty years. And you know what? I never got over it. I don't think I've ever admitted that to anyone before. Not even to Fran."

Emma started to reach out to him, but he turned abruptly and walked to a far cabinet where he removed a bottle of Laphroaig and poured himself a couple of fingers of scotch. He downed it in one gulp.

"I guess you never do get over something like that," was all Emma could find to say.

Jack nodded. "It was the end of everything, Emma. The end of my marriage. Sometimes, I wonder if it was the end of my life. Of course, Fran and I went on living. We had to for Cara. But, you know what? Instead of binding us together, it pulled us apart. She kept wanting to talk about it. I couldn't. Instead I buried myself in my work. She devoted herself to Cara. And to her friends. The ones who *would* listen. Cara was the only one who came out stronger. The day Johnny died, we were all crying and she said, 'Daddy, you'll see. I'm going to be a doctor. This isn't going to happen to anybody else's little brother ever again. I promise.' Poor kid, I think she's still trying to keep that promise."

Jack took a deep breath, and smiled. "Too much information, right Emma? Let's go."

On the way back to her house, Jack didn't bring his son up again. Seated next to him in his car Emma wanted reach over and give Jack a hug. But she knew it was a cheap shot. Taking advantage of his pain. Sympathy wasn't what he wanted. So she chattered away about the party. How perfect his house was. All the fun it would be. The words sounded forced and hollow.

When they got to her door, Jack kissed her lightly on each cheek. "*Ciao, bella,*" he said, as if nothing had happened.

"*Ciao,*" she replied. "Thanks for dinner." As she opened her front door, she heard the wheels of his Tesla crunching on the pebbles of her drive. She couldn't bring herself to look back.

7

MONDAY MORNING – UNDER THE BUS

Emma awoke the next morning, pulled her fleece muumuu over her pajamas and went downstairs to make coffee. Bundled against the Blissburg morning chill, she sat on her back deck, dunking a Claud's fig and pistachio biscotto into the coffee she'd poured into her favorite Marimekko mug.

How little we understand each other, she thought. *Even our closest friends. After nine months, I hardly know Jack Russo. Did I think we were close simply because I told him everything that was on my mind? A running verbal tweet of my random thoughts, opinions and deepest fears?* The idea embarrassed her.

Then, again, she reminded herself, it was Jack who once said he could tell her "anything."

"You know Emma," he began after they'd spent an hour over dinner discussing *8½,* a movie they both adored, "I married my high school sweetheart. And, don't get me wrong. I was a lucky man. She was a wonderful woman. But she didn't get Fellini. In fact, and I hate to say it," he laughed, "I think the only books she read were store catalogues." He paused as though considering what he was about to say. Then he shrugged, "I have to admit, once in a while I used to wonder what it would have been like to meet someone…I mean, later in life. When I was older. Someone I connected to. You know, in the head."

"And that didn't happen?" Emma had asked. "I mean, you must have met a lot of very bright women over the years…"

"Sure I did," Jack readily replied. "But I didn't *let* anything happen. I couldn't. I couldn't do that, you know, to Cara, to Fran. I loved them." He squinted sideways at Emma. "And don't get me wrong. Forty years of marriage doesn't mean I was a saint. I was not always a good boy, Emma. Once in a while I played around. I just made sure it was never with anyone I was actually gonna fall for."

Emma had winced. She'd heard the excuse before. And by the sheepish look on Jack's face when he spoke, she knew he understood that she did not approve. Nonetheless, at the time she'd appreciated his honesty, the heads up.

"By the way," he'd added before she could reply, "I'm not trying to excuse my conduct. And you can bet I've never told *that* to anyone else before." He laughed again. "What is it with you, Emma? I feel like I can tell you anything."

Oh my, Emma now mused, remembering her response to his confession of infidelity. In that one statement, with the artistry of a con man, she now realized that he had sealed her confidence in him – in them. At that one moment, she'd felt sure she knew everything there was to know about Jack Russo.

Now she realized just how wrong she had been. She'd been falling in love with a man she hardly new. A man who kept secrets from her.

She stood up abruptly from her chair on the deck, gathered her mug and the plate of biscotti, and went inside. *Time to get on with my life*, she whispered to herself.

That day, getting on with her life meant showing up at her Monday morning meeting with Steve Zimmer at the free legal clinic to discuss the Gomez matter. As she dressed, Emma mulled over the approach she would take. On the one hand, she wasn't going to let her son-in-law, Piers, bully her into interfering with Steve's lawsuits and jeopardizing her job.

On the other hand, she was going to try to keep an open mind with regard to Steve's proposed litigation. Maybe her son-in-law was right about settling the workers' grievances. Maybe they *were* trumped up. As for the wrongful death action against Curt Randall? In her heart of hearts Emma simply was not convinced Curt Randall was a murderer.

Emma decided to try to dress professionally that day. So Steve, her boss, would take her seriously.

Fine for Steve to dress in shorts, wrinkled T-shirts and flip flops, she mused - the better to identify with his downtrodden clients. Steve was a member of the California Bar and a graduate of UC Berkeley's prestigious School of Law.

Emma, however, was a paralegal. In the late sixties, many years before, she'd chosen to *marry* a lawyer instead of going to law school herself. Her father, a well known civil rights advocate, agreed with her choice.

"It's a man's game, Emma," he'd said. "Like baseball. The rules are made by men, for men. There's no sense in a woman trying to play on that field. She can't complete – at least not a womanly woman," he added. "Women lawyers aren't...you know...feminine."

Not "feminine."

Emma smiled. Her father was not a highly successful trial lawyer for nothing. He knew exactly where to land the knockout punch. After hearing her father's comment, Emma fled law school like a stray escaping the pound.

"Mark'll go to law school," her father had explained.

Mark was Emma's younger brother. At the time he was fifteen. Interested solely in wildlife and sixteen year old blondes.

In fact, however, her father was right. Mark did go to law school.

And hated it. He practiced law for five years. Then married a girl from Costa Rica and moved there to start a successful eco tourist lodge in the rainforest around Braulio Carillo National Park. He and Emma Skyped a few times a year. She tried to visit every two or three. Mark, however, returned to California only twice. For each of their parents' funerals.

Now Emma perused her wardrobe. Shorts were out. Sweat pants as well. And forget about colors. Only highly successful female partners at big established firms wore colors. Three thousand dollar red wool Akris suits or cobalt blue Armanis with themed Hermes scarfs and three-inch heels. The rich fabrics and vibrant colors screamed success. The *I'm so good I don't have to dress like a man* kind of success.

Deep down, Emma admitted she admired these women. The ones who didn't take their fathers' advice. Or the younger ones, like Julie and Cara, whose fathers were actually proud of their daughters' success.

That day, for her *take me seriously* meeting with Steve, Emma picked gray cotton twill slacks and a black and white striped, short-sleeved cotton knit sweater. She thought of it as the *make sure no one notices me* look. Instead of her beat up loafers, she wore black Final Call Ferragamos – without one of the goofy pairs of socks her grandson gave her for Christmas. It was hard to be taken seriously wearing socks with purple and blue dinosaurs on them.

A few minutes later, driving north on 101 to the legal clinic, Emma rehearsed what she would say in her meeting with Steve. Over the years she'd developed a certain analytical style. Old friends like Mary loved it. Jack bore it patiently.

Emma described it to herself as stream of consciousness. But she knew it was more like a sea than a stream. Driven by its force of logic like a strong tide. Building to an irrefutable crashing conclusion.

Piers once described it as an oil slick, slowly surrounding you till you were trapped.

Whatever the style was, Emma knew Julie hated it. Steve did too, often interrupting her mid-first-sentence with questions like, "so what's your point?"

That morning in the car on her way to the meeting she tried to articulate her "point." As usual, it wasn't easy.

There were numerous points. Steve would only have patience for one. So somehow Emma had to combine all her points into one big irrefutable truth. She rehearsed her presentation in her head.

Point number one: Curt Randall probably did not kill Santiago Gomez.

Despite Emma's confidence that this was true, even she had to admit that three pieces of evidence suggested that Curt did kill Gomez. First, his own bloody knife found hidden in his garage. Second, his anger with Gomez over the lawsuit. Third, his threat at the Chatham Club. Means. Opportunity. Motive. It added up to a strong case.

On the other hand, Emma reminded herself, *people who actually know Curt Randall don't believe he's a killer.*

In fact, lots of evidence demonstrated that was true. First, he was eighty-eight years old and battling lung cancer. Everyone who'd seen him recently agreed that Curt Randall did not have the strength to kill a strong, thirty-something farm hand. Even if he took Gomez by surprise.

Second, Curt had an alibi. His housekeeper saw him asleep in front of the television wearing his oxygen mask when she left his house the night Gomez died. Teresita had sworn Curt was asleep in the very same chair in the very same position when she arrived at his house the next morning. He'd never moved.

Third, Emma noted, those who knew Curt well believed the old man simply didn't have the will to murder. He'd been depressed and broken for years. Ever since his son died in the Viet Nam War. The old man was mean, but not violent. According to them, Curt Randall wouldn't hurt a flea.

Point number two, Emma continued. *Plenty of people besides Curt Randall wanted Gomez dead.*

First on the list was Gomez's cousin, Jose Diaz. *The two recently came to blows,* Emma reminded herself. *When Gomez tried to force Diaz to join the class action. Piers even suggested that Gomez was blackmailing his cousin.*

There was also the husband of the woman Gomez seduced. *Surely,* Emma thought, *a jealous husband has a motive to kill.*

And what about Randall's nephew? *What if the Gomez lawsuit bankrupted the old man's estate? Did Curt's nephew and heir kill Gomez to stop the suit? And then frame his uncle for the murder?*

Finally, Emma wondered, *what about the prune fanatics? Would Silas Bugbee go so far as to frame Randall to stop the plum ranch sale?* The look in Bugbee's eye when he talked about the "slaughter" of the trees had certainly unnerved her. Emma asked herself, *is the plum sucker capable of more than tears?*

Point number three, Emma concluded. *Regardless of who killed Gomez, settling the farm workers' grievances out of court made sense.*

Did all out war ever achieve a better result than an agreement? she asked. *More importantly, if Randall didn't kill Santiago Gomez, then Steve's wrongful death action could destroy an innocent old man.*

Before Emma finished rehearsing, she'd pulled into the parking lot in front of the free clinic. Unfortunately her attempt to articulate one universal "point" had raised more questions than answers.

Emma turned off the engine knowing she wasn't prepared for her meeting. But it was 10:05. She had no more time to rehearse. She got out of the car, locked it and entered the building.

As she strode past the reception desk, Emma noted that Barbara had embarked on a new romance. This one was titled *Rid Hard and Put Away Wet.* Its cover featured what looked like a buxom bar maid galloping over dusty Western terrain chased by a fierce looking posse.

Barbara looked up, "Steve's been wondering where you were. Says you have a ten o'clock.

"Well, I'm here, aren't I?" Emma answered before opening the door to Steve's office.

Steve gave Emma a big smile when she walked in the door. "Boy, this Gomez thing is heating up fast," Steve said. "The sooner we lodge a wrongful death action, the better. Yolanda Gomez is completely on board. What kind of punishment is a life sentence for a sick, eighty-eight year old murderer? I want money for the widow and children."

Emma started to argue that Randall was innocent, but Steve cut her off.

"I know, Randall's out on bail," he said. "But if you recall, Emma, the standard of proof in a civil suit is the 'preponderance of the evidence,' not 'beyond a reasonable doubt' which is the standard for a crime. I agree there could be a 'reasonable doubt' as to whether Randall killed Gomez. But I'll bet my bottom dollar that Randall's bloody knife, his threat to kill Gomez, and Gomez's late night visit to Randall's Sonoma ranch provide more than a preponderance of evidence to win a civil action against him."

Steve paused to let that information sink in.

"So here's my question, Emma," he continued. "Who do you know at the Chatham Club who might have heard those threats Randall made against Gomez?"

Emma immediately thought of Jack.

Steve watched her hesitate for a few seconds before adding, "What about that guy you're seeing? Jack? Jack Russo? He's a member of the club. I hear he hangs out there all the time."

How, Emma wondered, *does Steve know about Jack?*

She shook her head, but Steve ignored it. "Here's the other thing I need you to do," he continued. "I know it's asking a lot, but I just don't have time or the money to do this any other way. Besides," he glanced up quickly to smile at her again, "you know how much I trust your work."

Without letting her reply he added, "I need you to drive down to

Coachella with me this week. You can check out other possible suspects - the jealous husband and that blackmail thing – while I get a handle on how much money we can reasonably get for the wrongful death of a seasonal worker. I've talked an old friend down there from Coopers into helping us crunch the numbers for free."

Emma's head was spinning. Using Jack as a witness to Randall's threats was totally out of the question. As for accompanying Steve all the way to Coachella – Piers would go ballistic if he heard about that.

"Steve," Emma finally answered. "Don't you think you should slow down a little. I mean no one knows for sure that Randall killed Gomez. As you just said, there are lots of other suspects – both in Coachella and right here. In fact…"

As Emma spoke, she felt the ocean of information in her head swell out of control. But she could not stop herself. "Just yesterday," she continued, "on the Sunday Stroll, Silas Bugbee – you know, from the permits department – hauled me aside to…" Emma realized she was exaggerating, but she had to get Steve to postpone filing that suit, "to rant about Curt Randall's sale to the Chinese. Lots of people are furious about it. Bugbee was so angry, why he almost threatened me. Thinking that somehow I could, just, you know," she sputtered, "stop it by talking to Piers."

Emma watched Steve's face shut down. Then he hugged his arms across his chest like he thought he might explode.

Suddenly Emma realized that nothing she'd said made sense. Even to her.

"He…he mentioned something about the due diligence, too," she added, grasping at straws. "Something about HoCo finding some kind of poison in one of Curt's water tanks. He said that might finally wake people up. Start some sort of protest over the sale of the…"

Steve opened his mouth to interrupt her. Emma knew exactly what he'd say. She stopped speaking abruptly.

"What's your point, Emma?"

The gathering wave of information in her head suddenly collapsed. She tried to press on even as her mind went blank.

"My point is, Steve, there are a lot of," she hesitated, "of plum fanatics, like Silas Bugbee or even Peppino at Buchanon Vineyards who would like to...to block the sale of the plum ranch. And I wouldn't put it past one of them to...to frame..."

"Whoa!" Steve cried, interrupting her. "Stop right there, Emma. Do you even know what you just said?"

Emma's face flushed red. She covered it with her hands. How *could* she know what she'd just said? She was too flustered to think straight.

"Please correct me if I'm wrong, Emma," Steve began in the voice of someone speaking to a small child. "I *think* your theory is that Curt Randall, who was found with the murder weapon hidden in his garage, *did not* kill Santiago Gomez because the prune fanatics or some eighty year old vintner killed him in order to block the sale of Luther Burbank's historic plum trees to the Chinese. Tell me that's not your point, Emma. Please! Because, again, correct me if I'm wrong, I don't see any connection between saving plum trees and the death of a seasonal farm worker whom Curt Randall publicly threatened to kill? So I repeat, Emma. What's your point?"

Of course, Emma thought, *Steve's right. There is no connection between the plum trees and Gomez's death. What was I thinking?* Emma took a deep breath and tried to stay calm.

"Actually, Steve," she finally said, backtracking to where her argument had fallen apart, "the part about the prune lovers was only one of my points. A very small point – a subsidiary point. More like an informational point, if you will. I should never have led with it."

Steve winced.

"So my point, if I can limit myself to just one," she continued, "is that I'm not sure Curt Randall murdered Santiago Gomez, and that if he didn't, this wrongful death action you are planning to file is a big mistake."

"O...K," Steve said guardedly, "*my* point is that I need to find out if any of these other theories about who killed Gomez hold water. I'm talking about the viable theories. Like the husband of the woman Gomez allegedly seduced. Or his cousin whom he allegedly blackmailed. And I hoped, maybe, just maybe because you work..."

"Volunteer."

"...here that *you* would help me find those answers, Emma."

Emma nodded. "My other point," she added, "is that on the chance Randall didn't kill Gomez, we should explore settling the worker grievances out of court. Getting the Gomez family what they are entitled to without putting a bitter old man in his grave."

Steve listened to Emma and rubbed his chin. Then he nodded his head up and down a few times very slowly.

"Of course," he finally said. "You and Piers have been talking. And he's convinced you to take the family's side – the side the family bread is buttered on, I mean. OK." He nodded his head again in a parody of patience. "I get that. But I have to say, Emma, I thought you were better than that. I thought you had a mind of your own."

"You see," he added with a drawn out sigh, "one thing your son-in-law forgot to explain to you, when he was convincing you to throw the farm workers' cause under the bus, is that a private settlement really doesn't do the farm workers' 'cause' any good. Thousands of laborers are being exploited by big agro business. Throwing a little money at a few desperate farm workers and their families is not going to change that. All that is going to change that is a lawsuit big enough to attract the attention of voters and legislators in Sacramento and Washington; so that this country changes its policies towards seasonal workers. But what do you care about that, Emma, so long as Piers can buy your daughter a brand new Porsche?"

"That's not fair, Steve," Emma cried stomping out of the room.

8

MONDAY AFTERNOON – PLUM SUCKERS'
REVENGE

Emma stormed out of the office to her car, furious with Steve for his cheap shot.

What did he know? Piers had bought Julie a BMW SUV for her birthday, not another Porsche. Though why a family of three needed a big car like that was more than Emma could fathom. Of course, she'd held her tongue about it at the birthday bash Piers had recently thrown at The French Laundry. Her friend, Jack Russo, wasn't even invited to that, she'd fumed. But the party probably cost more than the BMW. So why spoil it?

When Emma started her car, however, she inexplicably burst into tears. There was another reason she didn't go to law school, she chastised herself for the thousandth time. It wasn't her father. It was because she couldn't think straight!

She'd just turned on to the highway when her phone rang. She saw it was Jack and waited till the call went into messaging. Something about their conversation the night before still troubled her. Undermined her confidence in him – in them. How could she have thought he was her best friend in the world and not known about his son? Forget playing hockey in the Olympics. The forty years of marriage to a saint. How could you really know someone who neglected to tell you something as important as that?

A few seconds later the phone beeped and she heard Jack's voice on Blue Tooth.

"Hi. It's me," the voice said.

Emma grimaced. Jack's messages annoyed her. They always began with "It's me," like there was only one "me" in the world.

"I heard something today at the Santa Rosa Chamber of Commerce breakfast," he continued. "You probably know about it already, but you mentioned that Piers has been playing his cards close to the vest. Anyway, give me a call."

He paused for a second, like there was more, then added. "I also wanted to mention...I feel a little awkward. About last night. About not telling you about Johnny. I been thinkin' about it. Like, somehow, I betrayed him by not telling you. Like I forgot, or something. But I didn't forget, Emma. I think about him every day. Even now, I think how he'd be. What he'd be doin'. Thirty-four years old. It's just that..."

The phone beeped, ending the message.

Emma's stomach lurched. *Darn the stupid machine,* she thought. Then she reminded herself that it was she who had stubbornly refused to take the call. She briefly considered calling him back, but decided against it. Not the best subject to discuss in the car heading for what she knew was a dead zone between the clinic and her house. Still, he'd asked her to call....

When she got home to her landline, she dialed Jack's number. The call went straight into phone mail. "Hi. It's Jack. Leave a message."

She hung up. He'd see she'd called.

EMMA HAD PICKED up the Blissburg Herald off her front porch when she came in, along with the day's mail. After hanging her jacket on a peg in the front hall, she sat down in the kitchen to sort it. The Herald appeared again at the bottom of the pile. A front-page story immediately caught her eye. The headline read, "Burbank Society Plans Plum Protest."

Emma read the short article. It informed the citizens of Blissburg that the Luther Burbank Society was planning a protest in the Blissburg plaza that day at 2:00 p.m. Following the protest rally, the LBS, as it was known, would present a petition to county officials to block the sale of the historic Randall Ranch. Home of the oldest Santa Rosa plum trees in the world.

The petition further demanded that the county investigate rumors that high levels of arsenic had been found in water at the property, fueling speculation that wells on the property, and possibly the water table itself, were contaminated. At a minimum, the petition demanded that the county seek a temporary restraining order blocking the sale of the property until the safety of the water table had been secured. The article quoted Silas Bugbee, president of the LBS, saying: "This is not just about historic plum trees anymore. It is a matter of life and death. No less than the health of Blissburg's citizens and of its unborn children is at stake."

Emma rubbed her temples. She had no doubt that the purpose of Jack's call was to inform her of the rally. She glanced at her watch. It was already after 1:00 p.m. So much for testing the *malfatti* recipe that afternoon. She grabbed a tub of yogurt out of the refrigerator and gulped it down. Then she pulled her coat off the hook in the front hall and starting walking up Blissburg Avenue towards the plaza.

When she got there, the first thing she saw was at least ten news vans with satellite dishes parked around the square. Well over a hundred people had gathered at the bandstand on the far west end of the square. At least another hundred were jammed around the fountain. It was more people than Emma had seen gathered in one place in Blissburg. Way more than for the Tuesday 'locals night' summer Dixieland concert. She always thought of *that* as a big crowd.

She also noticed that many protestors that day carried placards. They read everything from "Save the Plums," to "We love you, Luther Burbank," to "Five Prunes a Day Keeps the Doctor Away," to "Seasonal Workers Deserve Shade and Water," to "Water Is Our Sacred Right."

Someone had even found an old broken Howdy Doody doll dressed in jeans and a red checked shirt that they'd hung from a small noose. A sign on the doll's back said "CR." Emma marveled that with the doll's reddish brown hair painted white, it looked remarkably like old Curt Randall.

Interestingly, too, unlike the Tuesday night Dixieland retirees dressed in North Face, Levis and running shoes and sitting in their Costco camping chairs sharing salami, cheese and bottles of wine, this crowd was young, aggressive, vocal, and from the look of it, not local. Far from wearing fleece vests and running shoes, many men in the crowd were barefoot, dressed in tie died T-shirts and badly torn jeans. A small contingent sitting around the fountain looked to Emma like they'd stepped off the pages of *Little Women*. Girls in long ruffled skirts and men in knee length, cotton frock coats, their long hair tied back in ponytails. In the center of this group, Emma spotted Silas Bugbee.

She was about to walk over to engage him in conversation when a middle aged man with dreadlocks and a bullhorn jumped on to the bandstand after conversing briefly with a man in a suit standing in the wings. The man with the bullhorn addressed the crowd. He was shirtless, even in the late afternoon chill, and wore thin sackcloth, string pants - obviously, Emma noted, without the benefit of underwear.

"OK, everyone," he cried into his megaphone like a cheerleader. "Who knows why we're here today?"

"Plums!" someone yelled out.

"Farm workers!"

"Prunes," someone else screamed.

Many in the crowd laughed and hooted.

Then a small group of gray hairs dressed in old baseball uniforms with the words "Prune Packers" written across the front, started up a chant, "Twist my arm, break my back. But please don't mess with my digestive tract." This resulted in lots more shouting and laughing.

When the chanting and hooting finally ran its course, the man with the bullhorn continued. "Let's face it, folks, we here in Blissburg love our plums and we love our prunes."

This statement was followed by more laughter.

"But," the man continued, "what we care about most, what keeps the plums growing that give us the prunes that make us regular folks," he made an italics sign with his fingers when he said "regular." "Is our water!" he concluded.

At the sound of the word "water," all the disparate groups gathered in the square finally coalesced in one voice. "Clean Water! Clean Water! Clean Water!" they chanted.

It took a full five minutes for the noise to die down.

Then the man put the bullhorn to his mouth again. "Look," he said – and Emma could not help but admire his folksy, crowd pleasing manner, "a lot of us here are angry about a lot of things today."

"Yeahhh," somebody in the crowd yelled.

"And we have a right to be mad!" the man with the bullhorn exclaimed.

Now the crowd went a little wild. A few of the prune packers started doing a war dance brandishing imaginary tomahawks in the air. A lot of people in the crowd yelled, "Yeahhhhh," again.

"But there is one thing that binds us all together today," the man continued. "That's clean water."

"Clean Water! Clean Water! Clean Water!" the crowd chanted in unison.

"We have a report," the man shouted over the crowd. Emma could tell he was eager to move the rally along, "The water on the Randall Ranch is polluted. The water tanks have significant levels of arsenic. And guess what? We don't even know how far it goes. The wells, the water table, the irrigation systems, your dinner table? Now there is also a rumor that Curt Randall and his lawyers..."

A number of people in the crowd booed.

"Are trying to hush up this report. Trying to push through a very lucrative deal to sell that land to Chinese investors. Well, let me tell you something, that deal may be good for Curt Randall and his lawyers..."

More booing.

"But it ain't good for YOU!" The man with the megaphone stretched out his arm and pointed his finger at the crowd like some latter day version of Uncle Sam rallying the troops during World War II.

"Let me ask you something," the man continued. "Do you think the Chinese give one dried prune about pollution?"

Everyone in the crowd yelled. "No!"

"That's right," the man with the megaphone yelled. "They don't care! And do you think the Chinese give a plum about your drinking water?"

Now everyone in the crowd yelled, "They don't care! They don't care! They don't care!"

"Well," the man on the bandstand screamed, "what're ya gonna do about it?"

Everyone in the crowd was still yelling, "They don't care," so the man answered his own question. "This is what you're gonna do. Sign the petition to stop the sale of Curt Randall's plum ranch until we find out what is really goin' on at that ranch."

That's when about twenty people started to circulate throughout the crowd with pens and petitions. Emma recognized a few, including the local yoga instructor and a girl who worked at the Plaza Bakery.

It looked like most of the people at the rally were signing up – except for an Hispanic looking young man whom Emma noticed trolling the plaza tearing down 'Save the Plums' signs as fast as the demonstrators could plant them.

Indeed, Emma was tempted to sign the petition herself. If there *was* pollution on the Randall property, Emma didn't see the sense in letting the Chinese deal with it. Maybe the man with the megaphone was right. Did the Chinese really care? Look at Beijing!

Walking back home after the rally, Emma saw Jack hailing her from the other side of Blissburg Avenue. He sprinted across the street to join her.

"Wow," he said. "This place is jumpin'. Never seen anything like that before – not here in Blissburg. Reminds me of Nam."

"Nam," Emma repeated, thinking to herself that the Viet Nam War was another part of their past she and Jack had never discussed. "So, what did you do during the war?" she asked.

"After I graduated from college, I got drafted!" he replied. "Whaddaya think I did? I wasn't goin' to medical school. Or the seminary," he snorted. "Though a lot of my Harvard classmates did get outta the draft that way."

"What about the Peace Corps?" Emma asked. Her ex husband, Andy Bodreau, had sat out the war building fish ponds in Togo. A stint that translated into one badly flooded apartment early in their marriage when his oversized fish tank cracked in an earthquake.

"You know, Emma," Jack answered. "It sounds crazy, now. But I was twenty-one (I skipped a grade in grammar school) and all my buddies back in Providence were signin' up. *Signin' up*. We're talkin' *volunteering* to fight that war. Well," he shook his head. "I sure wasn't doin' that. But I wasn't gonna run, either. When I got drafted, I went. They sent me north, behind enemy lines."

He stopped talking and chuckled. "When I got my orders, they showed me a map. And this guy put a little red pin on it and said, 'you're goin' here.' And I said, 'no I'm not. That pin is in Cambodia. This here is called the Viet Nam War, remember? Look at a *real* map. That ain't Viet Nam.' And he says, 'Don't give me none of your Harvard lip, boy. You are goin' exactly where I tell you to!'"

Jack shook his head at Emma. "Oh boy! That's when I knew I wasn't cut out for the army. I was sixty-three days in a foxhole somewhere in Cambodia. Long enough to make me hate every frickin' day of that war. I counted them off with a rock in the dirt. I didn't shower for fifty-eight days. I was scared stiff all sixty-three. Then my commanding officer taps me on the shoulder one day. 'Russo,' he says. 'You're goin' home. Tomorrow. On a helicopter with the stiffs from the MASH unit.' I said, 'What? You're messin' with me.' He said, 'Shut up and pack your stuff.'"

"Actually," Jack corrected himself, "he didn't say 'stuff,' he used another word. An hour later, I was sitting in a chopper with body bags piled five feet high like so many cords of wood, and a gunner next to me firing rounds out of the open door." Jack shuddered involuntarily. "Next thing I knew, I was eatin' a plate of pasta in my mother's living room – my dad was already dead. That night, I proposed to Fran. And resolved that no one was ever again tellin' me what to do."

"What happened?" Emma asked. "Why'd they let you go?"

Jack laughed. "The Olympics. The coach was Ma's cousin. They drafted me for the Olympic team. And the rest, as they say, is history."

They walked a little further without speaking, while Emma digested what Jack had just said. She never ceased to wonder at how different their past lives were – he serving in the army while she was protesting the war on the Berkeley campus.

It was Jack who broke the silence.

"So, Emma," he said. "Did you sign that petition?"

She glanced sideways at him. Wondering if he were serious.

"No," she scoffed. "How could I with Piers representing Curt Randall in the deal?" She shook her finger at Jack. "Not because I wasn't tempted to, mind you. Clean water's important. Do *you* want Chinese growers polluting our water table?"

Jack frowned. "Look, Emma. As far as I'm concerned, Curt Randall can sell his plum ranch to anyone he dang well pleases. And don't get me wrong. I'm not sayin' *I'd* sell Luther Burbank's trees to the Chinese. I honestly don't know what I'd do if I were in Curt's shoes. The point is, I'm not in his shoes. So I'm sure as heck not gonna judge him for what he decides to do. And you can bet your life I'll defend his right to do whatever he wants with his property."

With that, Jack touched his forehead with the fingers of his right hand mimicking a salute. "See you Wednesday? Lunch at Willie's?" he said. But before he turned to walk back towards the plaza, he seemed to think of something.

"By the way," he squinted at Emma with a puzzled look. "Did you happen to notice who was standing on the bandstand today talkin' to the guy with the bull horn and no underwear?"

Emma shook her head.

"Rob Peters," Jack replied with a shrug. "Whaddaya make of *that*?"

Emma cocked her head to one side. "Who?" The name didn't mean anything to her.

"You know," Jack answered. "Curt's nephew. The heir. The one who'll lose a fortune if all Curt's money goes to the dogs."

Emma raised her finger to her lips and looked over her shoulder. "Shhhh! Jack! You're not supposed to know about that."

"Yeah. OK." Jack waved her concern away with his hand. "But don't you think that's kind of...funny. I mean, I've watched Peters in action plenty of times on the Historic Preservation Commission. I've never seen him vote a project down. He's the one vote every developer in the county can count on. What I'm sayin' is, Rob Peters has no problem with the Chinese buying his uncle's ranch so long as the sale proceeds end up in his pocket one day. So," Jack shrugged, "what's goin' on? Why's he suddenly on the side of the plum suckers? I think I'll poke around a little and find that out."

Jack turned on his heel and headed in the direction of the plaza. Emma continued home. As she walked along Blissburg Avenue, it crossed Emma's mind that Jack had not finished explaining about his son. She wondered when they might have the opportunity to address *that* sad topic again.

9

TUESDAY – LOOK WHO'S COMING TO LUNCH

The morning after the clean water rally, Emma had an 11:30 a.m. appointment with Peppino Pieri to work on her cookbook *What a Pair!* She wondered what the old vintner would choose for her spaghetti *Trapanese,* one of Jack's favorite recipes. *Trapanese,* or Sicilian pesto sauce, originated in Trapani, Sicily where Jack's family traced its roots. Instead of the more traditional pine nuts, this Sicilian version of pesto consisted of crushed almonds along with crushed ripe cherry tomatoes.

The other two menus she would discuss with Peppino that morning were based on Bolognese specialties: turkey with white truffles and veal roast with rosemary and thyme. She guessed the Sicilian dish might require a bold red. The two Bolognese dishes perhaps a white. Emma looked forward to exchanging ideas with Peppino, her new wine mentor.

First, however, she had to prepare the turkey and the *Trapanese.* She'd cooked the veal roast the night before.

By 8:00 a.m. Emma had finished her coffee and dressed. Then, donning her new favorite Loretta Caponi apron with an artichoke embroidered on the front pocket, she began to cook. The apron was a Christmas present from Jack - though Emma guessed that this Rolls Royce of kitchen linens must have been suggested by Cara, his daughter. The height of good taste, but utterly impersonal. Emma supposed that was the way Cara wanted it.

She set to work whirling two cups of cherry tomatoes in the blender for the pesto. Then she added basil, crushed garlic, toasted almonds, salt, olive oil and red pepper flakes, and whirled it again. After refrigerating the sauce, she began working on the turkey breasts.

Filetti di tacchino con truffi was a trickier recipe than the pesto. It consisted of turkey breasts cooked in white wine with Parmesan cheese, prosciutto and white truffles. Emma's grandmother was celebrated for this dish that she served to her very best customers. More recently, Emma had sampled it in Bologna while researching her first cookbook.

Promptly at 11:00 a.m., when everything was ready, she packed up the tasting dishes and drove to the Buchanon's estate where Peppino would pair the food with the perfect Buchanon wines.

Emma's weekly meetings with Peppino took place in the family kitchen of Barry and Lexie Buchanon's home. Every time Emma went there, she remembered last year's fateful City Opera fundraiser. The night the world of Opera's favorite soprano, Natasha Vasiliev, was murdered. The night that first destroyed and later clinched Emma's reputation as a food writer. The night she first met Jack Russo, the man who'd saved her life.

Like many of Sonoma County's most important estates, the Buchanon Estate and Vineyard was located about a mile off Silver Creek Road. The well-maintained drive wound up the side of a hill covered in grape vines, secured by three coded security gates the last of which was a stunning sculpture in the shape of metal clouds. They parted when the right numbers were keyed into the security pad.

Emma's heart skipped a beat every time she opened that last gate. In fact, everything about the Buchanon Estate seemed magical to her. From the sculptures, to the ancient redwood groves that separated the main house from its complex of guest houses, to the man-made brook and cascade of swimming pools that descended the hill at the rear of the house.

Emma had no sooner parked her car in one of the guest parking spaces, when Lexie Buchanon, herself, appeared at the front door with Morena, the Buchanons' live-in helper. The Buchanons always seemed to anticipate the arrival of guests. Emma invariably found at least one of them standing on the front porch ready to greet her when she arrived at the home. She assumed that some sort of elaborate security system must alert them, in advance.

"We'll help you get your stuff in, Emma," Lexie called jogging down the steps with Morena in tow.

Lexie's petite, taut figure was complemented by her aubergine cashmere sweat pants and a thin ash rose silk tank top. *Lexie stays in perfect shape*, Emma thought, reminding herself that the thirty-something had been a personal trainer and masseuse before she married one of her customers, the seventy-something Barry Buchanon.

And despite rumors that Lexie was a gold digger and sometimes abusive boss, over the past year Emma had seen the young woman's good side. Her generosity to those less fortunate in the Blissburg community. Her unexpected acts of thoughtfulness exemplified by her lending a well-manicured hand carrying in the lunch that day. In fact, after Emma singlehandedly solved Natasha Vasiliev's murder clearing Lexie as a prime suspect, Lexie had adopted her as a kind of surrogate mother.

They'd become so close that over the past month Emma's weekly food pairing sessions with Peppino had evolved from informal tastings for two at the Buchanons' kitchen counter to sit down events - often for as many as eight or ten guests. The transformation began with Lexie and her yoga instructor - it seemed that Emma's weekly wine tasting coincided precisely with the end of Lexie's lesson – and had recently included Barry Buchanon himself and anyone else who happened to be visiting him at the vineyard that day.

Emma didn't really mind. She always tested a full six-serving recipe of each of the dishes she would pair that day for her cookbook. There was no reason the extra food should go to waste.

Emma loaded Lexie and Morena's arms with plastic containers of veal, turkey and pasta sauce. Then the three of them climbed the few steps to the front porch and entered the Buchanons' home.

"You got my text, didn't you?" Lexie asked as they entered the sleek stainless steel and marble kitchen. They deposited the containers next to an enormous wooden bowl Morena had filled with tomatoes and local salad greens.

Emma nodded. Something about the cookbook. A meeting after lunch to schedule a photo shoot.

"Yeah," she replied. "I texted you back. I'm free all afternoon."

"Yummy," Lexie opened the container of Trapanese and inhaled. "So..." she paused, looked thoughtful for a minute and said, "We'll pick out a date for the shoot and brainstorm locations. Barry's thinking some photos of the three of us toasting, like, one of your entrees over by the pool. And maybe Barry cutting grapes. And some shots of Barry and me sitting down with friends to dinner..."

"For the cookbook, right?" Emma cut in. "You mean photos of you and Barry eating the dishes paired with the wine we feature in the book? Like the Barefoot Contessa does." She thought a moment. "Isn't that a little premature. I mean, we haven't even..."

Lexie was shaking her head. "No. Not for the cookbook, Emma. These are publicity shots. You know, like for your web page, Facebook, that kind of thing."

"Facebook," Emma shook her head. "I'm not on Facebook. I don't *want to be* on Facebook. And I don't have a web page. It's just not, you know, me."

"What?" Lexie laughed. "You *have* to be on Facebook, Emma. You wrote a book. You're a brand, for gosh sakes. You mean you're not using social media for marketing? That's crazy!"

Brand indeed! The thought made Emma cringe.

"Thanks, Lexie," she replied. "But honestly, I'm doing just fine marketing without Facebook. I'm too old for social media. Too private. It's not my bag."

"Nonsense," Lexie answered. "Our PR consultant will *insist* you market *What a Pair!* on Facebook. And on a web page."

Lexie appeared to have forgotten that Buchanon Vineyard's PR person was none other than Julie Larkin, Emma's daughter. Julie had been pestering Emma to get on Facebook and Twitter all year.

Lexie's face assumed a determined look. "That's it. You are opening a Facebook account today. Right after lunch. No ifs, ands, or buts. Oh," she added, "BTW, did I mention who is coming today?"

"No." Emma replied, glad to change the subject from Facebook. "But no worries. I made plenty of food. Pesto for eight," she added filling a pot with water to boil the pasta. "Veal and turkey for six. With Morena's yummy salad, we're all set."

Lexie wrinkled her nose. "The guys from HoCo are coming. Again. Frankly, I've had it up to here with those sexist pigs." She made a sideways chop with her hand across her neck. "All they talk about is business and women's big," she pointed to her chest. "Excepting, of course, that hunk who looks like a movie star. I'm not fed up with him." She made a large "o" with her mouth and licked her lips before resuming her righteous feminist rant. "But what does Barry care about the objectification of women? You know Barry. Give him a whiff of money and he's stoked. And, believe me, from what I can see, the Chinese reek of money. We're talkin' megabucks. Even more than Barry." She added, "Did I tell you? Summer bailed."

Summer, Emma knew, was Lexie's yoga instructor and a local political activist. Emma guessed she provided Lexie with her feminist sound bites. Emma remembered seeing Summer in the plaza passing out "Save the Plums" petitions after the rally the day before. No surprise she was boycotting the Chinese.

"And you know Peppino," Lexie continued. "He refuses to be in the same room with anyone from HoCo. Barry's so mad about how Peppino's treating them, he's ready to fire the dear old man." She rolled her eyes. "As if that's gonna happen. Barry knows as much about making wine as I do about..."

Lexie's voice trailed off as she searched for a way to finish the sentence.

"So that'll be," Emma cut in, performing a quick tally in her head, "seven of us." She glanced at the food on the counter. "We have more than enough." Then she added. "If we eat at 12:30, Peppino and I will have plenty of time to decide on the wines."

Which they did. But when she and Peppino sampled the *Trapanese* in the breakfast room a few minutes later, to Emma's dismay the old man merely shrugged. Clearly the Sicilian pesto was not the Tuscan winemaker's thing.

"I prefer my pesto with pine nuts," he dismissed it. "As for a wine," he threw his hands up in a gesture that said, *Who cares? Anything will do for this slop.* Then quickly selected Buchanon's *Piccina* made with mostly *Sangiovese* – Blood of Jove - grapes."

The veal and turkey, however, elicited groans of pleasure from the old man.

To Emma's surprise, Peppino selected '*Squisito,* a Buchanon *Pinot Noir* for the turkey. And Buchanon's *Philosophe,* a Dry Creek Valley *Grenache, Syrah, Mourvedre* blend, for the veal. Half an hour later, Peppino took his leave.

"Em-ma," he said. "You will have to excuse me. I'm sure Signora Alessandra has told you that I will not be joining you for lunch today. *I Visigotti ,*" he shrugged.

Emma nodded. "You mean the barbarians...Seriously, Peppino, the Chinese are hardly that."

"*Si, si*," Peppino sighed. "I know. They are an advanced civilization that predates the Etruscan rustics and the Roman thugs. But wine! *Dio mio*," he cried. "At least leave the wine to us."

Emma laughed. "Think of it as payback, Peppino. After all, didn't Marco Polo steal their noodles?"

But Emma could tell the old man was not amused by her joke. Wine, to Peppino Pieri, was quite simply not a laughing matter. He turned to leave, his face not even brightening with a smile.

WHEN EMMA RETURNED to the kitchen to add the pasta to the pot, she found it already cooked. Barry, it seemed, had engaged a catering service to help serve lunch by the pool that day. No less than three uniformed wait staff in the kitchen drained pasta, heated the turkey breasts and sorted starched Provencal linens, white *faience* plates and crystal. Soon a second catering truck appeared in the service driveway with goodies: lunch rolls; celery root *remoulade*; potato salad; watermelon salad with hot house tomatoes, basil and feta cheese; and a delectable array of tarts from the Plaza Bakery downtown.

The simple "tasting lunch" had been transformed into a feast, laid out on hand painted French platters. Emma's veal dish was sliced and served cold. The truffled turkey breasts laid out warmed to perfection.

Just before the preparations were complete, Lexie showed up in a skimpy Nan Lepore sundress and four-inch sling back heels. Minutes later, Barry appeared with his four Chinese guests. They were exactly the same four businessmen Emma and Jack had observed at dinner two nights before.

Emma glanced at her reflection in the French door windows and wished, for the first time in months, that she'd selected something dressier than blue jeans and a baggy T-shirt to wear.

Barry immediately motioned everyone to the buffet table where the wait staff served lunch. Against Lexie's urging, Emma held back, motioning the foreign contingent to fill their plates first while she observed them.

The four Chinese men, Emma noted, were exceptionally well dressed that day. The tallest of them – Emma guessed he was at least 6' 4" – was gorgeous. Surely, Emma noted, this was the hunk Lexie had "objectified" a few minutes before.

He was dressed in a silk knit polo shirt with stripes in shades of blue, orange and smoky gray. His starched cotton khakis fit his trim figure like a glove. His dark brown crocodile belt and matching crocodile loafers made Emma wish they weren't an endangered species.

Two of the other three men wore handkerchief thin, expertly tailored linen shirts – one dark French blue, one gray. The fourth man, who was stocky and much shorter than the other three, wore a beige striped sear sucker suit with a tan linen shirt and a blue and green silk printed tie. *Barbarians, ha!!!* Emma laughed. These men were the epitome of good taste by anyone's standard. Next to them, dressed in baggy bottomed chinos cinched under a swelling midriff, Barry Buchanon looked like Bilbo Baggins.

When all were seated, Barry raised a glass of his own Lexie Reserve to the company. Emma found the toast confusing. Barry characterized HoCo's imminent entry into the California wine industry as a milestone in Chinese-American relations. Something akin to Richard Nixon's 1972 visit to China.

After Barry had finished, it was Lexie's turn to propose a toast. Casting a bold glance at the tall, good-looking man seated across the table, Lexie lifted her glass and to Emma's surprise toasted "Alexander Wang."

Barry and his guests exchanged confused glances before Barry added, "Emma, you must meet our distinguished friends."

The men, whose formal manners rivaled her friend Jack Russo's, rose at once to greet her.

"Cheng Bo," Barry introduced the really good-looking man seated next to him. "Huang Ho," he continued indicating the shorter man in the sear sucker suit. "Chen Fung and Jing Lew," he added indicating the two men in the linen shirts.

When they had finished shaking hands, the men resumed their seats and, while eating, talked among themselves. No one addressed Emma or Lexie. It was as though they weren't there.

Emma observed Lexie try to break into the conversation twice, but everyone ignored her.

That's when things got messy. Lexie downed her first two glasses of wine, each in one gulp. Then Emma watched the young woman's expression harden from a pout into a sulk. She downed a third glass of wine between birdlike bites of watermelon salad. Poured herself a fourth. Threw that back. Blinked. Cracked her neck right and left. Then composed her face into what Emma knew from past experience was a dangerous, devil may care smirk.

"Enough business talk," she announced in a loud voice, licking her lips at the tall man seated across the table. "I hear Chengboy over there is a Clint Eastwood fan."

"Bo," the man replied. Then he added with a laugh, as though trying to placate the hostess by playing along, "Go ahead, make my day."

Emma held her breath. Did he mean to egg Lexie on, she wondered, or was it simply the only Clint Eastwood line the man knew?

"I just might do that, Chengboy," Lexie replied getting up from the table and stalking its perimeter in her four-inch heels like a tigress circling for a kill.

"Bo not boy," Barry cut in, casting a nervous glance at his wife. "His first name's Bo. It's backwards in China. Remember?"

Emma's eyes followed Lexie too, wondering if she were about to come off the spool. It had happened before.

But Bo appeared to enjoy the repartee. He laughed, "Or backwards in the US, depending on how you look at it. Right, Ho?"

Ho had pushed his chair back from the table as Lexie circled. Now he patted his knee – obviously inviting her to sit down on it. Emma got the feeling that the president and namesake of HoCo didn't want to be left out of any action with the hostess.

"His friends call him Bobo," Ho explained with a giggle.

Lexie abruptly stopped stalking and froze beside Ho's chair.

"OK, Blondie?" Ho crooked his little finger at Lexie. Emma noticed that his pinky nail was alarmingly long.

All four of the Chinese men burst out laughing. But apparently Lexie was too young to recognize the allusion to Clint Eastwood's 1960s character in *The Good, the Bad and the Ugly*. Emma could almost see the hairs on Lexie's neck stand up.

"How dare you call me Blondie, Huang?" she snapped.

"Ho," he replied. "Ho. Ho to you."

"Not funny, Huang!" Lexie yelled. Then she stormed into the kitchen.

Barry started to get up from his seat, but seemed to think better of leaving and sat back down. "Women in America," he shook his head. Then addressing the men at the table he added, "Ever hear of *Women's' Lib* in China?

"Woo...man leeb," Mr. Huang repeated, giving each syllable equal weight. Of the four men, Emma had noted that he was the least proficient in English. "*Ni...ne to Fi...ve.* Dor...ree Pah...ton. Whhwaaa. Beeega merr-on," he motioned with his hands on his chest in the shape of two melons.

Now, as the only woman left at the table, it was Emma's turn to feel uncomfortable. At her old San Francisco law firm, the Anti Harassment Committee had scheduled a full day training session addressing just this sort of bad behavior. But as far as Emma recalled, the best response to such prohibited language that anyone came up with at the training session was a loud, "Ewwwww." And if that didn't work, a report to the Risk Management Committee.

Somehow, "Ewwww," didn't sound right under the circumstances. Besides, who knew what "Ewww" might mean in Chinese? Uncomfortable as it was, Emma decided to keep her mouth shut and see what happened next.

Barry glanced at her, but registering no response on her face, joined in the laughter that quickly erupted round the table. Causing Emma to wonder whether this was what all high level international food industry lunches were like.

At that moment Bobo's phone must have vibrated. He pulled it out of his pocket and then excused himself to take the call. Ho continued to communicate, with the help of hand gestures, about his favorite American actresses. Emma decided to duck back into the kitchen to see where Lexie went.

Lexie wasn't in the kitchen, so Emma made her way towards the guest bathroom to sort things out in private.

As she walked past the breakfast room, however, she happened to glance out the double French doors into the side yard next to the house. There, she noticed a long, black limo pulled into the guest parking area to the left of the herb garden. Bobo stood near it conversing with another man. This fellow, however, wasn't Asian, and he wasn't dressed in a hand made suit. He was wearing overalls and a bandana tied around his forehead. Emma couldn't see his face clearly, but she thought he was the man she'd seen tearing down posters at the rally the day before.

Emma combed the ground floor of the Buchanon's house still looking for Lexie. When she returned to the lunch table a few minutes later, their hostess was still missing. Bobo was back in his chair. Mr. Huang spoke intently to Barry repeating a word that sounded like "prumran." It took Emma a few seconds to get the hang of it. But when she finally figured out that "prumran" meant "plum ranch" and "cut ran *daw*" meant Curt Randall, the rest of the monologue more or less fell into place.

Huang Ho, Emma realized, was explaining to Barry that a judge in Santa Rosa had issued a temporary restraining order – Huang called it a T WAR RO - stopping the sale of the Randall property. Mr. Huang wanted to know how such a thing was possible in America. Punctuated by much snide laughter (as opposed to the giggles that accompanied the melon talk) the gist of the speech appeared to be that Huang and his lawyers thought the T WAR RO was a joke.

Mr. Huang ended his monologue with a derisive "Ha!" He folded his arms belligerently across his chest. Then he waited for Barry to reply.

That's when Barry glanced across the table at Emma, his eyebrows raised as if to say *what on earth was that all about*?

"He's talking about the plum ranch sale," Emma replied. "Apparently, after that rally yesterday, a judge in Santa Rosa issued a TRO – temporarily stopping the sale of the ranch until more testing can be done. You know," she added, "to see how far down the pollution goes."

"You understood that?" Barry mouthed, looking impressed.

Emma nodded. She hadn't ridden the 55 Sacramento bus to work through San Francisco's Chinatown all those years for nothing. "He says he's not worried though. He thinks the judge's order is a joke."

"Ask Ho how long he thinks it's going to take for the sale to go through," Barry replied to Emma. "Now, with the murder investigation. Won't the delay cost HoCo a bundle?"

Emma didn't need to rephrase Barry's question for Ho. Bobo replied instead in perfect English.

"It won't take long," he brushed any concerns aside with a graceful wave of his manicured hand. "We have good lawyers. But as far as poor old Curt Randall's murder charge goes, I'm afraid the old man did us a favor when he murdered that poor young Mexican."

"How so?" Barry asked.

"He's desperate to sell the ranch now," Bobo laughed. "He needs cash to cover his legal expenses. I'm sorry to say that, far from costing HoCo a bundle, this most unfortunate crime may have provided us with an opportunity to purchase the property at an even better price."

Of course, Emma noted, Mr. Cheng didn't sound sorry at all. *Poor Piers*, she thought to herself. *He must be going nuts.*

10

TUESDAY AFTERNOON – GHOST WRITER

As soon as Emma could leave the table, she ducked back into the kitchen and packed up her empty food containers. Morena had already washed them, so Emma hoped to make a quick get away and avoid dealing with Facebook.

She was just leaving the kitchen via the breakfast room when Lexie caught her. She'd changed into tight stretch jeans and a blue and white T that looked like someone had slashed it strategically with a knife.

"Where do *you* think *you're* going, *Ms.* Corsi?" she greeted her, still sounding a little tipsy. "*You* have a Facebook lesson today."

Emma wracked her brain for a reason to beg off, but she realized she'd already told Lexie she was free all afternoon. Finally, she simply decided to tell the truth.

"Lexie," she sighed. "I don't know how else to say this. I'm not going on Facebook. In fact, I hate Facebook. The whole idea of it. Of branding yourself. Of turning your life into some kind of blog. Of having to read other people's blogs about themselves. Who needs it?"

Emma watched Lexie's eyes bug out. "You hate Facebook?" she

began. From the tone of Lexie's voice Emma wondered if, by mistake, she'd said she hated Bambi, or the Dalai Lama, or ET.

"Well," Emma snorted, "hate is a strong word but…" she didn't finish the sentence. The truth was she *did* hate Facebook. "But," she repeated trying to recoup, "well, it's not like I hate Mark Zuckerberg. I mean, I loved that movie about him, *Social Network*. Honestly, I think he does a lot of good things. I just hate his product, if you know what I mean. Like I admire JLo, too, but I wouldn't wear her clothes."

Lexie had cocked her head to one side. She blinked a couple of times.

"Emma," she finally said putting her hands on her hips. "Facebook isn't something you love or hate. It's something you *use*."

For a second, Emma wondered whether, in those few words, Lexie had just defined her own thirty-something generation.

"But I *do* hate it, Lexie," Emma nodded slowly. "And that makes it impossible for me to use it."

Lexie sucked her breath in and squinted at Emma, as though she'd discovered a defect in a favorite old blouse and wondered if she could continue to wear it. Then she blew the breath out and swatted her hand in the air.

"Nonsense, Emma. You just don't *understand* Facebook. Let me explain it to you. Then, when you know what it is, well…you won't love it or hate it. You'll just *use* it. OK?"

Emma tried to smile. She realized there was no way she could refuse Lexie's offer to help her *understand* Facebook. Not without looking like the Pope challenging Galileo's theory that the earth revolved around the sun.

"You're right, Lexie," she finally said. "I *don't* understand Facebook. Why don't we give it a try?"

Emma followed Lexie out the French doors in the breakfast room across the side flower garden to a little bungalow that Emma soon realized was Lexie Buchanon's private office. For a young woman whom Emma had dismissed as an airhead, the office was surprisingly well organized. Far better organized, Emma noted, than Emma's own little office off her farmhouse kitchen.

The twelve by fifteen foot room was painted in sponged Tuscan yellow and lined with closed cherry cupboards. Each was labeled: shopping, Russian Arts Archive (an organization Lexie chaired), household, art, Kathy (Lexie's personal assistant), yoga, Poops (Lexie's Sydney Silky terrier), vacation - just to name a few that caught Emma's eye. Two original Hockney landscapes hung on the walls. A cherry desktop with leather inserts was immaculate, except for a 27" iMac and one bundle of mail placed squarely in front of it.

Emma gazed around the pristine space. She'd worked with lawyers whose offices looked like that. And wondered if their owners' minds were tidy or empty. She had never figured that out.

Lexie had pulled a seat up for Emma next to her ergonomic Herman Miller Embody chair, pushed aside the mail and turned on her iMac. Watching Lexie's fingers move across her keyboard at lightning speed, Emma soon realized she was not dealing with an amateur. Lexie was up and running in seconds – and logged on to her Facebook page.

Because Emma did not belong to Facebook, she had never seen a Facebook page before. Lexie's consisted of an adorable photograph of Lexie smiling holding what appeared to be a tranquilized tiger cub. Behind it was another photo of an expanse of rolling vineyards probably taken somewhere on the Buchanon Estate, but it could have been France just as well. Under that, to Emma's dismay, was an array of boxes, tags, images, superscripts and subscripts that was more confusing than CNN.

Lexie scrolled down the page while images erupted on the screen and then quickly disappeared from view. Photos of Lexie with a Tibetan monk, buildings being blown up in Gaza, a luscious apple pie followed by dogs being tortured, Lexie at a Jay Z concert along with girls sold into slavery in Nigeria, someone's main course at a fancy Paris restaurant, a quotation from Ghandi, a young woman giving birth, a man holding an assault weapon, a family vacation at the seashore.

Above the photographs, vertical and horizontal stripes announced "photos of Lexie," "Lexie's album," "chat with Lexie," "about Lexie," "Lexie's timeline," "Lexie's friends." Everywhere little thumbs pointed up or down next to the word "Like" in what looked like a digital format of *Survivor.*

What happens if nobody likes you? Emma wondered. *Do you get voted off the Internet?*

"See," Lexie said, expertly clicking on her mouse, opening and closing menus. "These are my friends."

To Emma's amazement, there were 3869 of them. "Wow!" she exclaimed, wondering if she could count her friends on more than one hand, "You have a lot of friends. How do you keep up with them?"

"Easy!" Lexie shrugged. "Watch."

In a block labeled "messages," Lexie instantly typed in, "I'm sitting here at the vineyard with my best friend and world famous cookbook author Emma Corsi."

In a matter of seconds, Lexie had posted a selfie of her and Emma on her Facebook page. Lexie looked great. Emma looked dazed.

The message ended with, "Check out Emma's cookbook, *Dining with the Stars.* You'll love her yummy spaghetti sauce recipe. Sergio uses it at his restaurant, but guess what? You can save $24 by making it at home. (Sorry, Sergio. You may lose a few customers.) I can't wait for her new book, *What a Pair!* written with yours truly. I'll keep you posted..."

"See," Lexie said, not taking her eyes off the screen. "That's called marketing. That's how it's done. Now let's look at 'all about Lexie.' That tells my 'friends' everything I want them to know about me. It's like...like my product description."

Lexie scrolled down the "all about Lexie" blurb. Much to Emma's surprise, she learned that Lexie was a freelance filmmaker and producer specializing in Buddhism and animal rights. She lived in Blissburg, Paris, and Australia, had traveled extensively in Southeast Asia, loved Klezmer music and the Brandenburg Concertos, and Sydney Silkies. Her favorite movie was *A League of Their Own,* and her favorite book was Nelson Mandela's autobiography."

"Really?" Emma asked. "You liked the Mandela autobiography. That's a long book."

Lexie laughed. "It just says 'my favorite book.' It doesn't say I read it."

"I didn't know you were a filmmaker, as well," Emma added.

"Yeah," Lexie sighed still looking at the screen. "I have my own little company, Poops Productions. Barry bought it for me as a wedding present. So I'd have something to do. I make little videos." She laughed, "You know. Mostly of us."

"O...K," Emma replied. "*You* produce little videos of you and Barry. What's *my* product?"

Lexie snorted. She still hadn't taken her eyes off the screen. "You!" she scoffed. "*You* are the product. That's what's so cool. Now, thanks to Facebook, *everybody* has a product. Themselves. And thanks to Facebook, everybody gets to brand and market that product any old way they choose. It's like...like you're your own little corporation marketing your product. You. And you get to do what's good for business. *You.* Cause *you are* the business. After all, corporations are people, aren't they? Didn't the Supreme Court just decide that? Like it was in the papers, right? So corporations are people and people are corporations and everybody gets to do what's best for their own little selves. Cool, huh? I mean it's so capitalist. So American!"

Emma's head was spinning. She felt like she had just taken an advanced course in history, sociology, poli sci, economics, marketing, psychology and civics all rolled into one. And learned that she,

Emma Corsi, was a new American product to be branded and marketed like a pair of shoes. How had she missed that?

"OK." Lexie said the word with the finality of something settled, beyond discussion. "You understand, right? So now I'm gonna sign you up on Facebook."

Before Emma could protest, Lexie had opened another screen titled "Welcome to Facebook: Create an Account." Then Lexie shot a series of questions at Emma. Name, age, gender, address, date of birth, what music she liked, what movies, what books. She even asked for the names of Emma's family members and friends. Screens flashed, boxes appeared and disappeared. Still Lexie's eyes never left the screen. Five minutes later she sat back, cracked her neck a couple times, finally took her eyes off the screen to grin at Emma, and said, "You're all set. What do you think?"

To Emma's horror, staring back at her from the screen was a little box containing her photograph. Her face wore a scowl. She looked old and bitter. Under it, Lexie had pasted a photo she'd found on the Internet of Emma seated behind the auction table at the Opera in the Vineyard fundraiser from the year before. She was holding up a copy of her cookbook, *Dining with the Stars*. Under that was a caption. It read, "I love food and opera."

The "about Emma" category that Lexie opened next said Emma lived in an historic farmhouse in Blissburg, CA, wrote cookbooks, loved to cook, and volunteered for the Blissburg Free Legal Services Clinic where she found meaning in her life helping poor people get what was fair. Her favorite movie was *81/2*. Her favorite book was *One Hundred Years of Solitude*. She listened to the Beatles and Coldplay. And *loved* cats.

"I don't love cats, Lexie. I never said that. I'm allergic to them," Emma exclaimed. "And I never listen to Coldplay."

Lexie shrugged. "You gotta love dogs or cats, Emma. It makes you more...human. Or you could put something exotic, like snakes. And stick with Coldplay. The Beatles make you sound too...."

"Dogs," Emma snapped. "Put dogs. Labs. And, yes. I'll stick with Coldplay. Gwyneth Paltrow. Right? Just remind me of one of their songs."

"Don't panic," Lexie shrugged.

"I'm not panicking," Emma bristled. "Just tell me the name of one of their songs!"

"That *is* the name of one of their songs," Lexie laughed. "But we need to fix the photograph."

With a click of the mouse, Lexie erased the photo she had taken and mounted in the box, and added the photo from the fundraiser instead.

"You're good to go," she said exiting Emma's new Facebook page.

Before turning off her computer, Lexie paused for a second to review her own Facebook page one more time. Emma couldn't help noticing that there were already 342 "likes" under Lexie's posting about *Dining with the Stars*!

A few minutes later, Emma and Lexie had picked a date for the photo shoot. Then Emma drove home.

When Emma turned into her driveway, Julie was just locking up her office.

Julie's office was located in a Victorian cottage on Blissburg Avenue in front of the old renovated farmhouse where Emma now lived. Emma got out of her car. Then she and her daughter exchanged a hug under the old magnolia tree in the yard separating the two buildings.

"I'm off to pick up Harry." Julie glanced at her mother sideways. "Where've *you* been?"

"I've been meeting with Peppino and Lexie about the cookbook," Emma replied, bracing herself for some well-meant criticism.

Ever since Emma moved to Blissburg, Julie had complained that her mother needed to dress "professionally" if she wanted to be taken seriously.

"You mean the wine-pairing sessions?" Julie asked. "I thought you complained that those had turned into business lunches. With Barry and his rich friends." Julie looked her mother up and down and winced. "You went dressed like that?"

Of course Emma felt she had to defend herself. "Look," she began. "I'm the cook, right? I don't dress up. I get dirty."

"I thought Morena served lunch," Julie answered. She was never one to back off. "So who was there?"

All of a sudden, Emma felt trapped. She raised her eyebrows as though about to impart a secret. "I was just going to tell you. The HoCo people were there. And the truth is," she added a bit self right-eously, "I heard a lot more things dressed like this."

Julie looked skeptical.

"No one takes me seriously," Emma explained her newly invented theory. "They ignore me. Like I'm not there. So they talk. I'm sure the HoCo people had no idea that I was Piers' mother-in-law."

Julie glanced at her watch and then motioned with her head towards Emma's front door. "I think we need to go inside and discuss this, Mom."

Julie followed Emma up the stairs to the wrap-around front porch of the old 1850s farmhouse. Emma was proud of the fact that she lived in one of the oldest buildings in Blissburg. They entered the front hall, passing by the comfortable living room with its over-stuffed sofa and chairs, past the dining room with the original wooden wainscoting that Emma loved, and into the new cook's kitchen with its butcher block counters and professional Viking stove. They sat down on two stools at the counter, looking out over the huge garden where Emma's grandson, Harry, loved to play.

"Want some tea?" Emma asked.

Julie shook her head, all business. "I want to know what you heard from HoCo at lunch today."

Apparently Piers had told Julie all the details about the HoCo deal. When Emma described Huang Ho's reaction to the TRO, the order temporarily blocking the plum ranch sale, Julie shot back angrily.

"He thought it was funny?" she asked. "Seriously? He laughed?"

"He called it a joke. 'No big deal.' At least, I think that's what he said," Emma shrugged. "His accent is really thick, but I understood it a lot better than Barry did. Then he laughed about it and Cheng Bo, Huang Ho's right hand man, said their lawyers would take care of it - and that Curt had actually done them a favor by murdering Gomez."

"What?" Julie cried. "Mom, Curt Randall did not kill Gomez. He and Piers are spending a bundle trying to prove that. Without any help from the police, I might add. They are so convinced they have the killer, they don't even look at anyone else. Unfortunately Curt's made his share of enemies around here, acting the bitter recluse all these years. And from all accounts, he hasn't treated his workers well. Like he has a vendetta against Mexicans."

"Who told you that?" Emma asked.

"Everyone Piers has talked to about the murder," Julie sighed. "Mom, the police aren't the only ones convinced Curt did it. But you know Piers, once he believes in someone. He has doctors willing to testify that the old man simply didn't have the strength to follow Gomez up that trail and plunge a knife in his back." She shook her head. "I just hope he gets some proof – and fast. Otherwise Curt Randall is about to lose not only everything he owns, but possibly his life as well. He wouldn't last a week in jail."

Emma thought twice about telling Julie the rest of what Cheng Bo said. Finally, she decided she had to.

"Cheng Bo told Barry something else," she continued. "Not about the criminal investigation. It's about the plum ranch sale. He said that the reason Curt did them a favor was that, due to his skyrocketing defense costs, Curt Randall has now lowered the price of the ranch. Cheng Bo implied they'll make out like bandits."

Julie cringed. "That's exactly what Piers told me last night. The old man wants to unload the property as fast as he can. Says the place has been cursed ever since his son died. Piers is trying to talk him out of it. Hoping he can clear Curt's name. Fast enough to head off a fire sale as soon as the court lifts the TRO. Which may be soon. HoCo's lawyers are preparing a report detailing the expensive remediation they'll do to ensure there's no danger to the water table."

"Sounds like fancy legal footwork to me," Emma mused.

"Who knows?" Julie shrugged. "HoCo has enough money to paint the sky red if they need to."

Julie glanced at her watch again. Emma noticed she looked tired. *Too much stress*, Emma mused.

"Mom," Julie said. Even her voice sounded tired. "I have a few extra minutes. Maybe I'll take you up on that cup of tea."

Emma nodded. "Caff or no caff?" she asked putting the teakettle on to boil and pulling a flowered mug off the shelf over the stove.

"No caff," Julie laughed, "though I sure feel like I could use it." She paused. "So did you and the Buchanons make any headway on that new cookbook? I thought you were hoping to publish in time for Christmas."

Emma laughed. Her computer was sitting next to them on the kitchen counter. She often worked there in the afternoon while she was testing her recipes.

"I don't think I'd call it headway," Emma replied, booting up her computer. "I was going to check this out with you. I'm not at all pleased – and, by the way, I find it a complete invasion of my privacy."

Julie watched her mother struggle to open a site. Predictably, the young woman quickly grew impatient.

"Mom, I don't have all day," she said elbowing Emma aside.

Then she recognized the screen. "Facebook? Are you trying to log onto Facebook? I thought you hated Facebook. What's your ID?"

Emma rubbed her temples. She was starting to get a headache. "I don't know," she clicked on her cell. "I thought I wrote it down here..."

"On your cell?" Julie exclaimed. "You should *never* keep IDs and passwords on your cell phone. I've told you that a million..."

"OK! OK! I didn't know where else to put it. What am I supposed to do?" Emma exclaimed. "Tattoo this stuff on my behind!"

Julie pretended to gag. "Just tell me your ID."

"Julie123, capital J," Emma said.

Julie shook her head. "No, Mom. That's your password. And by the way..."

"I know. I know," Emma snapped. "Never use your child's name as an ID. It's just...well, at least I can remember it..."

Julie was still shaking her head. "Mom," she repeated. "Julie123 is not your ID. I need your ID. That's different from your password."

"I didn't know I needed to remember the ID," Emma shrugged

Suddenly Emma grabbed her mouse back and started to close her computer. "Let's forget this," she said. "You're being abusive."

Julie grabbed it back. "No. I want to see your Facebook page."

Julie typed something onto the Log In screen.

"Your ID's your email address, duh," she said. "Julie 123 is your password."

The site magically opened and Emma's new Facebook page appeared on the screen. Her flattering Opera in the Vineyard photo smiled happily back at them. Emma noted, with relief, that she didn't look half bad.

After multiple more clicks, Julie looked sideways at her mother. "Mom," she exclaimed, "this is great. I've been telling you to do this for years. Who helped you?"

"Lexie," Emma replied. "It took her about five minutes."

"She's good," Julie said, sounding genuinely impressed.

She'd scrolled half way down the "about Emma" column when her smile changed to a frown. "What's this about Labs? Suddenly you love Labs? You were all over Piers and me when we bought Sunny. And Coldplay? I bet you don't even know who Coldplay is?"

"Gwyneth Paltrow," Emma replied. Then something on the

computer screen caught her eye. "Thirty-two friend suggestions? Julie, who are all these people?"

"Don't worry," Julie replied. "They're just suggestions of people who Facebook thinks you might want to invite as friends."

Julie scrolled down the page some more. "Here," she pointed to the screen. "See? These are people who have seen that you're on Facebook. They are *inviting* you to be friends. Wow! There are four of them already."

Emma repositioned the screen so she could see it. "Who?"

"Jack," Julie answered. "Of course. You know Jack Russo'd be on Facebook. And some woman named Patti Banks..."

"Ohhhh," Emma replied, letting the Jack comment slide. "I went to grammar school with Patti. I haven't seen her in years. I wonder what she's up to..."

"There's one way to find out," Julie clicked a button on the screen.

"What did you just do?" Emma asked.

"*You* just friended her."

"Great!" Emma snorted. "I never really liked Patti. Now I get to find out what she had for breakfast! Oh, look," she added, clicking "confirm" after Jack's name, "here's Louise, the librarian at my old law firm, Dunn & Munster. We were great friends until she moved to Seattle." She clicked the confirm button again and continued to scroll.

"OMG!" she shouted seconds later. "Remember Clare Braun, Marisa's mother? You and Marisa were inseparable until Marisa transferred to that school in Marin. I love Clare. I wonder how she's doing?" Emma clicked the "confirm" button another time. This was starting to be fun.

Julie had tilted the screen so she could look at Clare Braun's invitation. "Hey, ask her what Marisa is up to. I'd love to..."

Suddenly Julie stopped speaking. A new invitation had just popped up – along with a message.

"Who's this?" Julie squinted at the screen. "Someone named Dan Worthington wants to be your friend. He's posted a message. Wow. This is weird."

Emma grabbed the computer away from Julie. "Dan Worthington!"

Amidst a blur of boxes and bubbles, she finally located the message. It read: "Dear Emma, Kim left. This time for good. I need to see you. After all these years you're still in my heart. I hope we can reconnect."

Emma felt her own heart stop beating. Dan Worthington had been the love of her life. Her soul mate. The man who, after Andy left, she'd thought could make it all worthwhile – heartbreak, divorce, loss. Her old college classmate who broke up with his wife and reconciled, all in the space of Julie's high school semester abroad. Thankfully, Julie never knew of the affair.

"Mo-om," Emma heard Julie's voice through a fog. "Mo-om! What's going on? Who is this guy? What's the matter?"

Emma could feel the color rise to her cheeks. Julie would notice. Emma struggled to pull herself together.

"Nothing," she shook her head, willing herself to stay calm. "Nothing's the matter. It's...it's," she tried to think of some excuse. Something that would satisfy her suspicious daughter.

"I'm a little upset," she finally answered. "I do recognize the name. He's...he's someone I used to work with," she lied. "I mean," she scrambled not to implicate anyone at her old firm. "Opposing counsel. Someone who propositioned me once," she added. That would sound OK. "And..." she swallowed, "and I reported him. Years ago. Once in a while he tries to contact me and, you know, it upsets me."

Emma let out a deep breath. A necessary fib, she told herself, slipping her hands into her lap. They were shaking.

"Then why does he say 'reconnect?' I mean, if it was a one way street?" Julie replied.

Emma took another deep breath, and tried to shrug. "You know how it is, Julie. Men never think it was a one way street."

Julie looked satisfied. At least for the moment. "Well, it's no big deal, Mom. You don't have to accept his invitation to be friends."

Julie started to hit the "Delete" button, but Emma pushed the computer away.

"So, you're sure. All I have to do is push 'Delete Request'?" Emma asked. "I think I want the satisfaction of doing that myself."

Then she closed her computer. "In fact," she added, "I've had more than enough Facebook for today."

Julie was looking at her watch again. "Mom, I really have to go in a couple minutes, but there's something I want to tell you – and I think that now is as good a time as any. In fact, I've probably waited a little too long already, so I hope you won't be upset."

Emma felt her heart contract. Her expression changed from shock to worry. "Are you OK? Is Harry OK? Is Piers OK? Oh, honey, tell me I don't have to worry!"

To Emma's relief, Julie burst out laughing. "Mom, no! You don't have to worry. You're going to be really happy about this. You've been bugging me about it for years. I'm having another baby. I figured you knew already with all the weight I've gained. I've been eating like a horse. But everything's fine. It's just that, at my age, Piers and I really wanted to get all the test results back before we told anyone – even you."

Emma leaned over to give Julie a big hug.

"Anyway," Julie continued, "we got all the results last week and everything's fine. We are so thrilled. It's another boy. I'm due in September. I just hadn't found a good time to tell you."

All Emma's worries vanished into thin air. She hugged Julie again. "You know this makes me happier than anything in the world," she said.

Julie nodded, "Me, too!"

"And I want you to take it easy," Emma added.

"I know, Mom. I know." She kissed her mother's cheek. "Now I gotta run. Oh, by the way, let's keep it our little secret for a while. Harry doesn't know. We're not telling him for a few more weeks. I'm afraid this will be a big adjustment for him."

"I'll say," Emma laughed.

Emma saw Julie to the door. "Careful on the steps," she called after her as she made her way to her car.

Then she walked back to the kitchen, wondering how she could have missed all the signs: the weight gain, the fatigue, no caffeine, the SUV for goodness sake! Why didn't she guess weeks ago that her own daughter was pregnant? And why didn't Julie tell her? Share with her own mother the joy of the good news as well as the stress of waiting for the test results?

Once again, Emma raised the question. How well do we know each other? Even our own families, not to mention those whom we think are our closest friends.

Emma pulled a little leftover *Trapanese* sauce out of the refrigerator. It was Jack's favorite dish. She had planned on calling him when she got home, to see if he wanted to share a quick pasta dinner with her.

She glanced at the clock. Too late now.

Her computer still sat on the kitchen counter. Before heating the leftover sauce, she lifted the lid. Then she thought for a moment.

Her opened Facebook page stared back at her on the screen. "Friend Requests." "Dan Worthington." And to the right of his name, two boxes: "Confirm;" "Delete Request."

Emma clicked the "Confirm" button and, for some reason, held her breath.

11

WEDNESDAY – CONFLICT OF INTEREST

Wednesday morning, Emma woke up to a phone call from Steve.

"Hey, Emma. Hope I'm not calling too early. Did you get my email?" he began.

In fact, Steve wasn't calling too early. Emma glanced at the time on her cell phone. It was 8:30. Also, in fact, she was still asleep when her phone rang, having spent a restless night. *Why do I feel so frazzled?* she'd asked herself in the middle of the night unable to relax and fall asleep.

Too many competing emotions. That's what Emma told herself before taking an Advil PM at 4:00 a.m. Joy and excitement about the birth of the new baby. Anxiety about the book deal. Irritation with Steve. Concern about the murder. And now, Dan.

That's the problem, she realized. *That's the emotion I cannot name. After twenty plus years, how do I feel about Dan?*

"Hi. Are you there?" Steve's voice interrupted her.

She pinched her arm to wake herself up and cleared her throat.

"Hi, Steve," she answered. "I haven't got your email yet; but no, you aren't calling too early. What's up?"

"I know I sound a little desperate, Emma; but frankly, I am," Steve replied. Then he added without a pause. "I really need your help. I've been swamped with the Esquivel immigration hearings all week. I'm on my way to Alameda for another one today. And I scheduled meetings on the Gomez case down south Thursday and Friday. The point is, I'm still hoping you can help me out with that. No one else from the office can go."

Of course, Emma reminded herself. *Steve is calling about the murder investigation.* Steve's trip to Coachella to prove Curt Randall killed Santiago Gomez. Emma kicked herself for not getting back to Steve about it sooner.

"Sorry, Steve. I can't go. I'm a volunteer, remember?" she replied. "I can't just drop everything..."

"Because of Piers, right? Conflict of interest stuff," Steve cut in. "Look, Emma. I'm sorry about my reaction the other day. I get it. I see the bind you're in. But here's the thing. I know about the conflict of interest. It's out in the open. We're waiving it. I need help. I need to find answers to the same questions Piers is asking. Who killed Gomez? I know Piers has hired some fancy investigators to look into it. I need to satisfy myself about a few things before we file the wrongful death suit."

Steve paused. When Emma didn't answer he continued. "You know I trust you, Emma. To keep an open mind, no matter what. I need that. So please, drive south with me tomorrow and let's see what we can dig up. We'll talk more when I get back to the office later this afternoon. OK? Oh, and I need someone to interview Gomez's cousin this evening. The one who found Santiago's body. I can't. It's my wife's birthday and I promised her I wouldn't miss the party. If I do, all hell will break loose..."

Emma bristled. Darned if Steve didn't bring up his wife's birthday. Of course she wanted to help him with something like that. But her mind was too fuzzy for a rational reply. Besides, she was still mad at Steve for his comments about Piers and Porsches.

"Steve, look," she replied. "I can't commit to a trip now. But I'll think about it. I promise. We can talk more this afternoon. When you're back from Alameda."

"Around 4:00," Steve replied.

"See you then." Emma hung up the phone.

She went downstairs to her kitchen to make coffee, but abruptly decided to check Facebook, instead. She started to log on at the dining room table, her heart filled with equal parts of anticipation and dread. Before she clicked the log in button, however, she stopped herself. Her hands were shaking. She returned to the kitchen, made coffee and sat down to think while it brewed.

What is the matter with me? she asked. *What am I afraid of?*

She answered her own question. *Maybe I'm afraid of losing control. I did it once before and it broke my heart.*

But Dan was my soul mate, she replied. *The only man I was sure I could happily spend the rest of my life with.*

So why worry? she reassured herself. *If he writes back, I'll either pick up where I left off with the love of my life. The handsome architect who dumped me* – Emma had to admit he had dumped her – *and ran home when his wife decided she wanted him back. Or I won't. Either way, we'll both survive. We did before.*

The coffee was ready. Emma poured herself a cup, topped it off with milk and grabbed one of Claud's biscotti. Then she returned to the dining room and clicked on her Facebook page.

Yes. There was a message. Her heart skipped a beat. It was from Dan. This one was private. It read:

Hi Emma,

I know this sounds crazy. All those years ago, we both agreed that I'd never break up my marriage over you. But Kim's gone – this time for good. She moved to Santa Fe with a guy she's been seeing for years. I guess I just didn't want to know.

The divorce is final. No more screwing around this time. The kids are madder'n heck, but, at 35 and 37 I guess they – we – will all survive. They are fine. Alice has two kids of her own. John's an architect now in D.C. Ha! What a surprise!

I can't tell you how many times I've picked up the phone to call you since I transferred to the Denver office so Kim and I could try to rebuild a life together. But I knew it wasn't fair. I didn't have anything to offer you.

Now I can't help hoping that maybe I do. I've never forgotten you. You don't forget your soul mate once you are lucky enough to find her

I can't believe I found you on Facebook. Or that you are living in Blissburg, CA. I always thought you were an urbanite like me, a committed city girl. I know things change. And by the way, congratulations on the new career. I've been reading about your cooking on the Internet.

Listen, Emma, I REALLY want to see you. To see if, finally, things can work out the way I always thought they were meant to. I know. Too bad we didn't figure all this out years ago, before we let other people steal our hearts. But maybe better late than never.

Just name a date. We have a $150M arena in San Jose that brings me to northern California twice a month. Say the word, and I'll be on my way to Blissburg. How wonderful that sounds!

VERY VERY TRULY YOURS,

Dan

Without even realizing it, Emma started to cry. She wiped her nose on the sleeve of her muumuu. She didn't even try to dry her eyes. It was the message she'd been waiting for. Waiting for over twenty years. But instead of being happy, the message had made her sad.

Don't rock the boat! It takes a long time to get happy! a voice warned inside her head.

Emma sipped her coffee staring at the screen, wondering what to do. Then another message popped up on her screen. "Hey, we're friends on Facebook! Lunch? The Trough? Noon?" It was Jack Russo.

Emma felt her stomach lurch. Something was still bothering her. *What is it?* she asked herself again.

But this time she knew the answer. It was Jack. Jack Russo was what was bothering her. She and Jack had been carrying their relationship around like Humpty Dumpty for almost a year. Now she was afraid – more afraid than she wanted to admit - that Humpty Dumpty was about to fall apart.

She quickly accepted Jack's lunch invitation.

Then she emailed her boss, Steve. "I'm good to go tomorrow. We'll talk later this afternoon."

Finally, without stopping to think any more about it, Emma posted a private message for Dan.

Hey Dan,

Great to hear from you. I mean it. And of course, I'm sorry about you and Kim, but I hope it is all for the best.

I have to be out of town for a few days on business. When I get back, we'll figure out a time to meet.

Meanwhile, lots of love and thanks for getting in touch.

Emma

She was about to post the message when she thought of something. She revised the second to the last sentence to read. "When I get back, we'll figure out a time *and place* to meet."

Then she let the message go.

Emma wasn't sure why, but after working for an hour or two on her book, she took more care than usual dressing for her lunch with Jack that day. She ironed her green and blue flowered Liberty print blouse – a gift from Julie – took a clean pair of loden green slim jeans out of the closet and slipped her feet into an old pair of two inch Ferragamo heels. She even put on a little mascara and eyeliner to highlight her pale blue eyes.

She looked herself over in the full-length bathroom mirror and smiled. Then she grabbed her small black shoulder bag and started walking to the plaza.

When she arrived at The Trough, Jack was already sitting at their usual table in the shade checking his email. Emma knew what was on his mind that day. Their dinner on Saturday. The one she was supposed to cook. The one he'd purchased for $5000 at the Opera in the Vineyard fundraiser the year before. At that price, Emma agreed he had a right to be concerned.

"Hi," Jack glanced up and smiled as Emma approached the table. "You look terrific. Going someplace special after lunch?" He stood up to pull out Emma' chair.

The question cut Emma to the quick.

Is he saying I don't think our lunches are special? she asked herself. *The ones he pays for every week?*

She knew she'd let her appearance slide the past few months when they were together. Suddenly she felt guilty.

But then, again, she told herself, *Jack never acts like he notices.*

Now, it seemed, perhaps he did.

"Lunch with you *is* special," she answered, blushing at the awkwardness of her reply.

"'The lady doth protest too much,'" Jack laughed quoting Shakespeare.

Emma turned to glance at him and then sat down, too embarrassed to think of a clever reply.

"Do you want some wine?" he asked. "I ordered myself a glass of *Sancerre*."

Emma shook her head. "No. I have some work to do this afternoon."

They studied their menus to fill what seemed like an unaccustomed pause.

After the waiter took their orders, Jack broke the silence.

"So about dinner," he began. "Sorry," he paused. "Am I making too big a deal out of this?"

"No. No!" Emma exclaimed. "You have every right to. It's an expensive dinner," she laughed. "I really want it to be great."

For the next few minutes, they discussed the menu: *malfatti*, veal scallops, green beans, salad and his favorite, Bavarian cream, for dessert. Then shopping – she'd already ordered the veal. The rest, she told him, she'd pick up fresh at the Saturday Blissburg Farmer's Market. Everything was under control, except for a few things to buy at Pete's. She'd make the Bavarian cream for dessert the night before.

Jack mentioned that Peppino had already delivered the wine. He would take care of drinks. Celina would set the table. Emma promised to bring flowers.

When they were finished, Jack leaned back in his chair. "That does it," he said with a satisfied smile. "Emma, we make a good team."

She shook a warning finger at him. "Save that for the after-dinner drinks," she said, more nervous about the dinner than she'd let on.

They were drinking cappuccinos when Jack changed the subject. "So," he squinted his eyes at her tilting his head from side to side, "how's the cookbook coming? You gonna make the deadline for Christmas sales?"

Emma smiled. She realized that Jack always remembered to ask her about herself. What was on her mind. What she was doing. It was an endearing trait. She wondered if she showed as much interest in him. Aside from talking about his grandchildren, she realized that Jack said little about himself.

"Funny you should ask," she replied. "I had lunch yesterday with the Buchanons. Guess who was there?"

Jack shook his head.

"The Chinese. Bo, Ho, Fung and Lew. I think I got that right," she laughed. "Assuming we're on a first name basis." She rolled her eyes. "Lexie went off the spool again. Women's Lib. She said the Chinese were sexist pigs and right she was. All Ho wanted to discuss was his favorite actresses' melons. Tell me. Is that what these super-important power lunches have been about all these years? Is this what we women have been missing?"

Jack shrugged. "'Fraid so. That and all the dough. But, believe me, things have changed. Look at my daughter. The research she does in her lab is worth billions and she's taking home a chunk of it. Things may not have changed so much in China, though.

"Here's the worst part," Emma continued. "Cheng Bo told Barry that Randall is falling apart over the Gomez investigation. No surprise," she added, "given the murder charges against him. Paying for his defense costs must be costing him a bundle. Piers won't talk to me about it – because I work with Steve. But I gather he has his hands full trying to convince Randall not to sell the ranch to HoCo for a song to get some cash."

Jack looked over Emma's shoulder and squinted as though he were thinking. "I just don't think the old guy did it, Emma. Last time I saw him, which was only two weeks ago, he could barely lift himself out of a chair." He shook his head emphatically. "Nah. Something else is goin' on."

"That's exactly what Piers thinks," Emma agreed. "Lots of people hated Gomez. Including the husband of the woman he was seeing and the cousin that Piers says Gomez tried to blackmail..."

"By the way," Jack interrupted. "I did some poking around myself the other day. About Rob Peters. Curt's nephew." He lowered his voice. "The one who'll lose a bundle if Curt changes his will. It seems Rob's borrowed a lot of money. On the assumption that he's the sole heir. Now I hear Rob's investments are belly up. Some big wine venture that failed. People at the club say he's goin' around town bad mouthing Curt. I guess Rob tried to borrow money from him and Curt refused."

"So you think that's why he was at the rally? Because he's mad at Curt?" Emma asked.

"Maybe," Jack said.

"That doesn't explain Gomez, though," Emma replied.

Jack shrugged. "Look. If Peters really *is* the sole beneficiary of Randall's estate, he couldn't have been too happy about the Gomez suit. A judgment in a class action could cost Randall millions. Not to mention attorney fees. Suddenly," Jack snapped his fingers, "there goes the estate. Depending on how desperate Peters is for money, who knows what he might do?"

Emma nodded. "You mean, kill Gomez to stop the lawsuit, and then frame Curt for the murder?"

Jack threw his hands up. "As far as I can tell, *someone* is trying to frame Curt. Hey, by the way," he changed the subject. "You're on Facebook now."

"Kicking and screaming," Emma laughed. "Lexie insisted I join. Nice of you to friend me."

"I like the photo. From the auction, right?" Jack asked. "That night I met you."

"Glad you like it." Emma paused. "Let me ask you something, Jack. Why are *you* on Facebook? I don't get it. Why do you want to know all those dumb things people post about themselves? Does a busy guy like you really have time?"

"Not that busy anymore, Emma," Jack rolled his eyes. "For me, it's a good way to keep up. With my daughter. With business. With organizations I support. With friends I left behind on the East Coast." He laughed. "I'm a sociable guy. My daughter said it would be good for me. And guess what? She was right. Now I'm in touch with people I haven't seen in years."

"People you haven't seen in years," Emma repeated. "Let me ask you something else," she paused.

A little voice in the back of her head told her to stop, but she ignored it.

"Did you ever hear from someone...I don't know...someone out of the blue? Someone from your past that really surprised you?"

Jack was draining the last of his cappuccino. He put down his cup. "Whaddya mean? What kind of surprise? Like a good surprise? Like someone from my past I'd been...I don't know...hoping to hear from? Like an old girlfriend kinda surprise? You hear of that happening when people go on Facebook. Is that what you mean?" He cocked his head, stared into her eyes and squinted. Like he was trying to read her mind. Then, before she answered, he shook his head. "No, that never happened to me."

Alarms started ringing in Emma's ears. She dropped her eyes and blushed.

"Did it happen to you?" he asked.

"What? What do you mean?" Emma stammered. "Did what happen?"

She guessed, by then, her face had turned three shades of red.

"Nothing," he smiled perfunctorily. "I mean it as a compliment. I'm guessin' a nice woman like you, divorced for many years, probably has some guys in her past. You never talk about them, that's all." He nodded slowly. "You talk about a lot of other stuff. But not that. So I wondered...Me, I was married for almost fifty years – to the same woman. I got nothin' to talk about. In polite company that is. Nothing except a few one night stands."

Jack signaled the waiter to bring the check. They sat in silence for a minute while he paid. Then he cast her a sheepish grin.

"I know that wasn't fair, Emma," he said. "You got secrets. I got secrets – well, not secrets. Just things I never told you. Like," he shrugged. "Like about Johnny. That's not a secret. It's just," he sighed. "It's just something that. Well, let me put it this way. It's something that, when I moved here, I realized I no longer had to explain."

The same pained expression crossed Jack's face that she'd seen the week before. He blew out a big sigh and then continued.

"After Johnny died, Frannie and I spent thirty years with people avoiding us. Like it was just too hard to watch our pain. It wasn't their fault. People just didn't know what to say. Frankly, when I moved, it was kind of a relief to be with people, like you, who just didn't know. But I see now I was wrong. You're too good a friend not to have told you." He plastered a smile back on his face and stood up.

"Let me know if you need some help over the next couple of days. You know, shopping for the party. I'll give you a call."

That's when Emma remembered. She hadn't told him she was leaving town.

In spite of herself, she winced. "Speaking of the Gomez murder investigation. I just promised Steve I'd drive down to Coachella with him. He's set up interviews with some people Gomez worked with there. He wants to answer some questions about the murder – satisfy his mind about who did it before he files the wrongful death suit. He needs me to help."

"Isn't that kinda hard?" Jack asked. "What will Piers say?"

"Oh," Emma stammered. "Steve said they'd waive any possible conflict of interest. Frankly, I'm hoping I can dig up some evidence to prove that Curt Randall didn't do it. Piers can't object to that!"

Jack looked skeptical. "When do you leave?"

"Tomorrow," Emma replied. "We'll stay Thursday and Fri…"

Emma stopped. All of a sudden, she realized that she was in a bind. If she and Steve stayed in Coachella Thursday and Friday there was no way she'd be back on Saturday in time to make dinner. She'd have to convince Steve to drive back Friday night.

"I mean," she corrected herself, "we're going down tomorrow and staying just one night."

"Kind of a long trip for one night. You driving?" Jack asked.

"Steve doesn't have the budget for anything else," Emma explained.

"You sure about getting back on Friday?" he added. "I mean, aren't you cutting it kind of close? Isn't there an awful lot to do?"

Emma tried to put on a confident face, meanwhile wondering how on earth she could drive to Coachella and still prepare that dinner on time.

She nodded her head. "No problem. Really. Don't worry. I've done it a million times. Saturday's great. I'll have plenty of time."

"OK," Jack replied, but he didn't look convinced. "If you're sure. You're the boss. Just let me know if there is anything I can do."

"Don't worry. I will," she waved. "And thanks, Jack. Thanks so much for the lunch. For everything," she added. Then wished she hadn't. It sounded too final. It sounded like she was telling him goodbye.

12

WEDNESDAY AFTERNOON – HASTA LA VISTA

After lunch Emma drove to the free legal clinic. Barbara had taken a long lunch. Something about a Western Romance convention in Windsor a few miles away.

The reception desk was empty. And the office was filled with its usual diverse population of clients: Hispanic workers trying to get a break, moms with children on their laps seeking restraining orders or trying to secure benefits, runaway teenagers seeking everything from welfare to divorces from their parents, dads trying to get to visit their kids. Emma's heart went out to them. Unlike her ex-husband, these folks had no money to hire high-priced lawyers to get them off the hook. *Thank goodness,* she thought as she walked past the sorry parade into her cubicle. *Thank goodness for people like my boss, Steve Zimmer.*

Once in her makeshift office, it took but a few minutes to locate the Gomez files. They went back quite a few years to when Santiago Gomez first visited the legal clinic to request help with a pay dispute he had with a former employer. A landscaping firm for whom he worked as a gardener. That suit resulted in a small settlement in Gomez's favor. It was followed, Emma soon realized, by more suits. An assault charge, later dropped, brought by a co-worker at the winery where Gomez worked after the landscaping stint. A suit against an insurance company for medical benefits in connection with the birth of his son. A suit against the winery for more back pay.

After that Gomez got a job at Curt Randall's plum ranch. That's when things appeared to settle down. For a while. Until Gomez's address changed to Coachella, California. There, Steve managed to hush up a harassment suit filed by a woman who worked in a local bar.

Then, only about a month ago, Gomez filed the unfair labor practices lawsuit against Curt Randall. The lawsuit alleged that Gomez worked as a fruit and vegetable picker at Randall Enterprises under conditions that violated both California and federal law. Specifically, the complaint stated that Randall Enterprises failed to provide Gomez with adequate water, shade and housing.

Eventually Steve hoped to file a class action representing all similarly situated workers on Randall's vast Coachella farms. But he'd had trouble getting workers to join the suit. Few were willing to jeopardize their low paying jobs.

And who could blame them? Emma asked herself as she read through the file. *Who wanted to risk their paycheck for years of litigation with no guarantees?*

Emma skimmed pages of Steve's "memos to the file" detailing Gomez's frustrating quest for support among his co-workers in Coachella. And, more recently, up north where a few Randall Enterprises seasonal workers, like Gomez's cousin, had resettled to find better work.

Then she quickly scanned Barbara's notes of every contact Gomez had with the legal clinic.

The last entries were dated the afternoon before the murder. Gomez had called the BFLSC around 3:00 p.m. and asked to talk to Steve. But Steve was in trial in Santa Rosa that day.

According to Steve's notes from later that night, he'd tried twice to return the call. But Steve didn't get through. His final note read, "into voicemail. L/m to call me back on cell."

That was the very last entry into Gomez's file. Gomez never did call Steve back.

Emma couldn't help wondering what Gomez called about the afternoon before he died.

It was almost 4:00. Steve would be back soon. Emma checked to see if Barbara was back from the Western Romance conference. She was. That day, her ample figure was stuffed into black stretch jeans and a tight fitting purple sweater.

"Barbara," Emma approached the reception desk gingerly. There was something about the bullet casings Barbara wore around her neck that put Emma on edge. "You know Santiago Gomez?"

Barbara's face looked stricken. She placed her hand on her heart. "Know him!" she sighed. "Honey, I may actually have been the last person to talk to him alive."

"Do you think someone talked to him after he was dead?" Emma replied.

Barbara swatted her hand. "You're so funny. You know what I mean. I asked Steve. He never reached him. He tried two or three times that night. So, maybe I was the very last person to talk to the poor guy before he was murdered. Kinda gives me the creeps."

"Did he say anything when he called?" Emma asked. "Like what he wanted?"

"Just that he wanted to talk to Steve," Barbara shrugged. "I wrote it down in the log. He wanted to talk to Steve and I told him Steve was in court all day, but that he'd call him back as soon as he could. You know Steve," she rolled her eyes. "24/7. It's like he's married to this place. I feel sorry for the wife. Frankly," she added, cupping her hand around her mouth, "just between you and me, I'm not sure things are exactly 'quiet' on the home front, if you know what I mean."

Emma winced. She'd been worried about that. "Thanks. I was

just wondering what that call was about. Probably the class action, but you never know," Emma paused. "I thought it might shed some light on the killer. I know the police are focused on Curt Randall, but..." she shrugged and turned to go.

"Curt Randall," Barbara repeated the name. "Wait a minute. Now I'm remembering. Gomez *did* mumble something about Curt Randall. Right before he hung up. I wonder if I mentioned it to Steve..."

"What? What did he say?" Emma asked.

"Something about talking to Curt. Either he *had* talked to him or he *was going* to talk to him. I forget. Anyway," she batted the memory away with her hand, "he hung up the phone before he said what it was."

Steve had just walked into the office. He stood beside them, his head cocked to one side. "Who hung up?" he asked.

"Santiago Gomez," Barbara replied. "That's why I don't know what he called about the afternoon before he died." She shivered. "It really does give me the creeps. To think, I was the..."

"What do you mean?" Steve said. "Did he say something else before he hung up the phone?"

"Just about Curt Randall," Barbara shrugged. "I think he said he had talked to him. Or maybe that he needed to talk to him. Yes. That was it. He said he needed to talk to him. And I thought to myself – of course I didn't say anything because it's not my place. I'm not a lawyer. So, I thought but didn't say, *he's a plaintiff. Plaintiffs don't talk to people they sue. Their lawyers do that.* That's why I said he should talk to you, Steve, and that you'd call him back as soon as you could."

"Which I did," Steve replied. "But I never got through. And he never returned my call."

Steve's face assumed the snide scowl that Emma was familiar with. "Anything else you forgot about the call?"

"No," Barbara replied. Her face still as stone. "I didn't 'forget,' Steve," she added making quotation marks with her fingers. "I assumed that whatever he was calling about, he'd tell you himself. I'm a receptionist, not a mind reader," she added.

Even Emma could tell there was nothing more forthcoming. Steve jerked his head in direction of his office.

"What was that all about?" he asked, taking a seat behind his desk and motioning to Emma to sit down on the other metal chair crammed into his room.

"I reviewed the Gomez file," Emma answered. "You know, before our trip. To get up to speed. And I noticed that Gomez called the office the night before he died. After that, it didn't look like you reached him. It looked like he never called you back. Next thing, he was dead."

Steve nodded. "Exactly. I assume he called about the class action. He wasn't having much luck signing people up. People up here were afraid to join the class. Afraid they'd lose their jobs."

"That's what I assumed, too," Emma answered, "until I saw Barbara's note about his call. Then I started to wonder. What if he had something else on his mind? Something that might give us a clue. About his murder. So I asked Barbara what she remembered..."

"She said he wanted to talk to me," Steve cut in.

"That's what she told me, too," Emma answered. "At first. Then I mentioned Curt Randall. That I didn't think he murdered Gomez..."

Emma watched Steve's eyebrows knit into a frown.

"Steve, you know I don't think Curt's the killer. He's old and sick. He can barely pull himself out of a chair. I agree with Piers." She didn't mention Jack. "You have to live with that."

"OK. OK." Steve made a circle with his hand for her to go on with her story.

"Anyway," Emma continued, "when I mentioned Curt's name, Barbara remembered that before he hung up, Gomez said he wanted to talk to Curt. That he needed to talk to Curt. Barbara remembered because, like she told you, she thought it was not kosher for Gomez to talk to Curt without his lawyer. That's why she said you'd call him back as soon as you could. Which you did."

"That's it?" Steve asked.

Emma nodded her head.

Steve sat back in his chair and blew out a deep breath. "It sounds fishy," he finally said. "Why would Santiago need to talk to Curt? They hated each other. And Santiago's been through enough litigation to know not to contact the other side." He thought for a minute. "So maybe Santiago was on his way to talk to Curt, *not* his cousin, when he was killed."

Emma shrugged. "About what?"

"Beats me," Steve said. "That's a question for you to ask the cousin. What was on Santiago's mind. You're going tonight, right?"

Steve looked at his computer screen and almost jumped out of his chair. Jees! It's almost five. I gotta run. If I don't get to that restaurant in Rohnert Park by 5:45, I really think Jesse will divorce me. In front of twenty of her best friends. Sorry Emma, do you can think you can manage?"

"What?" Emma said.

"The Diaz interview," he answered. "Santiago's cousin."

Emma drew her breath in sharply. The idea of confronting Jose Diaz made her nervous.

"What if he's the killer, Steve?" she said.

"Don't worry," Steve replied. "I thought of that. You're meeting him at a bar out Blissburg Ave. It's called the *Hasta la Vista Lounge*..."

Emma shuddered at the name.

"The place will be rocking," Steve laughed. "If Diaz is the killer, trust me, he's not going to put a knife into you in a crowded bar."

Emma wasn't convinced.

Steve reassured her, "The bartender's name is Poncho. Poncho Lopez. He's my friend. If anything looks fishy go tell Poncho. Better yet, check in with Poncho when you get to the lounge. I've done Poncho some favors. He'll watch out for you."

Steve then listed a series of questions he wanted Emma to ask Diaz. She copied them down on a legal pad.

"Call me right after you finish with Diaz. OK?"

Steve didn't wait for Emma to reply.

THE *HASTA LA Vista* Lounge was located on the south end of Blissburg Avenue right before the turnoff to 101. Emma passed it a hundred times on her way to San Francisco. It was the small, squat building next to the Mexican grocery with the barbecue outside. The one where the chicken always smelled so good. Emma remembered the barbecue all right; but whenever she passed, the lounge looked deserted.

At 8:00 p.m. when she parked her car across the street, the place was mobbed. A crowd of men wearing dark jeans, checked shirts and straw cowboy hats milled around the front of the building.

Emma had always liked the broad cross section of Blissburg's citizenry – old hippies, young San Francisco professionals with weekend wineries and $10,000 bicycles, farm families who had worked the land around Blissburg for years, and, of course, the Latino workers. That night, however, as she got out of her car the crowd of young men in front of *Hasta la Vista* made her pause. Collectively, they looked tough.

EMMA CROSSED the street and made her way through a wall of men. Some of the old ones whistled at her and yelled words in Spanish she didn't understand. She was embarrassed to admit that she found the attention flattering.

The first thing she did when she entered the lounge was approach the bar. A short, burly, dark-skinned man served drinks.

Emma noticed that with his long nose and full lips he looked like he'd stepped out of a Mayan ruin.

"Is Poncho here?" she greeted him nervously. The name Poncho didn't sound flattering.

The man tilted his head back and poked his chest with his fore-finger. "I'm Poncho," he answered not looking at all offended. "Who's looking for me, *mamacita*?" the man asked.

Emma cleared her throat. She wasn't sure what *mamacita* signi-fied, but like Poncho, she decided it wasn't offensive.

"Me, Emma Corsi," she said. "Steve Zimmer, who I gather is a friend of yours, suggested I talk to you about a situation."

Poncho squinted at her and nodded slowly. "Steve. OK. Steve's my friend. What's the *situation*?"

Emma cleared her throat again. "I'm meeting someone here named Jose Diaz. To ask him some questions about the Gomez murder. Steve represents the Gomez family in connection with the murder." She hastened to add, "He couldn't come. He had to attend his wife's birthday party."

Poncho replied with a short, explosive laugh. It sounded like the report of a shotgun. "Steve had to attend his wife's birthday party?" he repeated. He might as well have said, *what a wus.*

Then Poncho cupped his hands, palms up, and made a come hither motion with his fingers. "C'mon, lady. What did you say your name was?"

"Emma," she replied. "I work with Steve."

"Look, Emma. I got customers. See?" he looked down the bar in each direction. "I asked you what you want."

"Well," Emma stammered. "I want...." She swallowed and thought for a few seconds. "I don't want to have any trouble with Diaz. Steve said you'd keep an eye out for me while I interview him about the murder."

Poncho burst out laughing. This time it sounded like the roar of a Harley Davidson.

"Keep an eye out for you? For what? Because of Diaz? Like what's he gonna do? Knife you? Here at my bar?" He laughed again. "Diaz is afraid of his own shadow. He was sure as heck afraid of his cousin, Santiago Gomez, if that's what you want to know. I'll keep an eye on him for you. He's sittin' right over there."

Poncho motioned with his thumb to a table by a stone fireplace at the far end of the room. The young man seated there was so short his feet barely touched the ground. He was long faced and skinny. Emma guessed his whole body weighed about as much as her right thigh.

"Ohhhhh. Scary, *Senora!*" Poncho pretended to shiver. "But don't worry. Poncho will protect you!"

Seconds later, Emma had seated herself across the table from Jose Diaz. He was drinking a beer. When the waiter glanced at her she ordered a Corona.

"Hi, Mr. Diaz," she began. "I hope Steve told you that he couldn't meet with you tonight. I work with him. I'm here instead." She decided to skip any mention of the birthday party.

The young man nodded. "Jose," he answered. "Call me Jose. Steve said you have some questions. About my cousin's murder. You know," he eyed her nervously, "the police have already questioned me. I told them everything I know. The old man..." he hesitated.

"Curt Randall?" Emma replied.

"Yeah, Randall," Jose nodded. "He's the one who did it. Randall didn't like Santiago. I didn't like Santiago either. No one did. But I didn't kill him. Randall did."

Emma's heart sank. "How do you know that?" she asked.

"Because my cousin called me, that's why," Jose replied. "He called me when I was eating dinner with my family. He said he was on his way to Randall's house to tell him something. He didn't tell me what, but he said Randall wouldn't like it. Wouldn't like what he had to say. But that maybe now the old man would 'respect' him. That was the word he used. 'Respect.'"

"He didn't tell you what it was about?" Emma said.

"No," Jose replied. "But he sounded worried. And I thought that was strange. Because Santiago, he was tough. He never sounded worried. He said something about him being in some kind of danger. That after he talked to Randall, he would come to my house and explain."

Emma nodded. "But he never came."

"Yeah," Jose replied. "I waited up for a while. Finally I went to bed. I figured he changed his mind." He shook his head. "To tell you the truth Ms..." he paused.

"Corsi," Emma supplied.

"Ms. Corsi. I told the police this. I was relieved he never came. Santiago was always trouble. Even when we were kids. I didn't want to get mixed up with him anymore. Then, in the morning, there he was. Dead."

"So you have no idea what he went to talk to Randall about?" Emma tried again.

Jose shook his head. "How should I know? I never heard from him after that call. But you see, don't you? Whatever it was, Randall didn't like it. So it must have been about that lawsuit. The one Santiago wanted me to join. He was threatening Randall and Randall killed him."

Emma's heart sank. It seemed like a noose was closing around old Curt Randall's neck. She perfunctorily ran through all Steve's questions.

Where was Jose the night of the murder?

Jose's wife would testify he was home all night with her.

What had he and Santiago argued about?

Gomez threatened him for not joining the lawsuit.

"Why didn't you want to join?" Emma asked.

Jose shrugged as though the answer was obvious. "Because I

finally had a good job, decent wages and housing for my family," he explained. "Why mess that up? I work hard. Finally I have a job where I can support my wife and children. Joining the class action would just get me fired." Jose shook his head. "Look, old man Randall hates us Mexicans. Always has. I see the hatred in his eyes every time he looks at me. But he needs us. And he treats the Sonoma employees fairly because the winery folks up here won't have it any other way. Unlike the workers down south at Randall Enterprises," he added, "who kill themselves for less than a living wage."

"But Randall couldn't fire you for joining a lawsuit," Emma explained. "Not legally."

Jose just laughed. "People like Randall can do whatever they want."

"What was Santiago threatening you with, Jose?" Emma asked. She'd saved the big question for last.

"What do you mean?" Jose lowered his voice.

"He was threatening you with something," Emma answered. "Something he thought would somehow make you agree to join the suit."

Jose took a deep breath and looked away. "I smuggled my wife's cousins and a few friends over the border. A year ago. Santiago threatened to rat on me if I didn't cooperate."

Suddenly anger flashed in the young man's eyes. "I'm here. I work hard. My kids are here. They go to school. They will grow up in the U.S. and become American citizens. Santiago was trying to destroy that – so he could be a hero." He pounded the table, then glanced quickly at Emma as though surprised by his own act. "I wouldn't join. I told him that. He got mad and we argued. Randall heard the shouting and sent someone to break up the fight."

"Did you do anything to him?" Emma asked. "Did you hit him?"

Jose dropped his eyes and seemed to blush. "I kicked him," he said. "Where it hurt. What else could I do? Santiago was way bigger than me. He always was."

Emma was done with Steve's questions. But there was still one thing she didn't understand.

"Jose," she said, "you've told me you didn't kill your cousin. And that your wife will swear you were home the night he died. But why do you think Curt Randall killed him? A lot of other people did not like your cousin. I've even heard rumors that Santiago was involved with another man's wife..."

Jose nodded. "Down south. It's true. I heard Armando Carillo threaten to kill him. One night in a bar. For fooling around with his wife."

He thought for a moment.

"There's something else," he added. "I told the police, but I don't think it's connected to Santiago's murder. The night my cousin and I had the fight he told me his old friend Louis Cardenas had dropped out of the lawsuit. Louis was making trouble. Telling people the lawsuit was no good. That Santiago was only out for himself. Santiago was mad. Said he'd like to make Louis squirm."

"Where can I find Cardenas?" Emma asked.

"In Coachella. He works for Randall Enterprises." Jose shrugged. "Look, *senora*. Like I said. All I know is what my cousin told me. Santiago said he was on his way to see Curt Randall on the night he died. If that was where he was going, then Curt Randall killed him."

"All that may be true," Emma nodded. "But you and I both know that Curt Randall is sick. So sick he can barely lift himself out of a chair. How can you be so sure he's the killer?"

Diaz laughed. "Sure, Randall is old and sick. But less than a month ago I seen him throw a rock at one of my kids. Just for chasin' a baseball inside the old man's yard. Are you tryin' to tell me that, if my cousin got him mad, old Randall couldn't run him through with a knife?"

Emma shuddered.

A few minutes later she was back in her car. The first thing she did was call Steve.

"Hi. It's me," Emma replied to Steve's greeting when he answered his cell. "I mean, it's Emma," she corrected herself. "Emma Corsi."

"I know. I know," Steve sounded annoyed.

"Sorry to bother you during the bir…"

"No problem," Steve cut in. "So. What happened? Make it fast. They're lighting the candles…."

Emma took a few seconds to organize her thoughts.

"Diaz says his wife will support his alibi that he was home the night Gomez died. He also said Randall threw a rock at his son a few weeks ago."

"Threw a rock? What's your point?" Steve asked.

"The kid was chasing a ball into Randall's yard," Emma explained. "Diaz said Randall had plenty of strength to chase the kid away. He also says Gomez called him the night he died. He was on his way to Randall's. To 'tell him something he didn't want to hear.' Gomez said he'd meet Diaz later that night to explain. Gomez never showed up. Diaz found Gomez's body on the footpath to Randall's house early the next day."

"What about the jealous husband?" Steve asked.

"Armando Carillo," Emma replied. "He threatened to kill Gomez for fooling around with his wife."

"Where?" Steve added.

"'Coachella. Not here."

"And the blackmail?"

"Diaz admits it," Emma replied. "Last year he smuggled some relatives over the border. Gomez threatened to blow the whistle if Diaz didn't cooperate. It's a motive, all right. But somehow, I just don't think Diaz is our killer."

"Why do you believe him?" Steve asked.

Emma thought for a minute. "Because he's half my size and acts like he's afraid of his own shadow."

Then Emma remembered the flash of anger in Diaz's eyes when he talked about his cousin.

"But what do I know?" she added. "He was capable of anything if he thought his family could be deported."

"I gotta run," Steve said. "We can discuss this more in the car when I pick you up. Seven sharp."

"Steve, wait." In the background, Emma heard people singing *Happy Birthday*. "I have to be home Friday no later than..."

But it was too late. Steve had already hung up.

13

THURSDAY MORNING – TWO FOR THE ROAD

Emma was not an early riser. Waking at 7:00 a.m. was hard. Being ready to go anywhere at 7:00 a.m. was close to impossible. She packed herself one change of clothes - black jeans and a short sleeved flowered print blouse. Coachella would be hot. Then she went to bed. As she fell asleep, she assured herself that come what may, she and Steve would drive home Friday night. In plenty of time for her to organize her dinner for Jack.

The next morning, true to his word, Steve's Subaru rolled into Emma's driveway at exactly 7:00 a.m. To her dismay, he was stuffing the last bite of a sausage, egg and cheese McMuffin into his mouth as she pulled open the door to his car. A red cardboard container of hash browns lay uneaten in his lap, and a large McCafe coffee sat in the beverage container by the steering wheel.

Darn! He's already eaten, she thought to herself. She'd had no time to make coffee.

Steve must have noted the desperate look in her eyes. "Sorry, have you not had coffee?" he added, placing a protective hand on his.

Emma shook her head. There was no way she was driving more than half way to Mexico without some caffeine.

"I'll need some," she stated.

Steve frowned. "There's another Mickey D right off the highway past Petaluma. I'll pull into the drive thru."

Emma shook her head again. "I don't do Mickey D." She mentally added *and neither should you. Why didn't do-gooder lefties get the food thing?*

Steve rolled his eyes in an optical version of *this is going to be a really long day.* Then he leaned back in his seat and said, "OK. What *do* you do, Emma?"

"Plaza Bakery," she said.

Steve looked at his watch. "Jees! The line there will be out the door. We don't have time...." He glanced at her face and stepped on the gas.

The line at the Plaza Bakery *was* out the door. Twenty minutes later, Emma emerged with a large latte and a still warm sour cherry *gallette.*

Steve glanced at her and winced as she took a bite that deposited a snowstorm of pastry flakes on the passenger seat of his car. "Those are loaded with cholesterol," he remarked, "in case you didn't know."

"At least it's *local* cholesterol," she replied.

They drove eating and drinking in silence for another twenty minutes. Till they hit the Santa Rosa rush hour traffic and abruptly slowed to a halt.

"Darn," Emma mumbled noting that a large squirt of foam had sloshed out of her coffee cup down the front of her shirt. As she searched for a Kleenex in her purse, another dollop splashed onto the beige fabric seat of Steve's car. "Sorry," she said.

Steve cringed. By then, he had finished his hash browns and emptied his large McCafe.

"How was the birthday party?" Emma added, hoping to distract him from the mess she'd made with her coffee.

Steve replied with an abrupt shake of his head. Like a pitcher rejecting a catcher's hand signal.

"Tell me more about your conversation with Diaz." Steve clearly didn't want to talk about the party. "The way I see it, you got three important things. Correct me if I'm wrong."

"First," Steve began, "Diaz had a motive to kill Gomez because Gomez was threatening to blackmail him if he didn't join the class action. But Diaz has an alibi for the night Gomez died. And your instincts tell you he isn't the murderer. I think it's because you believe he's..." Steve winced, "too small."

Steve stopped speaking and glanced sideways at Emma. They had emerged from the Santa Rosa rush hour slowdown and entered the Petaluma bottleneck.

Emma nodded. "Go on."

"Second," Steve continued, "a man named Armando Carillo also had a motive to kill Gomez who'd fooled around with his wife. In fact, Carillo threatened to kill Gomez. But he lives near Coachella and nothing places him at the scene of the crime. BTW, I arranged a meeting with him this afternoon. As far as Carillo goes, we have motive but, so far, no opportunity or means."

Steve glanced at Emma who nodded again.

"Third," Steve concluded, "Diaz will testify that Randall hates Mexicans. That less than a month ago, he had enough strength to throw a rock at Diaz's son to get him out of his yard. That the night Gomez died, he told Diaz he was on his way to Randall's house to tell Randall something he didn't want to hear. Gomez intended to meet Diaz later that night. But Gomez never showed up at Diaz's home. The next morning, Diaz found Gomez's body near Randall's house."

Steve glanced at Emma again. "Was there anything else?"

Emma thought for a minute. Then she pulled out of her purse some notes she'd made.

"Did I mention that Diaz said his cousin sounded worried when he talked to him on the phone?" she asked. "That Gomez said something about being in danger?"

Steve shook his head.

Emma consulted her notes again. "Oh, one more thing. There was someone named Louis. Did I mention him?"

Steve shook his head again.

Emma squinted at a name she'd written on her notepad. "Diaz said that a man named Louis Cardenas had dropped out of the lawsuit. He was making trouble. Telling everyone that Gomez was just out for himself. That the lawsuit wouldn't do the workers any good. Gomez was mad about it."

This time Steve nodded. "I've already talked to Cardenas. He withdrew from the suit a few weeks ago. Gomez was upset."

"But it's not a motive for Cardenas to kill Gomez," Emma replied. "More the other way around."

"Besides," Steve added, "Cardenas lives near Coachella. Same as Carillo. Even if he had a motive, nothing places him at the scene of the crime."

By then, the Subaru had crossed the Richmond Bridge and was traveling, at what Emma considered a reckless speed, east on 580 towards Livermore. They were cruising against the traffic now headed for the long, hot, flat stretch of Highway 5 that would take them south towards Los Angeles.

"So, where does that leave us Steve?" she asked. "Who are the suspects? What's the plan?"

Steve paused. "You know where I stand. Everything you've said points to Curt Randall. He hates Mexicans and he particularly hated Gomez for bringing the lawsuit. That gives him a motive. The night he died, Gomez was on his way to Randall's house to tell him something Randall didn't want to hear. That provides Randall with opportunity. And Gomez was killed with Randall's knife that was later found hidden in Randall's garage. That gives Randall the means. Motive, opportunity, means. I'd say the conclusion is inescapable that Randall is the murderer."

Emma was hard put to deny the logic of Steve's argument. Everything pointed to Randall. But she wasn't about to give up on her son-in-law's client yet.

"OK," she nodded. "I agree. Curt Randall had motive, opportunity and means. But just for the sake of argument, since we have an eight hour drive and nothing else to do, let's run through the alternatives."

Steve glanced sideways at her and finally smiled. Emma realized it was the first time she'd seen Steve smile in weeks.

"You got me," he laughed. "I'm trapped. I got nowhere to go."

Emma leaned over and pulled a pen out of her purse. "First, let's make a list of all the possible suspects," she said.

Steve began. "Curt Randall. Motive, opportunity, means."

"Jose Diaz," Emma answered. "Motive. He was being black-mailed by the victim. Opportunity. Gomez arranged to see him the night of the murder. Means. Diaz worked at the ranch and could easily have stolen the weapon to frame Randall."

"But you said you didn't think Diaz killed him," Steve shot back.

"I could always change my mind," Emma shrugged. "Now add Armando Carillo to the list. He had a motive. He hated Gomez for schtupping his wife."

"Schtupping?" Steve raised his eyebrows.

"Not a legal term, but it's descriptive. As for opportunity," she continued, "nothing places him at the scene of the crime; but nothing places him anywhere else."

"We'll interview him tomorrow and get his story," Steve replied.

"What about Cardenas?" Emma added. "Motive..." she hesitated. "Gomez threatened him for backing out of the suit. Maybe they argued and Cardenas killed him."

Steve shook his head. "No opportunity. Nothing places Cardenas at the scene of the crime. And what about the knife? Where did Cardenas get Randall's knife?"

"Maybe we just don't know that yet," was all Emma could reply. "Now add Silas Bugbee to our list," she continued. "He hates Randall for selling the Burbank plums to the Chinese. What if he thought Gomez's suit was the reason Curt needed to sell?"

"You mean the Silas Bugbee who works in the permits department?" Steve scoffed. "The guy who looks like he stepped off the set of *Walden Pond*? Who cries when you ask for a request form? No."

"He has a motive," Emma replied. "So he stays on my list. Finally, there's Rob Peters."

"Who?" Steve asked.

"Rob Peters. Curt Randall's only heir," Emma explained, careful not to disclose what Piers had told her about Randall's plan to change his will.

"If Peters suspected that all his inheritance might disappear paying off a judgment in the Gomez lawsuit, then Peters had a strong motive to murder Gomez. Particularly before that class action got filed. Peters lives in town so he had the opportunity. And he probably had access to his uncle's knife which gives him the means to commit the murder."

"Check it out," Steve replied.

"I intend to," Emma answered. "So, now that we have our list of suspects, what's our plan?"

The plan, Steve explained, was that he and Emma would meet with Armando Carillo later that evening after they checked into their Coachella motel. The next morning, Friday, Emma would meet with Gomez's widow while Steve met with the numbers man to figure out what the family could claim in the wrongful death action. Emma offered to follow up with Louis Cardenas. The man who'd dropped out of the lawsuit.

Steve had started to explain that he'd also set up a late afternoon visit with Gomez's brother and his family, when Emma interrupted him.

"Steve," she said, "I tried to tell you last night. I *have* to go back to Blissburg tomorrow."

Steve shook his head. "That's impossible. If we leave after dinner, we'll be driving all night.

"Then we'll drive all night," Emma replied. "You don't understand. I have to get back. I..." she stammered. "I promised someone. It's important. Really important."

"Can't be done," Steve scoffed. "What's so important that we can't leave Saturday?"

That's when Emma explained. Or tried to. When she finished, Steve wasn't convinced.

"Look, Emma," he began, "it's obvious this boyfriend of yours is very important to you. And yeah, I know he saved your life. But I got my marriage on the line. I got a wife at home who's madder than a hornet that I'm missing her nephew's graduation from nursery school tomorrow in order to help some poor farm worker's family. My whole marriage is going down the tubes over this case – and I'm supposed to worry about your boyfriend missing his $5000 home cooked meal? Sorry. I just can't get that excited about it. But if it means that much – and obviously it does – I'll tell you what I'll do. We'll leave at 5:00 am and I'll have you home by – what? 1:00 on Saturday? OK?"

But Emma knew that was not OK. She shook her head.

"We'll find an airport," she replied. "I'll fly home tomorrow night. Out of Palm Springs."

As she spoke, her fingers tapped on her cell phone. The last flight out of Palm Springs for San Francisco on Friday left at 7:00 p.m. It cost $400, but she'd be home by 11:00.

"You'll drop me at the airport? Right?" she asked.

She must have sounded desperate. Steve immediately agreed.

A few minutes later, he pulled into a hot dusty rest stop where he took a couple of Safeway turkey sandwiches and two bags of chips out of a cooler along with a soda and a bottle of water. They sat at a concrete table under the broiling sun and ate while Emma reserved the flight on her phone. A few minutes later, they were hurtling down Highway 5 again.

14

THURSDAY AFTERNOON – THE GOOD HOUSEKEEPING SEAL

It was well past 2:00 p.m. when Steve finally exited Highway 5 for the 210 towards Coachella. Half an hour later, they pulled into a Motel 6 on the outskirts of town.

Stepping out of the air-conditioned car, Emma felt like she'd slammed into a wall of hot air that knocked the breath out of her lungs.

"Ouch!" Steve grimaced when his fingers touched the scorched car door handle before grabbing her overnight bag from the back seat of the car.

"Hot," she stated.

"Hundred and one, according to my dashboard thermometer," he replied. "You travel light."

"One night," Emma answered. "Remember?"

Steve checked them into their rooms. Heading back outside to find the stairs to the motel's second floor, he called over his shoulder, "Meet you at the car in five. This is a pit and dump the bags stop. We're meeting Carillo at the Citrus Road facility in fifteen."

A few minutes later, Emma found her room at the far end of the first floor outdoor corridor. Its window faced the area assigned for parking semi trucks. She imagined their headlights illuminating the room's scuffed walls in the middle of the night.

She quickly erased that image from her head, dumped her overnight bag on the queen-sized bed's stained blue quilt, and entered the bathroom to wash her face. Then she changed from her T-shirt into a thin cotton short-sleeved blouse, grabbed her purse, locked her door and met Steve back at the car.

The heat had permeated its interior in just the few minutes they were gone. The air inside the car was now thick enough to chew.

They drove southeast of Coachella. In just a few minutes the town had disappeared. All they could see was fields in every direction.

"How do they grow things here?" Emma exclaimed. "It's so hot and dry."

"Wells," Steve answered. "Someone named Rector drilled wells here. Around the turn of the century. I read about it last night. At first, the place was called Woodspur because the railroad stopped near here to pick up lumber from nearby Indio – aka Indian Springs."

"And Coachella?" Emma asked. "Is that a Native American name?"

Steve shook his head. "The story goes that the name was a mistake. A misspelling of a Spanish word, *conchilla*. Which means little shells. Apparently Rector, who owned the land, wanted to name the town Conchilla after a bunch of little shells found in the sand around here. But whoever printed the town prospectus misspelled the name. The developers didn't want to delay the announcement, so Rector accepted the misspelled name and the town's been known as Coachella ever since. Funny, huh?"

"Sad," Emma shrugged, thinking of Blissburg's unlucky namesake – an eighteen year old gold seeker shot in a quarrel. And of California's random place names that seemed, suddenly, to mirror the state's reckless development: Weed, Cool, Yreka.

"Sad compared to the old Spanish names," she added. "Like the missions named after saints - or angels."

Steve shook his head. "All depends on your point of view, Emma. The missions exploited Native Americans. Now Randall exploits Mexicans. It's all the same. It's all sad.'"

A strong smell of onions had suddenly filled the car. She changed the subject.

"What on earth is *that*?" Emma asked.

"Must be the onion harvest," Steve replied. "Randall Enterprises grows a lot of onions around here."

Emma looked out the window. To the right and left, dirt roads crossed the narrow highway. They led across vast fields to dusty collections of houses, barns and what looked like old warehouses. Before long, Steve turned down one of them.

"Where are we?" Emma asked, wondering how a few hours' drive from San Francisco could have dumped her in what looked like an alien world.

"Randall Enterprises," Steve answered.

"Randall Enterprises?" Emma repeated.

He gestured with a hundred and eighty degree sweep of his hand. "As far as the eye can see," he said. "Literally, Randall Enterprises, your friend Curt, owns most of this valley. The land. The farms. The labor camps – now they call them 'employer housing' - those industrial buildings in the distance, the bungalows to the east, the ranches to the south. He owns it all."

"And Carillo? The guy we're interviewing. He lives here?" Emma pointed up the road towards a large block of wood and whitewashed stucco buildings. Some even had small front yards boasting flower and vegetable gardens.

Steve nodded. "Carillo lives in permanent worker housing provided by the company. There's not much of it left. In the eighties and nineties, worker protection laws required all employers who provided housing to meet new federal and state standards. Most growers just stopped providing housing rather than spend the money to upgrade their camps. Of course, that left the workers with no housing at all."

"So what do they do?" Emma asked as Steve pulled into a parking slot in front of one of the wooden, two story buildings.

"They live wherever they can," Steve answered. "Stables, garages, abandoned trailers, tents. Or cheek to jowl in overcrowded apartments in town. They don't get paid enough to rent on the open market – sometimes they aren't in one place more than a few months of the year."

Emma told herself Steve was exaggerating. "That's crazy. People in California don't live in stables. We have laws. Anyway," she added pointing again to the row of houses where they had parked the car, "these houses look fine."

And they did, Emma assured herself as they approached one of the wood dwellings with a particularly well-tended front yard. The two-story building had a front porch with a pot of lavender to the right of the front door. It sat under a painted ceramic medallion of Mary and Baby Jesus that hung on the wall.

When they knocked, a man who looked to be in his mid forties opened the door. His black eyes were set wide apart in his broad face. Under them, his flat nose and mouth looked crowded above an almost non-existent chin. He was not an attractive man, despite a full head of thick wavy black hair that was by far his most attractive feature. *Not a happy man,* Emma thought. Unlike her pint-sized friend from the *Hasta la Vista* Lounge, Armando Carillo was a man she preferred not to meet alone.

His home, on the other hand, was immaculate. *Senora* Helena Carillo, though allegedly unfaithful, was a good housekeeper, Emma noted.

Armando Carillo grudgingly motioned to her and Steve to come in.

They sat down on a brown velvet couch. Emma immediately

noted that its armrests were covered with bright woven textiles much like the ones she used to cover her furniture at home.

"These are beautiful," she exclaimed, fingering the intricate pattern of one of the textiles. "From Chiapas, right?" she added. "I have some fabric that is very similar."

Carillo narrowed his eyes mistrustfully and shifted them from side to side. As though her simple question were a trap.

Steve quickly intervened. "Listen, Mr. Carillo, we know you're busy. And we don't want to take up a lot of your time. As I mentioned on the phone, we are here in connection with Santiago Gomez's murder..."

"Yes, I know." The man's scowl grew darker. "You're here because you think *I* killed that no good dog." He took a menacing step towards Steve.

For a second, Emma wondered if she would have to intervene. And if so, how. Then an attractive young woman, probably in her thirties, entered the room.

"Armando," she said. "That is no way to treat these people. Excuse him," she added to Emma, before turning back to her husband. "Please, everyone sit down. I'm Helena, Mrs. Carillo. Can I offer you something? An *aqua fresca*? Caffe?"

Emma started to reply that an *aqua fresca* sounded great, but Steve cut her off.

"No need to trouble yourself," he shook his head. "And thank you. Thank you very much. We just need to ask you some questions about Mr. Gomez."

"About the way he treated me," the woman interrupted. "Yes, of course. That's why you're here," she added, motioning again for her husband to sit down. "I'm sure you are aware that Mr. Gomez... well..." she cast her eyes demurely to the floor. "That Mr. Gomez made, what shall I call it, some unwanted advances towards me. And that there were rumors, untrue rumors, that required my husband to take some action with regard to him. But I can assure you that nothing happened between me and that man. And that my husband, in my defense, did nothing more than speak some words to him. Angry words, to be sure. But just words."

Helena Carillo glanced at her husband again. Emma interpreted it as a command for him to be silent.

Then she continued. "Any number of people here can bear witness to this fact," she said. "Armando and Santiago argued. Some unpleasant words were exchanged – to defend my honor. That's all. Moreover," she turned to address Steve directly, "as we have already informed the police who were here, the day that Santiago Gomez was murdered, Armando was in the fields overseeing the onion harvest, providing the drinking water, signing the *tarjetas*..." She stopped speaking for a moment, apparently noticing Emma's questioning stare.

"The cards – you know, for the workers to show how many bags of onions they filled." She smiled and walked over to pat her husband's thigh, "My Armando is a foreman, you know. Not a laborer. He is a permanent employee of Randall Enterprises, year round. He represents Randall Enterprises with the labor contractors. That's why we live here." She laughed again. "You think he would risk all this," her eyes took in the living room, the couch, the coffee table, the flat screen TV, "on that dog Gomez? No," she shook her head, "twenty men saw Armando *here*, in Coachella when Gomez died. The police know this. If that is why you are here to talk to us, to accuse my husband, then you are sadly mistaken. Armando Carillo would not hurt a flea."

With that one statement, Emma thought to herself, the beautiful Mrs. Carillo lost all credibility. From the expression on his face, she was sure Armando Carillo would gladly have strangled both her and Steve with his bare hands.

Steve waited for a moment before he replied. Then, inexplicably to Emma, he appeared to abandon all thought that Armando Carillo murdered Gomez in a fit of jealous rage.

"I appreciate everything you've said," he began. "And I am sorry, *Senora* Carillo, that you believe that I have come to accuse your husband. As I explained to him on the phone, the police in Sonoma County are confident that they have found Gomez's murderer. I am confident of this, too. But I am filing a civil law suit against the suspect whom you know, Curt Randall, for money to compensate Gomez's wife and children for their loss." He turned to Carillo. "In order to do this, to remove all doubt as to who murdered Santiago Gomez, I need to confirm your alibi; and to ask you if there is anyone else, besides Curt Randall, who might have had a reason to hate Santiago Gomez enough to kill him."

After glancing at his wife who nodded at him to proceed, Carillo finally spoke.

"As for my alibi," he began. "A lot of people can swear I was here when Gomez died. Antonio Gonzalez...,"

"*Senora* Gomez's cousin," Steve interrupted. "The one whose family she now lives with?"

Carillo nodded. "Then...Louis Cardenas. I signed his tarjeta. The card has a date and the time. To keep track of the work. As far as knowing who else hated Gomez enough to kill him?" Carillo laughed rather harshly. "It's a very long list. Nobody here liked Santiago Gomez."

"What about Cardenas?" Emma cut in, recognizing the name from her conversation with Diaz. "Didn't he have a run in with Gomez about dropping out of the lawsuit?"

Carillo glanced at his wife who answered for him. "Cardenas and Gomez? They had an argument, yes, over the lawsuit. Cardenas is my cousin. I know. But like my husband told you. Cardenas was in the field picking onions when Gomez died. His tarjeta will prove that. So?" she shrugged. "If he was here in Coachella when Gomez died, well...he couldn't be two places at once, could he?"

Steve looked down at his cell phone where he had made a few notes. "OK. I know Gonzales lives with Gomez's wife. Where would I find Cardenas?"

Carillo lifted his shoulders in a leisurely shrug. Then he stood up and walked over to the couch where Steve sat. "Cardenas?" he repeated putting his hand on Steve's arm and slowly but surely guiding him up from the couch, across the room, and out the front door to the porch. "See that big building over there – the big barn? Behind that. That's where Cardenas lives. With the seasonal workers."

Emma had followed Steve outside. He was about to say goodbye, but Emma had one last question. Something *Senora* Carillo said was bothering her.

She turned to address the woman who now stood next to her husband on the porch.

"One more thing, Mrs. Carillo. You said that your husband was working in the fields picking onions the day Santiago Gomez died. But Gomez died at night. Where was your husband *the night* Gomez died?"

Before Emma had finished her question, Senora Carillo opened her big red lips and started to laugh. Even Armando Carillo finally cracked a smile.

"What? Because we're Mexicans you think we're stupid?" the young woman cried. "You think these dumb laborers are gonna pick onions in the bright sun? In this heat? And have a stroke? Lady! The onions. They pick them at night. After the sun goes down. They pick them on their knees. All night long. They wear little headlamps so they can see, and not cut their fingers off in the dark with the sharp little blades of their *tijeras*. Because lady," she laughed again and glanced at her husband, "no *gringa* like you at the big Whole Food, gonna buy an onion with Mexican blood on it." She laughed even harder. "Even though every onion in California is stained with Mexican blood!"

Senora Carillo spat the last words out of her mouth before entering her home and slamming the door. Emma watched Armando glance after her with a proud smile. Then, as Emma and Steve turned to walk to the car, she saw the Mexican pull a cigarette out of his pocket, light it and take a satisfied puff.

15

THURSDAY NIGHT – MORE SECRETS

"Nice goin'," Steve patted Emma on the back as they walked to the car. "Maybe next time you'll do a little homework before you start asking questions. Ever hear the rule, 'don't ask a question you don't already know the answer to?' Number one rule you learn in law school."

"Remember Steve? I didn't go to law school," Emma replied. "Besides," she muttered mostly to herself, "if you already know the answer, why bother to ask the question?"

Nonetheless, Emma wished she'd bit her tongue.

"OK," she added. "Carillo appears to have an alibi for the night Gomez died. But Carillo may be lying. And so far, the only people we have to corroborate what he said are Louis Cardenas, who is Mrs. Carillo's cousin and Antonio Gonzalez…"

"Who is Yolanda Gomez's cousin," Steve finished her sentence, "and has no reason to lie about the identity of her husband's killer. You will talk to him tomorrow and find out. Now, however, we are going to find Louis Cardenas."

Finding Cardenas turned out to be harder than finding his cousin. The dirt road leading from the employer housing where the

Carillos lived all but disappeared as Steve's Subaru made its way towards what looked like a big barn in the distance.

They drove as far as they could, then stopped the car a few hundred feet away from the sprawling, derelict building. Once again, a wall of hot air slammed into her as Emma got out of the air-conditioned car. So that walking the short distance from the car to the warehouse felt like swimming through hot mud. She studied the landscape to find some shade, but all around her she saw nothing but parched low shrubs. Shade for reptiles. *Senora* Carillo's *aqua fresca* rose in her imagination like a mirage.

Steve approached the dilapidated wooden building and peeked in a broken window. All he reported was what he called a *barracks,* row after row of mattresses covering the floor.

Behind the building, however, Emma found a series of low metal sheds. There, a man stood with his back to them, relieving himself noisily against the tin siding of one of the buildings.

Steve called to him. "Do you know Louis Cardenas?"

The man finished what he was doing, zipped up his pants and turned around.

He was of average height and stocky. A short stubbly beard covered half of his tanned brown face, and a blue bandana covered most of his curly black hair. His dark eyes, however, were remarkable for their thick, black lashes – so dark it almost looked to Emma like he was wearing mascara.

To her surprise, Emma thought she recognized the man, though at first she didn't know why. Then she remembered. He looked like the man she'd seen talking to Cheng Bo in the side yard of the Buchanon's home the day of her lunch with HoCo.

Maybe it's just the bandana, she thought, trying to wipe the surprised look off her face. But it wasn't the bandana that she recognized. It was the eyes.

"Who wants to know?" the man asked, ignoring Emma and staring sharply at Steve. The quick, involuntary fluttering of his well-delineated eyelids quickly signaled to Emma that the man was ill at ease.

"My name's Steve Zimmer," Steve answered. "I spoke with you a few weeks ago. About the class action. You'd decided to withdraw and..."

"Gomez is dead," the man replied flatly. "That's the end of it, isn't it? The police have the murderer. Curt Randall. What do you want with me?"

"I just want to ask a few questions," Steve replied. "You knew Gomez..."

"Look man," Cardenas cut in, "the police already questioned me. The night Gomez died, I was over there," he pointed to the fields behind the sheds. "I was picking onions, filling my quotas. I have the *tarjeta* to prove it. The police were satisfied. What else do you need to know?"

By now, Emma could feel herself drenched in sweat. The sun was so hot, she feared she might faint. She looked at Steve.

"Could we go inside somewhere? Out of the sun?" she asked

Again, her simple question provoked nothing but harsh laughter. "You wanna go inside, *Senora*?" the Mexican replied. "Sure, lady, let's go inside. Here," he approached one of the sheds. *"Mi casa es su casa,"* he muttered opening the door and steering her across the threshold.

Inside, the metal structure had heated up like an oven. Way hotter than it was outside. Light filtered in from one dirty window, hazily illuminating a mattress on the floor, a table and a broken wooden chair. There was only one room. No kitchen. No bath. *This man lives in a tool shed,* Emma thought to herself.

Before she fully comprehended what she'd seen, Steve dragged her out by the arm and directed her towards the car.

Then he motioned to Cardenas with a jerk of his head. "I've seen the *tarjeta*," he said. "I don't think you murdered Santiago Gomez. But if Curt Randall *didn't* murder Gomez, I need to find out who did.

Before I file a lawsuit. Maybe you can help me. Is there somewhere I can buy you a cold beer?"

At the mention of the cold beer, Cardenas' reluctance thawed a little. He thought about the offer for a few seconds, blinked a few times, then walked with Emma and Steve towards their car.

Once they were inside, Steve turned the air conditioning on full blast.

Steve glanced at his watch. "Given the time, why don't we grab some dinner too. Where should we go?"

Cardenas directed Steve back onto the highway headed east. Before long, they turned down a two-lane road, and stopped in front of a cantina that served Mexican food. No one had spoken during the course of the short ride.

Inside the restaurant, Cardenas nodded to a few of the patrons who eyed Emma and Steve with suspicion. No one, Emma noted, smiled.

Cardenas sat down at a table and immediately ordered a *Dos Equis* and a plate of enchiladas. Steve and Emma followed suit. It wasn't until the beer arrived that Steve addressed his dinner guest. His first question was not about Gomez's murder, but it was exactly what Emma had on her mind.

"Listen, Louis," Steve began. "Before we talk about Gomez, you gotta explain something to me. Why'd you drop out of the suit?" He shook his head in genuine confusion.

Louis remained silent, so Steve continued. "You're entitled to a better life. A life with dignity. By law, you're entitled to shade, running water, a toilet. That's all we are asking for in the lawsuit. Do you understand?"

Louis had taken a long slow drink of the beer. Emma watched him put the bottle down and focus his eyes on the table. Like he might fall off a cliff if he looked away.

"I need my job," he finally answered.

"You can keep your job," Steve replied. "Randall can't fire you for asking for things you're entitled to."

"Randall?" Cardenas laughed, still staring at the table. "What does he know? The contractors handle everything now. They find the laborers. Handle the payroll. Nothing's gonna change because of a lawsuit. From what I hear, they go on forever. Even if you win you lose. So," he added, "you take the best deal you can get."

"Who told you that?" Emma asked. "About the lawsuits?"

Cardenas clammed up. He wouldn't say.

Their food had arrived. Emma watched the Mexican wolf it down like he hadn't eaten in weeks.

"Do you have family here, Louis?" Emma asked. "Did your family persuade you to drop out of the suit?"

"No. No family here." Carillo shook his head. "I send my mother money in Mexico."

"I can get you *more* money," Steve replied.

The man continued to eat.

That's when Emma remembered Cheng Bo.

"But you do come north, don't you, Louis?" To Sonoma?" she asked. "On family business?"

The man glanced up quickly. "No," he said. His black eyes narrowed with suspicion. "What makes you ask?"

Emma shrugged. "Something *Senora* Carillo said. I must have misunderstood. I thought she said you went north a few days after Gomez died."

Steve looked at her questioningly. "I don't remember that," he said.

"See," Emma smiled. "I was mistaken. You never work in Sonoma, right? You only work here."

Cardenas eyed her for a few seconds. Then he repeated her words, "I never work in Sonoma. I only work here."

But Emma was sure she had seen him. Tearing down signs in the Plaza. Talking to Cheng Bo.

Cardenas grudgingly verified Armando Carillo's alibi on the

night Gomez died. Much as he disliked Gomez, he disliked Armando Carillo more. He called him a brute. A traitor who now worked for the growers. Who'd betrayed his people, misstating their hours, cheating them out of their pay. Turning a blind eye to illegal working conditions.

"As for my cousin, Helena," he added. "Sure she fools around. Who wouldn't with that dog of a husband. She should have left him years ago. But all she cares about is money."

It was dark and the temperature had plummeted by the time they left the restaurant. Emma shivered in her light cotton shirt. They dropped Cardenas back at the end of the dirt road, turned their car around and made their way to the Motel 6.

"So where does that leave you with your list of suspects?" Steve asked when he and Emma were alone in the car.

"Carillo and Cardenas both have alibis," Emma admitted. "Unless they're lying to cover for each other."

"What was all that about Cardenas coming north to visit family? Did I miss something?" Steve asked.

Emma shook her head.

"Cardenas is lying. I saw Cardenas talking to Cheng Bo a few days after the murder," she explained. "He may not have killed Santiago Gomez, but I'll bet the farm he has something to hide."

"Don't we all," Steve answered.

THAT NIGHT, lying in bed, Emma watched the truck lights turn into the parking lot in front of her room. Suddenly illuminating it, and just as suddenly going dark.

What did Steve mean that everyone has something to hide? she asked herself. *I don't. I don't have anything to hide.*

Then, for the first time all day, she thought of Dan Worthington. The affair she'd hidden for years. And suddenly she understood what Steve meant.

16

FRIDAY MORNING – HARD TIMES IN PUEBLODURO

The next morning Emma's cell phone woke her up at 8:00 a.m. It was Jack. Reluctantly, she took the call.

"Don't worry," she replied to his question regarding her whereabouts. "I'm on an early flight home from Palm Springs." Then, hoping to justify her absence, she added, "By the way, we're finding out all kinds of interesting things down here. And boy, were you right. Conditions in Coachella are…"

She stopped speaking, unable to find the right words to describe what she'd seen. "Third world" wasn't PC. Nor was it particularly accurate.

"Unhealthy," she finally finished her sentence. "No one should live the way these poor people do. Not even a dog," she added thinking of the overheated metal shed Louis Cardenas used as a home.

In answer to Jack's next question, however, Emma said only, "No. I have no idea who murdered Gomez. Everyone has an alibi."

Jack mumbled something about safe travels. They said goodbye and hung up.

Five minutes later, Steve called.

"I'm in the breakfast room," he announced. "They've got donuts, pastries and coffee. I suggest you join me – I don't think the Plaza Bakery has a branch in Coachella yet."

"Ha, ha," was all Emma could muster for his early morning sarcasm. "I'll be right down. By the way, I should also check out before we leave."

"Yeah," Steve replied. "I keep forgetting. I'm driving all the way home alone. We'll leave your bags in the trunk so we can drive directly to the airport when we're done."

A FEW MINUTES LATER, overnight bag in hand, Emma had checked out of her room and found her way to the motel's bleak little breakfast room. The cubicle was furnished with square metal tables and folding chairs. Notwithstanding the depressing décor, the dining room was surprisingly full – truckers in T-shirts, salesmen in suits – all of them greeting the two bright eyed wait staff like old friends.

Which, apparently, they were, Emma observed.

"See ya Tuesday, Sal," a portly man in his fifties called to one of the waitresses as he ambled out the door carrying a large sample case.

"As long as you're buying," Sal replied, waving a plump, jewelry-laden hand.

Soon after, a tall man wearing cowboy boots, a white T-shirt and a black denim vest entered the breakfast room and gave the second waitress a bear hug.

"Long time no see, Dottie."

"Visiting my daughter in El Paso," she replied. "Good to be home. How are those grandkids?"

It's a friendly place, Emma noted filling her cardboard cup full of coffee and joining the pastry line. *A transient subculture of familiar faces. A caravansary along a latter day Silk Road. With Chevys and Mack trucks instead of camels. Donuts and coffee instead of dates and tea.*

That thought somehow eased Emma's guilt when she grabbed a

huge glazed donut off the tray, eagerly anticipating the explosion of sugar in her mouth.

Steve was already well into his second chocolate donut and third cup of coffee. "Eat up," was all he said looking at his watch as she sat down. "You're dropping me in Coachella where I'm meeting the numbers guy at 9:00. Gomez's widow lives just a few miles out of town. It's a place called Puebloduro. I've plugged the address into my GPS so it'll be easy to find."

"Can't you drop me first?" Emma replied, rattled by the offer of the GPS. "I'm not comfortable driving around here alone."

Steve rolled his eyes. "You sound like my mother."

Emma took the comparison as unflattering.

"OK. I'll drop you there," he relented, rising from his chair coffee cup in hand. "But you may have to kill some time if you get finished with Mrs. Gomez before I'm finished with the numbers guy. He's doing me a favor. I'm taking all the time I need. I'm warning you. There won't be much to do in Puebloduro while you wait for me to pick you up."

"I'll kill the time," Emma replied, translating the name in her head. The word *duro* meant "hard" in Italian. And *pueblo* meant "town" in Spanish. It wasn't promising.

"You remember the assignment? All the questions to ask?" Steve asked.

Emma nodded. "Yes."

It took only a few minutes to drive from the motel to Puebloduro. At a glance, Emma noted, the place lived up to its name – a dirt road off the highway leading to a dilapidated trailer park. Along the way, Emma noticed a steady stream of women carrying large plastic bottles. Gaggles of children played happily enough on bare, treeless, unpaved streets. It looked like a scene from a refugee camp in a war zone.

"What's with the plastic bottles?" Emma asked as Steve pulled to a stop in front of the small, broken down trailer where Santiago Gomez's widow lived.

"The water here's contaminated," Steve shrugged. "There've been some stories about it in the news. People have to get their drinking water from a tank. That's what the plastic bottles are for."

"Doesn't the city do something about it?" Emma replied.

"City?" Steve laughed. "What city? This is a DUC."

"A what?"

"An Disadvantaged Unincorporated Community."

Emma's eyebrows shot up in surprise. "We allow that? In California?"

"Apparently in California *we* do," Steve nodded. "And you, lady, are lookin' at one." He drummed his fingertips on the steering wheel. "I gotta go."

But as Emma opened the car door, he tapped her shoulder. "You know what to say? Right?"

Emma nodded. They'd discussed it the day before. "I'm looking for three things. First, information about anyone Yolanda Gomez thinks might have wanted to kill her husband. Second, information about why Gomez went north to the ranch the week he died. Third, what Yolanda thinks her husband planned to tell Curt Randall on the night he died."

Steve agreed. "Then find out anything you can about the family, the kids, their circumstances, their needs." He motioned for her to get out of the car. "I'll call your cell when I'm done with the numbers guy. By the way," he added as she slammed the door, "thanks, Emma. Thanks for doing this." Before Emma could reply, Steve had driven away.

Yolanda Gomez's trailer looked more like a transport vehicle than a home. More like a trailer you'd haul animals in, or furniture or packed goods. There were no front stairs. Just a front door flush to the ground.

Two young children playing in the street eyed Emma suspiciously as she knocked. Then a woman with a careworn face and a toddler hanging on her long denim skirt opened the door. She had lots of black hair that she'd caught up in a bun. She looked to be about thirty and might have been beautiful had she not looked so sad.

"Yolanda?" Emma asked.

The woman nodded.

"Emma Corsi. I work with Steve Zimmer. He couldn't come today – he's meeting with a man who is helping to find out what you may be entitled to on account of your husband's death." Emma stopped, then added, "Though, of course, no amount of money can…"

The woman bit her lip and nodded again. "Come in," she said.

Emma entered and looked around.

There wasn't much to see. The trailer Emma entered appeared to have two rooms. The one in which she stood was a combined living room and kitchen with a refrigerator and hot plate. She guessed that a closed door led to a bedroom and, hopefully, a bathroom as well.

Once inside, Yolanda Gomez placed her forefinger to her lips. Then in a soft voice she said, "We must talk quietly. My brother, Antonio, he is asleep in the next room. He works at night, picking vegetables."

"I understand," Emma said. Then she felt foolish. What could she understand? Nothing she saw made sense. But she added, suddenly curious. "How many people live here – in the trailer."

Yolanda thought for a moment. "Including the baby?" she asked, sitting down and scooping the little girl into her lap.

Emma nodded again.

"Six," Yolanda answered. "Me, my brother and my mother – and the three little ones. But that's since…" Her voice trailed off.

"Six?" Emma repeated, throwing her hands up involuntarily in disbelief.

"Santiago and my brother both worked at night," Yolanda Gomez explained. "They sleep during the day. My mother and I use the bed while they are in the field. The little ones," she smiled. "They can fall asleep anywhere. During the day they are in school. Today, the bus broke down. So I tell them to play outside. So as not to wake my brother."

"I see," Emma replied.

"Can I offer you something? Coffee?"

Emma shook her head. What she really wanted was water. But according to Steve, that was scarce. She was about to jump into her questions, when Yolanda interrupted her.

"Mrs. Corsi, right?"

"Emma," Emma corrected her.

"Emma," the young woman repeated. "First of all, I want you to know how much me and my family appreciate all that Steve has tried to do for us. This is a terrible thing that has happened. We need all the help we can get."

Emma nodded.

"But I will be honest," the woman continued. "As you may know, my husband left what was a good job in Sonoma to come and work here. So he could be a part of the, what do you say? Lawsuit? At first, he convinced me it was a good idea. Curt Randall, he is not a nice man. I thought Santiago was doing the right thing. Moving here. Making the old man pay for getting rich off our backs."

"But now you don't think the lawsuit was a good idea," Emma sighed.

The woman nodded. "My husband was a hard man. Sometimes he treated me badly. I will be honest with you, sometimes I do not miss him. But this lawsuit? What has it got us? Nothing. And if we had stayed put, my husband would be alive. And we would still have a decent roof over our heads."

Emma's face must have betrayed the pain she felt hearing those words.

The woman shrugged. "I'm not blaming you or Steve. If Mr. Randall is breaking the law, like Steve said, he should pay. But it's still not a fight worth fighting. Not for people like us. Not for me." She looked at her daughter. "Not for them."

"OK," Emma nodded. "But if Curt Randall murdered your husband and Steve can get you money, that's OK. Right?"

Emma took the woman's shrug as a skeptical yes.

"Then here is what I need to know...."

She began with Steve's list of questions.

"First, was there anyone else, besides Curt Randall, that might have wanted your husband dead?"

Yolanda Gomez's answer to this question was more complicated than Emma expected. Much like Armando Diaz, she described her husband as a man haunted by trouble.

"It followed him like his shadow," his wife explained. "From the moment I met him. He fought with everyone. His family. His friends. He didn't have any except Louis Cardenas. He fought with his employers. With people he met in bars."

The young widow stopped speaking abruptly. Then as though to answer the question Emma did not ask she said. "Why did I marry such a man? I was pregnant. I didn't have a choice."

"You didn't have a choice," Emma repeated softly.

"About getting pregnant," the woman laughed bitterly. "And then, about getting married."

Emma felt a sharp intake of breath. This was not the story she had expected.

"In answer to your question," the woman continued. "A lot of people wanted to see my husband dead." Her voice dropped to a whisper. "Sometimes, even me."

In response to the look of horror that Emma felt cross her face, the widow added quickly, "I didn't kill my husband. I was here the night he died. Here with my mother. She will tell you the same."

Emma quickly ran through the list of other suspects. Yolanda Gomez confirmed each one's alibi. Armando Carillo hated Gomez but he was in the fields picking onions on the night her husband died. Her brother had seen him. As for Jose Diaz, Yolanda just laughed.

"Jose was afraid of his own shadow." She repeated the bartender's phrase. "He wouldn't hurt a flea. Couldn't. He was afraid of Santiago since they were kids. That is why Santiago thought he could bully him into joining the lawsuit."

"But he didn't," Emma replied.

"Apparently not." Yolanda squinted her eyes at Emma. "I know what you're thinking. Sure, Jose carried a grudge. But Jose is not a killer."

"What about Louis Cardenas?" Emma asked. "You just said Cardenas was your late husband's friend. Perhaps the only friend he had. Why did Cardenas drop out of the suit?"

Yolanda Gomez explained, "That is why Santiago went north, *Senora*. To answer that question. Louis and Santiago were friends since childhood. Then, suddenly, Louis drops out of the lawsuit. But that's not all. He convinces other workers to do the same. Santiago couldn't figure out why. All he knew was that Louis was traveling north. So he followed him to find out what was going on."

"Did he find out?" Emma replied, finally believing she was on to something.

Yolanda Gomez dropped her eyes. "I don't know," was all she said.

"What do you mean? What don't you know?" Emma asked.

"The last time I talked to him, all Santiago said was that Louis – that 'rat' he called him – had found a better way to...he used a not nice word...to screw Randall."

"And what was the 'better way'?" Emma asked.

Yolanda nodded. "That's what I don't know. Santiago never called me again. The next morning Jose called. He told me Santiago was dead."

Emma thought about everything Yolanda had said. Then she asked the third question. "On the night he died, Santiago told his cousin that he was going to Randall's house to tell him something Randall didn't want to hear. Something that would make Randall respect him. Do you know what that was?"

Yolanda Gomez shook her head. "No."

Emma continued. "Santiago also told his cousin that night that he was in danger. Do you know why?"

Again, Mrs. Gomez shook her head. "No."

Emma paused a few more seconds. Then she asked one more question. "Is there anything else you think Steve and I should know, Mrs. Gomez? Anything that might possibly shed light on who killed your husband?"

After Emma asked her question, Yolanda Gomez was silent for a long time. Emma could tell she was struggling with something. Something she knew, but didn't want to tell.

"Mrs. Gomez," Emma finally said. "It's important to a lot of people that we find out who killed your late husband. Please. If you have any more information, tell me. It could make the difference between an innocent man going to jail – or a guilty man going free."

Still, Yolanda Gomez remained silent. Her black eyes flickered around the room like desperate flies.

When she finally spoke, her voice barely registered above whisper.

"The last night I spoke to Santiago," she said, "he told me someone was paying Louis off. I don't know who. But you cannot tell Louis I know. He'll kill me if you do."

"Louis Cardenas would kill you?" Emma gasped. "Then Louis Cardenas would kill your husband, too."

"That's right," Yolanda Gomez nodded. "But he didn't. The night Santiago died, he was in the fields working, side by side with my brother. You can ask Antonio when he wakes up. Louis did not kill my husband. Someone else did."

· · ·

AN HOUR later Emma had asked Yolanda every question she could think of regarding the Gomez family: schools, health issues, special needs. Anything that might help Steve get a bigger judgment against Curt Randall.

Then Emma's phone rang. It was Steve.

"Hi," he said. "How's it going?"

"OK," she answered guardedly.

"I'm delayed," he added.

"What?" she said.

"Delayed. We got a lotta stuff to do. You're gonna have to kill another couple of hours."

"Couple of hours!" Emma gasped.

"It was your call to give me the car," Steve reminded her. "You didn't want to drive."

Emma took a deep breath. "OK," she replied. "Call me when you're done."

Steve hung up.

17

FRIDAY NOON – A GIRL NAMED MARIA

Emma clicked off her phone and looked around the small room where she and Yolanda Gomez sat talking.

"Steve's running late," she apologized. "I know you must have things to do. I've taken up enough of your time. Is there anywhere I can walk to get some lunch?"

Yolanda laughed. Then she shook her head. "If you wait a few minutes, maybe my mother can drop you somewhere. When she takes my brother to work. There's a cantina, but it's too far to walk. Especially in this heat."

Which, Emma knew, was true. Over the course of their conversation, the room where they sat had heated up like the inside of a furnace.

Yolanda had excused herself to make her brother some lunch when Emma thought of something. She knew it wasn't relevant to the Gomez murder, but it interested her just the same.

Yolanda had heated up some rice and beans and made some quesadillas. She offered a plate to Emma. Munching on the rice and beans, Emma asked Yolanda about her mother.

"My mother?" Yolanda replied. "She cleans houses every morning in Coachella. She takes the car." Yolanda glanced at her watch. "She'll be back very soon to drive Antonio to work. We couldn't manage any other way."

"How old is she?" Emma asked, surprised that the woman still cleaned houses.

"Sixty-five. She was old when she had me," Yolanda explained.

"Your mother's my age," Emma said, grateful she wasn't cleaning houses. "Is she from around here?" she asked.

"Down the road, in Thermal," Yolanda replied. "And guess who she worked for as a kid."

"Curt Randall?" Emma asked. She had already done the calculation in her head. At sixty-five, Yolanda's mother would have been close to Cory's age. Curt Randall's son who died in Viet Nam. "Did your mother know Cory Randall?" she asked.

The young woman put down the pan she was washing. "Sure," she said. "My mother knew Cory. I think she knew Cory well. She always said Cory was different."

"What do you mean?" Emma asked.

"Different from his father." Yolanda shrugged. "Of course, *I* never knew him, but according to Ma, everyone *loved* Cory."

This information took Emma by surprise. "Loved him?" she repeated.

Yolanda laughed. It was the first time she had smiled since Emma arrived. "Yeah. According to Ma, Cory was the opposite of his dad. Kind. Generous." She giggled. "And handsome. But if you really want to know about Cory Randall, wait till Ma gets home. She'll give you an earful."

A few minutes later, Concetta Gonzales walked into the trailer, followed by her grandson and daughter. Her eyes narrowed suspiciously when she saw Emma, creating an older replica of the look her eight-year-old granddaughter had given Emma when she arrived.

Yolanda quickly introduced Emma to her mother. But the older woman brushed by her to knock on the bedroom door.

"Antonio, get up," she cried. "You're gonna to be late. Am I the only one here who still works?"

Clearly, Emma thought to herself, Concetta Gonzales was a force to be reckoned with.

Yolanda handed her mother a plate of rice and beans. The older woman dug into it hungrily before finally addressing Emma.

"You're here about the lawsuit, right?" she asked. "You gonna get them some money?" She gestured towards her three grandchildren. "That son of ..." she stopped. "Well, he oughta be good for something, right?"

Emma nodded. "I hope so."

"Gotta do more than hope," Concetta nodded matter-of-factly. "So?" she asked, "did my daughter tell you everything you need to know?"

Before Emma could answer, Yolanda cut in, "Ms. Corsi asked me about Cory Randall, Ma. I told her you were the person..."

At that moment, Antonio opened the bedroom door. He grabbed his lunch off the hot plate and looked at his watch. "We gotta go, Ma." Glancing at Emma he added, "Who's she? That lady from Steve's office?"

"She wants to know about Cory Randall," Concetta answered.

Antonio had rolled his quesadilla into a napkin. "Time to leave, Ma. We're workin' on Indio Lane. It's a good hour's drive. I'm startin' early today."

Watching the mother and son prepare to leave, Emma's heart sank. Her curiosity about Cory Randall would not be satisfied that day.

But when Concetta Gonzales opened the front door to the trailer, she motioned Emma to follow her with an abrupt shake of her head. "You! What's your name again?"

"Emma. Emma Corsi," Emma answered.

"OK, Emma. You wanna hear about Cory Randall?" she said.

"Come on in the truck. I'm gonna tell you everything you need to know."

That is how Emma found herself jammed between Antonio Gonzales and his mother in the front seat of an old green Ford pickup truck, bumping over rutted roads out to the Randall Enterprises' Indio Lane farm.

When they dropped Antonio off at the field, Emma remembered to confirm he'd seen Louis Cardenas in Coachella the night Santiago Gomez died. Concetta confirmed her daughter's alibi as well.

"I'm no fan of Cardenas," Antonio shrugged. "But, yeah, he was there. There's no way he killed Yolanda's brute of a husband. As for my sister?" The notion of her needing an alibi made him laugh. "Why would my sister go to Sonoma to kill her husband? She could have done it a hundred times, without leaving home. I'd have handed her the poison to do it. Right, Ma?"

Concetta Gonzales nodded. "Yolanda was home, with me, the night Santiago died."

It was on the long, hot ride back to Puebloduro that Concetta Gonzalez then told Emma the story of Cory Randall. It had all the romance and heartbreak of a Latino soap.

"I met Cory the summer I turned fourteen," Concetta began. "He was fifteen when he first came here to work in the fields. Of course, everyone knew that, one day, he would take over the business. So he was important. *Mui importante.* Smart. And *guapo.* You know, handsome. Like a movie star." Concetta Gonzales rolled her eyes and patted her heart. "Not a Latino lover," she added. "More like Tab Hunter. Remember him?"

Emma remembered Tab Hunter well. The cute, blond, teenage heartthrob of the fifties.

"So you could say he was not really our type here in Coachella," Concetta shrugged. "But, of course, he *was* our type. Cory was every girl in America's type."

Concetta Gonzales stopped talking. Her eyes glazed over staring through the windshield. She remained transfixed so long Emma feared she might not continue.

"So what happened next, Concetta?" she finally asked.

Concetta gave her head a sharp little shake and glanced sideways at her listener. "What happened next? Well," she continued, "nothing, exactly."

Emma waited for Concetta to continue. Then her stomach sank. *Was that it?* she wondered. *Cory Randall was the cute son of the company's owner whom all the girls had a crush on? End of story?*

"Did you actually meet him?" she said.

"Meet him?" Concetta scoffed. "Of course I met him. We all met him. My brother lived with him in the men's barracks." She glanced sideways at Emma and snorted. "Now they call it 'employer housing.' It has to be up to code. A lot of good that did. Growers don't provide housing any more. Now the migrants..."

Emma feared Concetta would get sidetracked again. "But getting back to Cory."

"Cory," Concetta nodded sharply. "He was such a nice guy. Any time he got a little money, he took us dancing. Or to the movies. He had a car, too. When he turned sixteen. A red Corvette convertible. I drove in it a few times."

They were halfway back to the trailer park. Concetta turned to look at Emma. "You wanna stop for a beer?"

They'd sat down in an air-conditioned cantina and ordered drinks when Concetta resumed her story.

"Of course I had a crush on Cory." She shrugged. "Everyone did. But there was nothing romantic. He was a gentleman. A *real* gentleman," she repeated slowly nodding her head.

"So what happened?" Emma asked, afraid, once again, that the story might end there.

Concetta sighed. "What happened is that before we knew it, it was the sixties. And like I said, Cory was smart. So smart he got into Stanford, that fancy school up north. Of course, all of us thought,

That's it. Cory's never hangin' out with us Latinos anymore. But guess what? Nothing changed. Every summer, Cory came down to Coachella. Lived in the labor camp. Worked with us, side by side."

Concetta stopped talking again and seemed to consider something. Finally she said, "I guess I shouldn't say *nothing* changed. Two things changed. The first thing was Cory."

"How?" Emma asked. "Did he get snobby?"

"Snobby?" Concetta looked annoyed. "Cory was never snobby."

"Then what do you mean?" Emma said.

"Cory didn't get snobby at Stanford," Concetta repeated emphatically. "It was the sixties, honey. Remember? You're my age, right? What do you think happened? Cory got political. Chavez started the boycotts. Cory and his father argued over how old Mr. Randall was running the farm."

"I never heard them argue," Concetta added, "but that's what people said. Cory told us workers we should have better housing. Better working condition. He even encouraged us to organize. Mind you, all this while he was the grower's son spending the summer here working under exactly the same conditions."

"So, all of a sudden, Cory the all-America heartthrob, became Cory the saint," Emma cut in.

Concetta didn't like the comparison. She shook her head. "Cory wasn't like that. He was our friend, not a saint."

"So what else changed?" Emma asked.

"The other thing that changed was probably just as important. No," Concetta corrected herself. "In the end, sadly, it was more important." She took a deep breath, and again became lost in thought.

Emma waited for a few seconds for Concetta to continue. When she didn't, Emma finally exploded.

"What? What was the second thing?" she asked.

"The year Cory turned nineteen, a new family came to work here," Concetta replied. "The Hidalgos. They had five children. The middle daughter was my age, seventeen. She and I became friends. Her name was Maria. She was very smart. She wanted to be a doctor. Imagine! A farm worker wanting to be a doctor. And she was beautiful." Concetta laughed cynically. "You can imagine the rest..."

She stopped talking again and stared out the windshield.

Once again, Emma feared that the woman was not going to continue. "Please tell me what happened," she said.

Concetta let out a long sigh. "That summer Cory and Maria fell in love. I was with them the night they met. He looked at her and I saw the look I had always wanted to see when he looked at *me*."

"So?" Emma asked.

"So nothing," Concetta replied, "at first. Maria put him off. No one could believe it. She rejected the advances of the boss's son. Of course, that only made him love her more. When school started, he even drove down from Stanford on the weekends to be near her. And finally, I guess, she relented. By then she was in college in L.A. I didn't see much of her anymore."

"So what did they do?" Emma asked.

"You mean, what did Cory do?" Concetta shrugged. "The summer he turned twenty-one, he asked her to marry him. The guy was an angel. And...he was in love."

"So what happened?" Emma replied.

"I was very jealous of Maria," Concetta answered. "She knew that. And so she stopped confiding in me. Her mother had got a good job working somewhere in a hospital. They bought a house in another town. After they moved, I didn't see Maria. All I know – because everyone here knew – is that during that summer, Cory told his father he wanted to marry Maria Hidalgo."

"Oh my gosh," Emma exclaimed. All the pieces of the story suddenly fell into place.

Concetta turned to her again with tears in her eyes.

"I see it in your face. You understand," she said. "When Cory told his father he wanted to marry Maria, his father went crazy. He visited Maria's family. To their face, he called her a…I won't say the word. You know what he said. Then he told Cory he'd disown him if he ever saw Maria again."

"What did Cory do?" Emma exclaimed.

"Cory wanted to marry Maria anyway. But Maria…," Concetta hesitated. "She wouldn't let him do that. Her pride was hurt. You know. For the things the father had said."

"So that's why Cory went to Viet Nam," Emma finished the story.

Concetta nodded. "After his father forbid him to marry Maria, Cory and his father had a terrible argument. Cory left home and never spoke to his father again. Then he dropped out of Stanford, enlisted in the army, and died six months later."

"What about Cory's mother?" Emma asked.

Concetta swatted her hand. "Old Mrs. Randall did exactly what Old Man Randall told her to. Then she died of a broken heart."

"Wow!" Emma exclaimed.

While Concetta was finishing her story, she and Emma had left the restaurant, gotten into the car and driven back to Puebloduro. When they pulled up beside the Gomez trailer, Emma noticed Steve's Subaru parked nearby. Steve stood a few feet away talking to Yolanda. Now he motioned to Emma to get out of the car.

"What happened to her?" Emma asked, ignoring him.

"To Maria?" Concetta answered. "I don't know. Like I said, I never saw her again. But I've heard that Maria always blamed herself for Cory's death. Like it was her fault. That maybe, if she'd acted differently, he'd still be alive."

"What did Maria do? Did she become a doctor?"

"I didn't care to know," Concetta grimaced. "Maybe, I blamed her a little, too, for Cory's death. We never got in touch. I heard she got married."

"To whom?" Emma asked.

"Sounded like a *gringo* name. Miller, I think, like the beer. And I heard she had a son."

Emma thought for a second. "When? How old is *he*?"

Concetta shrugged again. "It was a long time ago. He must be in his forties. I even sometimes wondered...." Concetta let the sentence hang unfinished.

Steve was still gesturing to Emma to get out of the car. But she had one last question. "So you have no idea where she is now?"

"Maria?" Concetta asked. "Last I heard, she was working at some school. Near Riverside I think. But that was a *long* time ago."

"Doing what?" Emma replied.

Concetta shook her head. "I don't know. I don't even remember where I heard it. Like I said, I haven't spoken with Maria Hidalgo in...," she laughed, "in over forty years."

18

FRIDAY AFTERNOON – BREAKING THE COWGIRL CODE

Steve had waved goodbye to Mrs. Gomez and started to walk towards the truck. As Emma opened the door and stepped down out of the cab, he took her arm.

"Where have you been?" he whispered directing her towards his car. "You were supposed to be interviewing the widow, not touring the Coachella Valley with her mother. We're late for the next meeting."

"I've got some really important information," Emma whispered back.

"From whom?" Steve opened the Subaru door and all but shoved her into the car. "Yolanda or the mother?"

"The mother," Emma answered. "It's about..."

"Save it for later," Steve interrupted as he ducked into the driver's seat. "First, I want to know what you heard from Yolanda Gomez and her brother."

Emma quickly repeated everything she'd heard from Yolanda Gomez: that nobody liked her husband; that there were times when even she wished he were dead; that her brother hated him as well. Nonetheless, Emma assured Steve that everyone she'd talked to had an alibi for the night Gomez died.

"They could all be lying," Steve shrugged. "Lying to protect themselves."

"As for why Gomez went north," Emma nodded, "according to Yolanda, he wanted to find out why his friend, Cardenas, dropped out of the suit."

"Did he ever find out?"

Emma shrugged. "Yolanda thinks someone paid Cardenas off."

"Who?" Steve asked.

"She doesn't know," Emma answered. "But think about it, Steve. Any number of people had reason to sabotage the lawsuit..."

"Like who?" Steve asked.

"Randall's nephew, Rob Peters," Emma answered, thinking fast. "If the lawsuit sucked money out of the estate, he had a reason to pay Cardenas to sabotage it. And what about the Chinese?" she added. "Maybe they wanted to stop the lawsuit."

"Why?" Steve asked. "I thought the lawsuit made Randall desperate to sell?"

Emma threw up her hands. "I don't know. Maybe Silas Bugbee paid him off to block the lawsuit. So the old man wouldn't be so desperate to sell to the Chinese."

Steve shook his head. "Nah. Everything still points to Randall."

That's when Emma told Steve about Cory.

"I want to find her," Emma concluded. "I want to find this Maria Miller, or whatever her name is. I want to know what happened to her."

"Why?" Steve asked. The star-crossed lovers story had not impressed him. "I say, let sleeping dogs lie."

Emma didn't agree. "Maria had a son. He's in his forties. Don't you see? It could be Curt Randall's grandson. Don't you want to know?"

Steve rolled his eyes. "First of all, that grandson thing only happens in movies. Old movies. Forget about it. And even if Curt Randall has a grandson, the kid's half Mexican. Given what we know, Randall won't be happy about that. More likely, he'll go ballistic."

But Emma believed Steve was wrong. He didn't have children. He didn't know.

"Please don't get sidetracked on this soap opera," Steve warned as they drove through downtown Coachella. "We've got more important things to do."

AN HOUR LATER, Emma and Steve left Santiago Gomez's brother's house no wiser than before. Their interview had turned up nothing.

"Lets go to the airport," Steve said. "If we're early, we'll grab a bite to eat before you get on the plane. I'm guessing the food at the Palm Springs Airport will be OK. I hope so. I'm famished."

"No lunch?" Emma asked.

"No money," Steve replied.

"Is this investigation all coming out of your pocket?" Emma asked.

Steve nodded. "Another reason my wife's so mad."

"Then dinner tonight's on me," Emma announced looking at her watch. "Assuming there's time."

THEY WERE HEADED out Grapefruit Boulevard towards Highway 10. Traffic was light. Within twenty minutes they'd turned off the highway on to Date Palm Drive. From there it was just a few more minutes to North Gene Autry Trail and the Palm Springs International Airport.

"You probably don't even know who Gene Autry was," Emma noted as Steve followed the signs towards the short-term parking lot near the main terminal.

"He was a cowboy, wasn't he?" Steve answered. "Way back in the fifties. He had that horse, Trigger."

Emma shook her head. "Wrong. That was Roy Rogers. Gene Autry's horse was Champion. There was a TV show when I was little - *The Adventures of Champion*. Gene Autry was the star. He made up something called the Cowboy Code that I still live by: never shoot first, never lie, be kind to old people and children, and never go back on your word..."

Steve just rolled his eyes.

They'd gotten out of the car and entered the terminal. Steve shouldered Emma's overnight bag and searched for a restaurant while Emma checked her cell phone. Jack had called twice.

They were on their way towards Chili's, when the Departures screen caught Emma's eye. She hadn't thought to check her flight status. The weather in Palm Springs was crystal clear.

She quickly ran down the list of departures looking for "San Francisco." That's when she realized that a light on the screen was flashing next to her flight. For a second or two her eyes refused to believe what she saw.

Steve must have noticed the look on her face. His eyes followed hers to the screen. Next to "San Francisco/7:00 p.m." the word "cancelled" was pulsing.

"Whoops," she heard Steve say. "Looks like we may have a leisurely dinner after all."

That wasn't the reaction Emma wanted.

She covered her face with her hands. Then uncovered it quickly and glanced at the sign again, hoping it had changed.

"That's impossible. They *can't* cancel this flight. I *have* to get home," she muttered through clenched teeth.

Never go back on your word. Never go back on your word. Suddenly, all she could think of was the Cowboy Code. She'd given her word to Jack. She'd promised she be home in plenty of time. She covered her face with her hands again; and wondered what on earth she was going to do.

Seconds later she stood at the check-in counter arguing with the airline attendant.

"You don't understand," she answered after the woman told her San Francisco was completely fogged in. "I have to get up north tonight. What about Oakland?"

"Oakland's fogged in, too," the woman replied.

"San Jose?"

"The last San Jose flight tonight has already departed," the woman patiently explained. "The best I can do is put you on the 10:00 a.m. San Francisco flight tomorrow morning, assuming the fog clears."

"Well," Emma sputtered, her voice becoming a little too loud. "That's just not good enough! I promised someone! I promised I'd be there tonight..."

Later Steve told her she shouted something about the Cowboy Code. That's when he grabbed her by the shoulder, spun her around, and slashed his forefinger across his throat. Then *he* took over the questioning.

"You're out of luck," he finally turned to address her. "There are no flights leaving for the Bay Area tonight. The first available flight tomorrow gets you home around noon."

Emma started to protest, but Steve cut her off. "Look, Emma, there's nothing anyone can do. It's nobody's fault. There are no more flights. So here's a plan. It's 6:15. We'll have dinner, be back at the motel by 8:00. Then we'll get up at 4:00 and I'll try to have you home by noon. That's as good an offer as you're gonna get. So be quiet and take it. Now let's go eat."

Emma bit her tongue and followed Steve into Chili's.

They both ordered steaks. They weren't half bad. While she chewed the red meat, Emma thought about her next move. It almost made her choke, but she knew she had no choice.

. . .

STEVE AND EMMA FINISHED DINNER, checked her into the motel again, and were in their rooms by 7:45. Staring around at the grimy walls – *what was that oozing, through the wallpaper* she wondered – Emma doubted the room had even been cleaned. Then her cell phone lit up. The ringer was still off.

There were four new messages from Jack.

"Are you back yet? Do you need help?

"Call me."

"Are you OK? Why don't you answer?"

"I'm starting to worry."

She messaged him back. "No worries. I'm up to my elbows in wet spinach and ricotta cheese. Almost done. Call you in the morning."

So much for the Cowboy Code. She'd now violated three of its rules. She'd gone back on her word, lied, and just been unkind to a senior.

But that was the easy message. It was the next communication that she dreaded. She pressed a new number into her cell phone.

The recipient answered on the first ring.

"Hi, it's me." Emma caught herself. "It's Emma."

There was a pause on the other end of the line. Then a jaunty voice replied.

"Emma. Can you hold on a minute?"

Emma waited. She could hear a conversation in the background. A female voice. Then a rushed goodbye.

The jaunty voice spoke to her again. "To what do I owe this pleasant surprise? Julie tells me you're down south. Working on a case…"

Emma took a deep breath, then finally replied, "Yes, Andy, I'm down south. In Coachella, to be exact. In fact, that is the reason for the call. I need your help."

There was a short pause at the other end of the line. "Really?" her ex husband replied in a voice that sounded more intrigued than surprised.

That's when Emma explained about Curt Randall, about the lawsuit, and about Jack Russo's dinner.

"The poor guy's obviously been framed," Andy replied regarding the lawsuit.

Since his fraud conviction, Emma noticed that Andy was an expert on being framed.

Emma let the comment slide. "About the dinner..." she reminded him.

Andy hesitated so long that Emma thought her ex-husband was going to refuse. Then he sighed laboriously. "You should have told me sooner. I offered to help. What exactly do you need me to do?"

Emma had fought with herself over what to say next.

"Andy, I'm in a jam," she said. "You're the only other person who knows Nonnie's *malfatti* recipe. Remember? You and I made it together a few times. In the old days. Do you think you could make a batch for me tonight? I'll email the recipe..."

"Don't bother," Andy replied. "I copied it years ago. Before I moved out. I can make Nonnie's sauce, too," he added.

"You stole the *malfatti* recipe?" Emma shouted. For some reason she thought she was going to cry. "You wrecked my life *and* you stole the *malfatti* recipe?"

"Community property. What did you expect me to do?" Andy was completely calm.

"Nothing," Emma replied. Then she clenched her jaw and counted to ten. "Anyway, I'm not using Nonnie's sauce this time. Just sautéed fresh cherry tomatoes." She took a deep breath. "Are you sure you have the *malfatti* recipe? Two tablespoons of chopped yellow onion sautéed in butter. Add two pounds of fresh cooked spinach, chopped and squeezed dry. Sauté for five minutes with a little salt and pepper. Add a cup and a half of ricotta cheese, four egg yolks and a cup and a half of Parmesan cheese, nutmeg and a little bit of flour to keep it all together.

"No problem," Andy answered. "I've made it dozens of times."

"OK," Emma replied. She was squeezing the phone so hard her hand hurt. "But you know the little trick, right? You add as little flour as possible so the *malfatti* don't get tough. Just a few tablespoons. Then shape the mixture into little balls the size of small walnuts, roll them in flour and boil them till they float to the top."

"Got it," Andy replied. "I usually try not to use *any* flour except to coat them."

Suddenly Emma got worried.

"No!" she exclaimed. "Forget that. Use *some* flour, otherwise the *malfatti* will completely fall apart. If that happens, we're screwed. Play it safe. Use flour. When they're cooked, coat them with melted butter. Then refrigerate them till I pick them up tomorrow around noon. Will you do that for me? Will you do me that one favor?"

Before Andy answered, Emma thought of something else. "Wait. Aren't you still under house arrest? How are you going to shop?"

"No worries," Andy assured her. "They let me out to shop. There's an all night Safeway near my house. Send me a list. I'll pick up everything you need and deliver it to Jack's tomorrow morning."

This time Emma screamed. "No! You're not going to Jack's house."

"I can't believe you said that." Andy sounded hurt. "Of course I'm going. I want to. Why can't I?"

Emma thought long and hard before she answered. She needed Andy's help, but there was no way she could let him show up at that dinner.

Finally she skirted the issue. "You can't go to Jack's house because you're under house arrest."

Andy batted the excuse away. "It's a charity. They let me out for charity events. I'll call my probation officer. No problem."

"OK," Emma tried again. "Andy, there's another reason you can't come to the dinner. It's about Jack. Jack doesn't like you."

But Andy wouldn't listen. "Nonsense," he said. "Of course Jack likes me. I like *him*. We get along great. He's a terrific guy. C'mon, Emma. It'll be fun. Cooking together. Just like old times."

By then Emma was too exhausted to argue.

"We'll talk about this later," she said. "Meanwhile, just make the *malfatti*. I'll email you a shopping list." She was about to hang up, when she stopped. "Oh. And thank you," she said

19

SATURDAY MORNING – JUST FRIENDS

When Emma's alarm went off at 4:00 a.m., she was dreaming about *malfatti*. She stood in her old kitchen, the kitchen in the first apartment she shared with Andy. And she was making *malfatti*. She wasn't making *malfatti* with Andy. She was making them with Jack. But every time she tried to form one of the small spinach and ricotta balls, it fell apart. Nothing stuck.

The next thing she knew, the chimes on her cell phone rang her awake. Lying in bed, part of her wanted to call Andy to see how he was doing. It was 4:00 a.m. She didn't dare.

Instead, she stumbled out of bed into the same clothes she'd worn the day before and thrown on a chair. She brushed her teeth, took all her blood pressure pills, and zipped up her overnight case. She realized she'd forgotten to brush her hair, but also realized she didn't care. Finally, she looked around the room for a coffee machine. There was none. They'd get something on the road.

Standing by the car waiting for Steve, Emma started to shiver. The nights really did get cold, she mused. A few minutes later, Steve clomped down the stairs from the second floor looking miserable.

"I can't believe I offered to do this," was all he said as he unlocked the car and got in.

Once they were on the road he added, "You owe me big time."

Emma wanted to reply that it was Steve who was repaying *her* for accompanying him on a mad dash to Coachella. *But why bother,* she thought.

They stopped for coffee and rancid muffins at the first gas station they found. Then Steve gunned the car north. No one talked for the first two hours, till Steve found an open Micky D and turned into the drive through for bacon, egg and cheese McBiscuits, hash browns and more coffee. Emma didn't complain. Instead she fed Steve his McBiscuit while he drove, trying not to spill her coffee on the upholstery.

"So," Steve finally said when he'd finished eating all the breakfast, "what's your plan for dinner? Did you call your friend and cancel? Or did you just change the menu?"

"Neither," Emma answered. Then she told Steve about her phone call to Andy.

"Ouch!" Steve replied. "That's some favor you called in. Wait," he thought a minute. "Isn't your ex still under house arrest?"

Emma explained about charity events.

"Kinda awkward, huh? Your ex and your boyfriend?"

"Jack's a friend. He's not my 'boyfriend,'" Emma explained.

"Oh," Steve nodded. "What's that supposed to mean? No sex? Aren't you guys kind of old for that, anyway?"

"Yes. No sex. And no. I'm not too old for that." Emma blushed. "And don't get any ideas. I'm not propositioning you."

Now Steve blushed. "Believe me, Emma. I didn't think you were. It's just that...well, I'm wondering about men and women being friends. At my age at least, my experience tells me it doesn't work. Something always happens." He paused, "Doesn't it?"

Emma glanced at her driving companion. It was still dark. Hard to see his face, but she could tell he had something more specific on his mind than her Platonic relationship with Jack.

"Does it?" Emma asked. "I mean, does *it* always happen. In my case it hasn't. I'm not sure why. I'm conflicted myself. I think he's depressed about his wife," she added.

"Take *my* wife, for example…" Steve ignored her answer. "She's got this friend at work. At least that's what she calls him. *It's OK. Don't worry. No sex. He's just a friend.* That's what she says. Well, is it?" he asked.

"Is it what?" Emma asked.

"Is it OK?"

Emma took a deep breath. Then she decided to be honest. "Probably not, Steve. It's probably not OK. She's probably more involved. Is she…" she hesitated. "Is she unhappy?"

"My wife?" Steve replied. "I don't know. Who knows if anyone's really happy or unhappy?"

"Does she say she's unhappy?" Emma persisted. "One way or another, women usually let you know when they're unhappy."

Steve sighed. "Yeah, she says she's unhappy. She says it all the time. She wants kids, but she says we can't afford them. Not on my salary. Not if she stops work. She's a teacher," he added.

"And the 'friend'?" Emma asked. "Another teacher?"

Steve nodded. "They hang out a lot – after school. Doing things I don't have time to do, like going to museums, taking walks, grabbing a coffee and talking. Heck, they even cook together – now that I don't have time anymore. And she makes me eat the stuff."

"She's unhappy and she's having an affair, Steve," Emma leveled with him. "Do you love her?"

"Yeah," Steve nodded.

"Then you have to do something about it."

"Like what?" Steve asked.

He sounded so helpless, Emma almost wanted to cry. "Get her back!"

"How?"

"Stop working so hard. Be there for her. Take her to the places she wants to go. Win her, Steve. Win her the way you go about winning a court case. Find out what she needs and do it."

"But I don't have time, Emma," Steve answered.

"Then you don't really love her," Emma replied.

Steve nodded again. "And the money? What am I supposed to do about that? Quit my job. Quit doin' what I love so we can have kids?"

Emma shook her head. "Just tell her you want kids and that you want them now. You'll figure the money out. I did. Besides, children need love, not money." Then she added, "But if you don't love each other, don't have a kid."

Steve thought about that for a few seconds. Then he shrugged. "You did. Didn't you? I mean, you and your ex had a kid and stopped loving each other. Your kid turned out all right."

"That's true, Steve," Emma replied, suddenly feeling very old. "We stopped loving each other, but we loved each other when we made our kid. At least, start with that."

"And now, you cook together. And you get each other out of jams." Steve laughed. "I guess that's more than a lot of married folks do."

"I guess you're right," Emma answered. She'd never thought of it that way.

They drove in silence for a long time. Suddenly it dawned on Emma that Dan hadn't crossed her mind in two days. Once again, she wondered what to do. *Get through the dinner first; then figure it out* she answered herself.

Somewhere near the Harris Ranch Steve reviewed the progress they'd made in the Gomez case. He and the numbers man had calculated over a million dollars in damages caused by Gomez's untimely death. Closer to eight million with punitive damages as well. Steve mused that those numbers could stick. At least against someone as rich as Curt Randall.

"And based on everything we've learned down here," Steve concluded, "all fingers still point to him as the murderer."

"I don't think cousin Diaz did it," Emma acknowledged as they crossed the Richmond Bridge heading for Marin.

"The jealous husband had a motive," Steve added, "but he also has an alibi.

"So does Cardenas, the guy who dropped out of the lawsuit," Emma cut in. "The same alibi as the jealous husband's. Still, there's got to be a connection."

"A connection with what?" Steve asked.

"A connection between Cardenas and the murder," Emma explained. "I just don't know what. Someone paid him to sabotage the lawsuit. Someone in Blissburg: Peters, Bugbee, maybe the Chinese? I still think Randall is innocent."

Steve laughed. "Is this seniors solidarity week? Curt Randall killed Santiago Gomez because he hates Mexicans and he was mad about the lawsuit. Motive, opportunity, means. Dream on, Emma. We've got our man."

Half an hour later, Steve dropped her off at her door.

"Thanks for all the help," he said as she grabbed her overnight case and got out of the car. "And for the advice," he added with a sad smile.

"Take it," Emma replied. "See you Monday."

The minute she got inside she checked her cell phone. Jack had called again three times. Seconds later, the land line rang.

She answered. But it wasn't Jack whose voice greeted her on the other end of the line. It was Andy.

"Hi," he greeted her in his jaunty voice. "I'm over at Jack's setting up. When I explained the situation to my probation officer, he agreed to let me out for the whole day. I can't leave Jack's property though, and I have to be home by 10:00. So I thought I'd lend you a hand." He dropped his voice to a whisper. "And by the way, no worries about Jack. I explained everything to *him*, too. I like him. Everything's fine."

20

SATURDAY AFTERNOON – WHOLE LOTTA FOOD

The look on Jack's face when he opened his door, however, confirmed Emma's worst fears. Contrary to Andy's assurances, things were not fine. Jack stood barring the entrance to his house, like a scary goalie protecting the net, his face an expressionless mask of stone.

I've lost my best friend, she told herself and almost started to cry.

After staring at her silently for almost a minute, Jack finally said, "Your ex is in the kitchen cooking. You know where it is."

No *hi*, Emma acknowledged. No, *I was worried.* No peck on the cheek. No hug. *The relationship is over.*

Part of her wanted to explain why things got so out of hand. But excuses were pointless once you'd broken the Cowboy Code: not kept your word, lied and been unkind to a senior.

"Jack, I *am* sorry," she managed to say before walking around him and making her way to the kitchen.

THERE, she found Celina and Andy. They, at least, looked like they were having fun and glad to see her.

Celina eyed Emma curiously for a few seconds before greeting her. "Hi, *Senora* Emma," she smiled uncertainly. "Don't worry. We have everything under control. Right, *Senor* Andy?"

Andy stood at the marble kitchen counter with his back towards Emma. At the sound of Celina's voice, he turned, his face wreathed in a benevolent smile. "Emma," he began in his chirpy voice. "You're back. Safe and sound. So soon! I'm relieved."

He stepped forward to give her an awkward hug with his elbows. His raised hands were covered in spinach and flour.

At least, Emma thought, it was more of a greeting than Jack gave her.

"Look," he said backing away and gesturing towards the counter top where a vast wooden board lay covered in flour and neat little green balls. "I'm almost finished. I shopped this morning. I didn't want to risk having the *malfatti* sit overnight."

How thoughtful. At least they look good, Emma thought to herself.

"Now," Andy continued, "check the fridge. I think I found everything on your list. But if we're missing something, Celina has offered to run out and get it. What do you think?"

Emma dutifully opened the refrigerator, checking her mental list against its contents. A far as she could tell, everything was there. Even ingredients for the Bavarian cream. But scrap that recipe. Driving up from Coachella, she'd realized there wasn't time to make Jack's favorite dessert. She'd make hot *zabaglione* with raspberries instead. *No use telling Jack about that*, she shuddered.

Emma closed the refrigerator and turned to Andy with a weak smile. "I think you got all of it." Then she noted Celina's raised eyebrows and added, "Thanks."

Andy beamed back, like a five year old with a gold star.

"This is fun, isn't it," he said. "I was just telling my new girl-friend, Brigitte, how much fun we used to have cooking. Interestingly Brigitte doesn't cook, even though she's French. She says French girls *don't* cook these days. So, since I'm stuck with this," he pointed to his ankle thingie, "we eat at home and guess who does the cooking? I can't tell you how many of the old recipes I've recreated."

"I'll bet," Emma answered, trying to absorb a lot of new information at once. Not that Andy hadn't always had girlfriends. It was just that...

"How did you meet Brigitte," she asked. "I mean, while under house arrest?"

"She's the delivery girl. From Whole Foods." He raised his hands like Jesus multiplying the loaves and fishes. "That's how I got everything here so fast."

"Whole Foods! That must have cost a fortune!" Emma exclaimed. "I thought you were going to the 24 hour Safeway. What do I owe you?"

Andy shook his head. "Not too bad. Brigitte gets a 'family and friends' discount. I *was* going to Safeway till I realized Brigitte could deliver everything here by 8:00 a.m. Why pull an all-nighter when you can get that kind of service? By the way," he added, "you owe Brigitte a little thank you. Maybe a nice bottle of wine?"

Emma clenched her teeth. She realized that her face bore the same stony mask she'd seen on Jack's when she arrived.

"Sure," she said. Then she thought of something else that made her stomach lurch. "You mean you've been here – *here at Jack's house* – since 8:00 a.m.?"

Andy and Celina's exchanged a questioning stare. "Maybe 8:15?" Andy said.

Celina nodded. "8:00-8:15." Then she looked back at Emma and shook her head. "Is no trouble for Meester Jack," she added. "He no sleep anyway. Maybe kinda depress. Maybe about hees wife." She rolled her eyes. "No matter how early I come, he always up. I put the coffee maker on for 5:00 a.m. Is empty when I arrive. At 5:00 p.m. he fall asleep in front of the news. Poor Meester Jack." She lowered her voice and squinted her eyes knowingly at Emma. "I think he's lonely, *Senora.*"

Andy lowered his voice as well. "Classic signs of depression. Believe me, I recognize them. Happened to me after they put this thingie on." He pointed to his ankle.

"Oh," he added after a pause. "Wait till you see what Celina did out back."

Celina led Emma outside. The day was a glorious eighty degrees. There wasn't a cloud in the sky. You couldn't have asked for better weather for a party, Emma noted. If only...

Then she saw the table and let out a gasp. It had been set with French provincial placemats, white faience dishes, silver and cut crystal. Three bouquets of flowers cut from Jack's garden formed the centerpiece. Peonies, roses, dahlias, bearded iris, lilies and hydrangeas. All arranged in hand painted vases.

"It's perfect," Emma exclaimed. "You're a..." she couldn't think of the right word. "A magician," she finally said. Then she caught Celina by the arm. "How's Jack?" she added whispering.

Celina shook her head. "Not so good today. *Senor* Andy already here when I arrive." She winced, "You know. Trying so hard to cheer him up." She smiled shyly at Emma. "He such a nice man, *Senor* Andy. Too bad about the troubles." She pointed to her ankle.

When Emma returned to the kitchen, the *malfatti* were done. It was lunch time. Andy had brought his swimsuit and announced he planned to eat by the pool.

"Join me." He gave her a poke. "You must keep a swimsuit here."

"Sorry, I have too much to do," Emma replied.

"Whatever you say." Andy scooped a generous serving of the *malfatti* onto a plate. "These turned out great. Try some. By the way, you were right about the flour."

"Oh," he added when he returned to the kitchen to pour himself a glass of white wine. "Don't worry about Jack. As I said, we get along fine. He's a great guy. Just a little depressed. Maybe you can, you know, help him..."

That was the last straw.

"Just because you like someone, doesn't mean *they* like you," Emma shot back angrily. "There's another side to the mountain. But you never understood that!"

"Mountain?" Andy walked back towards the pool shaking his head. "Who said anything about a mountain?"

Hopeless, Emma thought. A few minutes later, she was taking her anger out on the veal. Pounding scaloppini. Filling them with *prosciutto.* Dredging them in flour. Coating them in egg. Sautéing them in butter and oil. And topping them off with Fontina cheese.

Next she Frenched the green beans, leaving them to soak in cold water until they were ready to cook.

Finally, she began the tomato sauce.

It was easy. Two cloves of garlic sautéed in oil. Salt, pepper and fresh cherry tomatoes.

By 5:00 p.m., everything was ready except for the dessert. Andy opened two bottles of wine to breathe. Emma prepared the hors d'oeuvres: *prosciutto* wrapped around wedges of cantaloupe, Mount Tam, a runny Cremont, Humbolt Fog and crackers.

Emma still hadn't seen Jack since he stonily let her in the front door. When she noticed his car gone, she asked Celina.

"He went to the club to play tennis," she answered. "Meester Jack goes there a lot for the company."

At 5:30 Emma drove home to change. When she checked her phone, there was an email from Steve.

"Emma, I did some poking around," the message began. "You were right about Peters. He's neck deep in debt. And the word around town is he hates his uncle. Says he cheated his mother out of her half of the Randall Estate. Including the plum ranch where she grew up.

"As for Cardenas," he continued. "He was here all right. A few days after Gomez died. Guess who told me? Cousin Diaz who ran into him at the *Hasta la Vista* Lounge. I asked him why he didn't tell *you.* Know what he answered? 'She didn't ask.'"

There was a second message, as well. This one from Dan Worthington.

Hi Emma – I trust your business trip went well. Hoping to see you soon. Thinking of you. Dan.

The message from Steve was intriguing. She'd been right about Cardenas. He'd been at the rally and lied to her when she asked.

As for Peters? He'd been cheated out of his birthright once. Emma wondered if he'd kill to save it now.

Emma finished dressing. She fished a Marimekko tent dress out of her closet. Then she grabbed Jack's Loretta Caponi apron and stuffed it in her purse, got in her car and drove back to Jack's house.

21

SATURDAY NIGHT – IN YOUR FACEBOOK

Jack's daughter, Cara, and son-in-law, Mike, were already there when Emma arrived. Cara greeted Emma coolly. *Nothing personal*, Emma assured herself. *That's her nature.*

Mike, on the other hand, was effusive.

"Emma Corsi," he exclaimed. "I've heard a lot about you. Not just from Jack," he turned to his father-in-law and smiled. "All good. All good." Back to Emma. "You're famous. That murder you solved. The courage."

"Crazy, if you ask me," Cara interjected.

Mike looked at his wife and frowned. They were an interesting match. Cara tall and thin, her long face dominated by dark almond-shaped eyes, framed with shoulder length black hair. Mike was equally tall - well over six feet – muscular, blond, and blue-eyed. *Night and day*, Emma noted.

"Cara?" Mike replied to his wife's comment. Emma could hear the "tut tut" in his voice. "I know you were impressed by Emma's courage. You said so at the time, though you may not admit it now."

Cara glanced at him and rolled her eyes.

It was still eighty degrees, but Emma suddenly felt she needed to put on a sweater.

"I'll just excuse myself and peek in the kitchen," she smirked, suddenly realizing she'd adopted Andy's jaunty tone. "I'm cooking tonight," she added flustered. Then she bobbed in what she later feared looked like a curtsey, and dashed into the kitchen.

To her relief, things there appeared to be under control. Celina, dressed in a black blouse, black pants and a white apron, had already prepared three trays of hors d'oeuvres. The cheeses were oozing ripe. The olives were fragrant. The *prosciutto* was paper thin and not too salty. The melons were orange and dripping juice. *Goodness knows where they're from*, Emma wondered. *Coachella perhaps*?

Andy had also prepared stuffed mushrooms. Emma tried one. They tasted delicious.

"Where are the *malfatti*?" she asked. "They should be room temperature before we heat them." She checked the counter. They weren't there. Emma feared they were still in the fridge.

Andy replied without looking up from a New Yorker. "They're in the microwave, honey. I'll zap 'em for three minutes before you all sit down."

"Microwave!" Emma exclaimed. "No way. I've never *zapped malfatti*. For all I know, they'll fall apart. We are *not* heating them up in a microwave. We're heating them in the oven in a pan."

"Relax," Andy answered. "I've done it a million times. The microwave's perfect for this sort of dish. Trust me."

"*Trust* you?" Emma almost exploded, but the doorbell rang. She heard her daughter Julie's voice.

There was no way Cara and Julie could meet without her acting as referee. "Talk about a three alarm fire," Emma muttered racing out to the hall.

When Julie entered the living room armed in a poufy knit Alexander Wang and three-inch Prada heels, Emma watched her stare at Cara like a tigress protecting cubs.

"Wow, great to meet you finally," Julie exclaimed pasting what Emma knew was a fake smile on her face.

"Nice of your dad to plan this," she added, squinting mistrustfully at Jack.

"Hi," Piers added, extending his hand to Mike. "I'm the son-in-law."

After that, to Emma's dismay, nobody said a word. Until the doorbell rang again. This time it was the Monroes, the couple who'd recently moved to Blissburg and opened a real estate office downtown. After they arrived, Emma noted that the guests sorted themselves into relatively peaceful factions. Julie and Piers chatted with Jane Monroe. Cara and Mike with Jane's husband, Bob.

Jack served drinks. He never said a word to Emma. He never smiled.

After assuring herself no one was about to explode, Emma returned to the kitchen.

Andy stood by the microwave. "I've zapped the first two batches," he announced.

At the sound of the word "zapped", Emma's heart lurched into her stomach.

Andy must have noticed her distress. "I said relax. It's under control. Go get everyone to the table."

The damage was done. Emma did as she was told.

"*A tavola*," she announced, immediately embarrassed by the affectation.

"So soon?" Cara asked, snaring a wedge of melon and *prosciutto*.

Mike grabbed a couple of mushroom caps and stuffed them in his mouth. "These are delish!"

Everyone followed her into the yard. To Emma's relief, there were place cards. Emma recognized Andy's script alongside three well-executed grace notes. *When did he have time for that?* she wondered.

Thanks to Andy, she and Jack were assigned opposite ends of the table. Jane Monroe sat to Jack's left and Julie to his right. Mike to

Emma's left; Piers to her right. Bob Monroe and Cara took the seats in between.

Once everyone sat down, there was no need to worry about awkward pauses. The food took care of that. Celina immediately appeared with individual plates of *malfatti*.

"Wow! My favorite," Cara exclaimed.

Jack beamed. Genuinely pleased.

Then the dinner conversation took an unexpected turn.

Emma stared down at her plate. The spinach and ricotta dumplings *looked* OK. At least they hadn't fallen apart. She gingerly scooped one up with her fork, along with some sauce. Then, bracing herself, she took a bite.

To her amazement, the *malfatti* were divine. Light as feathers, but they kept their shape. Delicately flavored, but they held up to the sauce. In fact, they were the best *malfatti* she had ever tasted. She dug into her small pile, wondering if the first bite was a fluke. But no. Every bite was perfect.

A hush had fallen over the table as everyone started to eat. Then, suddenly, the chorus began.

"Oh my gosh! What is this? It's fabulous!"

That was Bob Monroe.

"Wow, Mom! Your *malfatti* have never tasted so good. What did you do?"

"Emma, you outdid yourself," Piers added, then turned to Mike. Didn't I tell you my mother-in-law's a great cook?"

"I've never tasted anything like this," Jane Monroe exclaimed. "At first, I thought they were Brussels sprouts in tomato sauce. But this is different. "

"My wife *tries* to make these," Mike added, "but hers always fall apart."

Across the table, Emma saw Cara shake her head. "These are amazing," she said. "To Emma. What a cook!"

At that point, everyone raised a glass. Except for Emma. And Jack.

"C'mon Dad. Raise your glass," Cara said.

He raised his eyebrows at Emma.

She heard the question even though he never said a word. *You gonna tell them? Or should I?*

Emma laughed nervously and raised her glass.

"Don't raise your glass, Mom," Julie said. "We're toasting *you.*"

"No," Emma answered. "We're toasting..." She couldn't say it. She started to choke. Finally, she took a sip of water and continued. "We're toasting Andy. Andy Bodreau. He made the *malfatti.* He gets the toast. To Andy."

"To Andy?" the others replied – except for Jack.

Julie frowned. "I don't get it. Why on earth are we toasting him?"

"'Cause he made dinner," Jack shrugged. He looked like he'd just swallowed a toad. "Your mother got too busy to cook tonight. So your dad bailed her out. Andy!" He called. "Come out here. Your *malfatti* are a hit. Take a bow."

Andy poked his head out of the kitchen. Everyone, except Emma, gave him a cheer. The next thing she knew, he had joined them pulling up a chair next to hers. Across the table, Jack's eyes shot daggers.

The rest of the food that evening was good. Nothing, however, compared with the *malfatti.* As for the company, Jack and Emma ignored each other. Julie and Cara did too. Mike and Piers discussed baseball. The Monroes spoke among themselves.

Then, something unexpected happened. Emma heard Mike mentioned "Red Sox". Next thing she knew, he and Piers were engaged in what Emma recognized as a form of social shorthand. Like speed dating for East Coast preppies.

"Harvard?" Piers asked.

"Ninety-three."

"House?"

"Lowell."

"Prep?"

"Exeter."

"Choate."

"Coolidge?"

"Thad?"

That's when Emma heard Mike scream. Like a thirteen year old at a Beiber concert.

"Dr. Cool? You know Dr. Cool?"

For all the shock value he might as well have said, "Dr. Livingston, I presume."

"Of course I know Dr. Cool," Pierce replied. "Who do you think gave him the name?"

Mike rose from his seat and reached across the table.

"Then you must be Larky."

"And you must be Buck."

Mike, sit down!" Cara ordered.

Julie had also risen from the table. "I think I'm gonna be sick," she said before rushing out of the room.

"I'll go start dessert," Emma announced also leaving the table.

Later, above the rhythmic whipping of egg yolks, sugar and Marsala wine, snatches of conversation drifted into the kitchen.

"Let's send Cooley a selfie. "

"Cara. Over here."

"Julie? Where's Julie?"

"Why weren't you at the wedding?"

"Taking the bar."

Emma filled champagne goblets with hot yellow froth and garnished it with raspberries. By the time she returned to the table, Larky and Buck had bonded like atoms.

"No Bavarian cream," Jack noted sadly to himself when Emma set down his dish of *zabaglione*.

"No time," Andy called across the table. "Still a workaholic, aren't you, honey."

That's when even the Monroes got confused.

Jane gestured with her hand towards Andy. "Who *is* he?" she asked.

Everyone stared at their host

Jack raised his eyebrows and pointed to Emma.

"He's my," she hesitated.

Everyone waited.

"He's my, my partner," she finally said. "In my catering business."

Julie had returned to the dining room. "Mom, please!" She slapped her napkin down on the table. "Don't make this more embarrassing than it already is!"

For the first time in her life, she cast a sympathetic glance at Jack.

"Andy's my dad," Julie explained in answer to Jane Monroe's question. "He and Mom have been divorced for over thirty years. In fact, they never should have gotten married in the first place. But, for some reason, when my mother gets in a jam, which she often does," she glared at Emma, "he's the one she calls." She glanced around the table at Cara, at Piers, at Jack. "I'm sorry. This is so awkward."

Jane Monroe reached across the table and patted Julie's hand. "I understand," she said. "It's mortifying for children when their parents get divorced, but look at it this way. My parents got divorced. They hate each other so much they can't be in the same room. Believe me, that's way more awkward than this is. You're lucky your parents are still there for you - and for each other. You just don't know it."

A profound stillness settled over the dining room. Finally, Bob Monroe, who still looked confused, asked another question.

"Emma," he said. "What is it you've been working so hard on? You're a food writer, aren't you? Is it a new cookbook?"

Everyone at the table stared back at Emma.

"No, it's not a cookbook," she replied. "Cooking is sort of my hobby," she hesitated. "Actually, I'm a retired paralegal. And now I volunteer a couple of days a week at the, you know, at that free legal clinic here in town. I do little things for them, filing, intake memos..."

That's when Julie, the public relations guru, finally interrupted her.

"That's not true," she announced. "Mom never gives herself credit. Yes, she wrote a cookbook, *Dining with the Stars.* It's been very successful. You can get it on Amazon and at Annemarie's here in town. And she's working on another cookbook, *What a Pair!*, for Buchanon Vineyards. In addition to all that, however, she also volunteers at the Blissburg Free Legal Services Clinic, the BFLSC. And she doesn't *just* do filing. She's Dr. Watson to their crack senior lawyer, Steve Zimmer. In fact, she's the one who solved the famous, so-called, *saucy murder* last year."

"Wow," Jane replied. "I read about it in the San Francisco papers. The murder of that opera singer in one of the vineyards."

"That's my Mom," Julie nodded, smiling proudly at Emma.

For a moment, Emma thought she was going to cry. She glanced at Jack. He was staring at Julie with undisguised awe.

"So what are you working on now?" Bob asked. "Another murder?"

Emma glanced quickly at Piers. "You know all this already, Piers. I'm not disclosing any secrets." Then she briefly explained about the Gomez murder.

"But I still don't think Curt did it," Emma concluded with a shrug.

"Who do you think did?" Cara asked.

Emma shook her head. "I don't know. That's what I spent the last two days trying to find out down south in Coachella." She shrugged apologetically. "That's why I couldn't get everything together for this dinner tonight. So my sous-chef," she gestured towards Andy, "had to step in."

"Getting back to the murder case," Jane Monroe replied, "I know Curt. Bob and I tried to find a buyer for his ranch. We thought we had someone until HoCo scared them off with that inflated bid. If you ask me," she added, "Curt Randall is a sad old man who never got over losing his son. But he's not a killer."

At the mention of losing a son, Emma glanced at Jack. Cara looked at him too.

He had reached in front of Jane and taken his daughter's hand.

"We know all about that, don't we Cara?" he said. Then, to Emma's surprise, he looked around the table. "I lost my son many years ago. Of course you never get over it. But you can't let it poison your life the way Curt did. It's not fair. Not fair to them. To their memory."

Everyone was silent for a few moments after Jack spoke. Piers finally resumed the conversation.

"So who was the buyer you had for Curt's ranch?" he asked.

"A non profit. But they couldn't match HoCo," Bob explained.

Piers grimaced. "Now Curt's ready to dump the place for a song."

"'Cause of the lawsuit?" Jane asked.

Piers nodded, "The defense costs and the contamination report. The water tanks have high levels of arsenic. You know what that could mean. Government investigations, fines, cleanup costs."

"What are you going to do?" Bob asked.

"HoCo's pushing Curt to lower the price." Piers shrugged. "Curt wants to do it. He's up to his ears in legal fees already for the criminal investigation."

Bob and his wife exchanged knowing glances.

"You thinking what I'm thinking?" Bob asked.

"The Buxton property in Sunnyvale, right? That buyer was Chinese, too," Jane replied.

Bob turned to Piers. "We ran into a similar thing a couple of years ago up in the San Francisco office where we worked. Our realty company represented the seller of a property in Sunnyvale. A

Chinese buyer made a huge offer. Scared everyone else away. Next thing you know, the water on the property is contaminated and the purchaser asks for a discount."

"What happened?" Piers asked.

"I don't know," Bob said. "We left the office. Moved up here."

"What was the name of the buyer?" Emma asked.

Bob shook his head again "I don't think I ever knew. The broker handling the deal moved to Texas."

"I can find out," Jane offered. "It's crazy who you can dig up on Facebook these days."

That's when Julie caught her mother's eye, "Speaking of Facebook, Mom. What ever happened to that creep who wanted to friend you? What was his name? Dan? Dan Worthington? I hope you got rid of him."

Before Emma could field the question, Andy cut in. "Dan Worthington! Since when is Dan Worthington creepy?" He raised an eyebrow at Emma and laughed. "As I recall, you had a massive crush on Dan in college. What's happened? Have you two got a little somethin' going on again?"

Emma glanced across the table to see if Jack was listening. From the look on his face, it was obvious he'd heard.

The conversation, however, was interrupted by a high-pitched beep. Like a fire alarm. At first, everyone looked at the ceiling. Then Andy shot up from his seat.

"Whoops, that's me." He turned to Emma. "Must be 10:00. Sorry to leave you with all the cleanup. I gotta run."

A few minutes later, the party broke up. Emma returned to the kitchen while Jack retrieved people's coats and saw them to their cars. Thanks to Celina, the kitchen was already spotless.

When Emma tiptoed into the hall for her jacket, however, Jack was standing there.

"You OK to drive?" It was the first time he'd addressed her all night.

"Thanks. I'm exhausted. But I can make it home."

"Driving tired is like driving drunk," Jack cautioned. "I don't want to be responsible."

Emma shook her head. She was too ashamed and too tired to sort things out. "I'll blast the oldies station to keep me awake."

Jack did not say goodbye, Emma noted. Nor did he yell "Text when you get home," as he always did when she drove away.

22

SUNDAY MORNING – WHERE IS MARIA?

The next morning, Emma was still too tired even to think of the Sunday Morning Stroll. Besides, Jack was a regular, and he was the last person she wanted to see.

Yes, she acknowledged, thanks to Andy, the dinner had been salvaged. Thanks to Julie, some of her reputation redeemed. But she knew that by turning to Andy she'd betrayed Jack.

And of course there was still the Dan problem. Julie and Jack now knew that she'd lied about their relationship. Emma still didn't know what to do about that.

Why didn't I come clean about Dan in the first place? she asked lying in her bed. By her age, everyone's life was cluttered with wreckage. Shards of broken relationships too precious to discard. Too sharp not to handle with care.

That's what I'm doing, she assured herself. *Handling the wreckage of my relationship with Dan with care. But why?* she wondered. *It was over so long ago.*

Emma still owed Dan an answer to his email. She dragged herself out of bed. Made a cup of coffee. Sat down at her computer and wrote to him:

Dear Dan,

I need more time. This is all very sudden. I'm a little confused.
Emma

She had just hit the send button, when her phone rang. It was Julie. As usual, Emma's daughter got straight to the point.

"What's going on with you and Jack?" she asked after Emma said "Hello."

Before Emma could answer *that* question, Julie added, "And why did you lie to me about the Facebook guy? Were you two, you know, involved? Is that why you and Dad broke up? Is there something I don't know?" Her voice quickly grew angry. "Was my whole childhood a lie?"

That's when Emma decided it was time to come clean.

"First of all, Julie," she began, "no, there is nothing you *should* know. And, second, no. Dad and I broke up because Dad wanted to. Not because of Dan." She took a deep breath. "Dan and I connected later, briefly, while you were in France. His wife left. We had an affair. She came back. We broke up. End of story. I never thought there was a reason you should know."

Julie took a moment to reply. "You always preferred to play the Virgin Mother role, didn't you, Mom? I even wondered if you were gay. Like maybe that's why Dad fooled around."

"I just didn't want to complicate your life more than your father and I already had!" Emma cried. "So I kept it a secret!"

"Not that big a secret," Julie replied. "You were obviously miserable when I got home from France. I thought it was my fault for leaving. That's why I didn't apply to any East Coast schools."

"Please," Emma begged. "Don't lay that on me too!"

They sat in silence for a few seconds.

"So...what're you going to do about Jack?" Julie asked. "I mean, if you get together with this Dan guy - who I gather dumped you to take back his wayward wife – won't you hurt Jack? He looked miserable last night. Not that I blamed him between Dad showing up and the Dan thing."

Emma cleared her throat. She didn't know what to say.

"Mom," her daughter continued. "Hard as it is to admit this, Jack's actually kind of a cool guy in a weird way. Not to mention that his son-in-law and Piers have just become best buds. Talk about awkward! Piers now has us spending our summer vacation together."

"Look, Julie," Emma sighed. "I don't know what I'm going to do about Jack. Based on how we left things last night, I'm not even sure the decision is mine to make. You're right. I hurt him. I broke my promise…"

She was about to recite the rest of the Cowboy Code when Julie cut in.

"By the way, Mom. Speaking of dinner. Dad's *malfatti* were delicious! Better than yours, I have to say."

"I know," Emma replied testily. "He says he didn't use any flour, except to coat them. Frankly, I find that hard to believe." She caught herself. "Why are we even talking about the *malfatti*? The point is I hurt Jack. I lied to him about Dan. Now he knows it. He'll carry a grudge. He's Sicilian. They do that. I'm afraid I've lost…"

To her surprise, Emma felt herself choke up.

"I'm afraid I've lost a good friend," she concluded weepily.

Julie's answer was entirely unsympathetic. "You made your bed, Mom. Now *you* have to lie in it. Excuse the pun. Have you seen the Dan guy yet?"

"No," Emma answered. "I keep putting him off."

"Well, that should tell you *something*," Julie said after a pause. "Not that you asked for my advice. Do you *plan* to see him?"

"I don't know. I mean, *see* him? What's the harm in that?" Emma asked.

"Only you can answer, Mom," Julie replied. "Harry just woke up. I gotta go. By the way, your grandson misses you. He hasn't seen you for a week."

"I miss him too," Emma said.

"Then come for an early supper tonight. Oh," Julie thought of something. "Before I hang up. Are there any more skeletons in your closet I should know about, Mom?"

Emma decided to come completely clean. "Just the contractor," she said.

"Not that guy who fixed up the bathroom!" Julie exclaimed. "With the weird tattoo. Mom, that's such a cliché." She hung up.

EMMA PUT her phone back down and stared at her computer. Speaking of skeletons had reminded her of something she'd forgotten wallowing in the misery of her own sorry soap opera - Cory Randall and his forbidden love for Maria Hidalgo Miller.

She brought up the Google screen. Then she typed in two words "Maria Miller". After that, she typed the word "Riverside."

Six hits appeared on her screen. Three of them listed middle names: Erin, Theroux, and Lester. Emma eliminated those from her list. They weren't even Hispanic. She decided to call the other three. It was Sunday morning.

The first one on her list answered on the first ring. The voice on the other end of the line sounded old and frail.

"Hello," Emma began. "I'm looking for someone named Maria Hidalgo Miller."

"I'm sorry," the voice answered. "Who?"

"Maria Hidalgo Miller," Emma replied.

"You have the wrong number." The voice sounded angry. "There's no one here by that name."

Emma tried the second name on her list.

"Hello. Is Maria Miller there?"

"This is Maria Miller," a younger voice answered. Emma could hear a child screaming in the background.

"OK," Emma replied. "By any chance, was your maiden name

Hidalgo? I'm trying to locate a Maria Hidalgo Miller who used to live in Coachella, California?"

"What do you want?" The woman's voice turned cold. "Is this some kind of debt collection racket? Who are you?"

"I'm…" suddenly Emma wasn't sure who she was. A curiosity seeker? Some kind of voyeur?

"I'm a cousin of someone who used to be called Maria Hidalgo," she lied. "Our aunt died and I'm looking for Maria in connection with a will."

Emma hoped her lie would give the real Maria an incentive to cooperate.

"Look," the woman answered. "I'd love to inherit some money from a long lost aunt, but my name is Mary Miller. No Hidalgo. There are no Hidalgos in my family that I'm aware of. So I think you have the wrong Mary. Goodbye."

The final Maria Miller on Emma's list turned out to be a lawyer in the city of Riverside. She was thirty-one years old.

Next, Emma tried Maria Hidalgo. There were twenty-five of those. Eleven had listed numbers. Emma tried them all. One was a twenty-year-old dental assistant. The next few didn't answer the phone. Emma left messages. Another was a retired naval officer who grew up in Florida. Yet another wasn't home, but her son said she was a nurse's aid. That story sounded promising until Emma discovered that the woman was recently arrived from Mexico and didn't speak English.

The last Maria Hidalgo was at Mass. She turned out to be eighty-six. Maybe Curt Randall's lover. Certainly not Cory's.

Looking for Maria Hidalgo Miller in Riverside was like looking for a needle in a haystack. *There must be another way to tackle this,* Emma told herself.

She tried a different search. This time she entered "Universities and colleges in Riverside County, CA."

Interestingly, her search yielded only three: Las Lomas University, a junior college and the University of California at Riverside. On her first try, Emma found a Mary Miller working at Las Lomas. A quick search of the Las Lomas website located a Mary H. Miller working in food services there. The department had a phone number listed. Since food services was open seven days a week, Emma gave the number a try.

Someone picked up the phone on the third ring.

"Hi," Emma began, "I'm looking for Mary Hidalgo Miller."

After a rather long pause, the voice on the other end of the line said, "I see someone here named Mary H. Miller. I don't know what the 'H' stands for."

"Can I speak to her?" Emma asked. Her heart had started thumping like a bass drum in a marching band. Something told her she was getting close to pay dirt.

"Can you hold a minute?" the voice asked.

"Sure."

While Emma waited for what seemed like an hour, she imagined all the classic stories of lives ruined by forbidden love: Romeo and Juliet, West Side Story, Lancelot and Guinevere, Ali McGraw and Ryan O'Neal. *Where was Maria Hidalgo?* Emma asked herself. *The Latina who dreamed of becoming doctor? Was she clearing tables now?*

Emma's thoughts were interrupted by a new voice. This one belonged to a woman. "Maria's on leave. Who's calling?"

This time Emma decided not to lie about a will. Instead she said, "I found a wallet with her name in it. It has a little money. I want to return it to her."

"That's kind of you," the woman replied. "Let me give you her cell number. She's had some hard times. She can use a little help."

It took only a few minutes to get Maria H. Miller on the line.

"I'm looking for Maria H. Miller. H as in Hidalgo."

"Yes, this is Maria H. Miller," the woman said. "Is something wrong?"

It crossed Emma's mind that this woman was used to bad news. She tried to sound reassuring.

"Nothing's wrong," she said. "I was hoping to ask you some questions. About someone named Cory."

"I know Cory," the woman replied. "Is there a problem at day care?"

"Day care?" Emma repeated. That didn't sound right.

"You're calling from day care, right?" the woman asked, her voice now tinged with worry. "I know I'm late, but I'll pay the bill. I talked to Linda about it already. See, I'm still on maternity leave; and my husband got laid off, and ..."

Emma's heart sank. "Listen, Maria. I apologize. I've made a mistake. I'm looking for Mary Hidalgo Miller. She's about sixty-five years old and she used to live in Coachella."

The voice on the line immediately relaxed. In fact, the woman laughed. "I'm Mary Hearn Miller and I'm twenty-five. You got the wrong number." She hung up the phone.

Darn! Emma thought, clicking off her cell. It was well passed 2:00 and she was still in her pajamas. She wandered into the kitchen and ate a tub of yogurt.

Then she picked up her cell again and telephoned Jack. She was glad when her call went straight into voice mail.

"Listen Jack," she began. It wasn't the friendliest of greetings. "This is Emma. I'm calling to apologize. For the past week or so I've done everything wrong. I'm sorry. You're a wonderful friend. You deserve better from me. I know I screwed up. But my job is important to me. And there's another reason I left town. It has to do with Dan. The guy I lied about. Who contacted me on Facebook and wants to reconnect. The truth is, I don't know how I feel about him. That's why I couldn't explain. But I do know how I feel about you. You're the best friend I've ever had. It means everything to me to keep it that way. So, if you can...

The phone beeped. "If you are satisfied with your message press 1. If you wish to delete it…"

Emma hung up.

She sat down in front of her computer again and looked at her watch. In an hour she had to leave for dinner at Julie's. She stared back at the screen for a long time. Finally she decided on one more try.

She brought up Google on the screen. Then she typed in the words: "University of California Riverside". When the Home page popped up she located a little box in the right hand corner. It was labeled "custom search". One of the categories was "people". In that box Emma typed "Mary Hidalgo Miller."

To Emma surprise, she got a hit. But the name was different from the name she'd typed into the box. The hit was for a Mary Hidalgo-Muller. This Mary Hidalgo was connected to some sort of lab. Emma's heart started to pound. She clicked on the name.

Seconds later a photograph appeared on her screen. The woman staring back at her was about her age. She had bobbed black hair streaked with gray, large black eyes and clear tanned skin. She looked confident, but stern. No doubt a beauty in her day, Emma noted.

She quickly realized, however, that the biography printed next to the woman's name was even more impressive than her looks. Maria Hidalgo-Muller was a PhD MD who chaired the biology department at the university. She'd taught there for thirty years, specializing in infectious diseases. She was the author of numerous books and articles, and the recipient of dozens of awards.

Emma quickly checked a few other sites verifying and elaborating on Maria Hidalgo-Muller's CV.

There was an email address attached to her website, but Emma decided to phone Maria Hidalgo at the biology department instead. It was Sunday. The department was closed. That phone call would have to wait. Besides, it was almost time to leave for supper with her daughter.

Emma shut down her computer. Then she sat there, thinking, for a long time. Maria Hidalgo had not let Cory's death destroy her. Her life was a success.

Emma remembered what Jack had said the night before about honoring loved ones. About not letting their death poison the lives of those they loved. Who, she now wondered - Curt or Maria - had honored Cory's life best?

23

SUNDAY EVENING – GUESS WHO'S COMING

When Emma rang the Larkin family's bell at 4:00, Piers opened the door.

"Come on in, Emma." Her son-in-law bent down to give her a hug.

Emma marveled that on a Sunday afternoon, Piers still looked well dressed. *Did the housekeeper even iron his jeans?* she wondered. Every hair was in place. His white Nike running shoes looked like they'd been to the dentist.

"Julie and Harry are caught in traffic," Piers said. Then seeing her face fall, he added. "Don't worry. Julie phoned. They'll be home in half an hour. Frankly, I'm kind of glad to have this time alone together. Want a glass of wine?"

Emma figured Piers was loosening her up to talk about the Gomez case. "A little early for me," she shrugged. "But sure, why not?"

A few minutes later, Piers appeared in the living room with a tray of goat cheese and filled her glass with his favorite '07 Jordan cabernet. At $90 a bottle, she tried to restrain herself from chugging it down.

After they'd clinked glasses and taken a first sip, Piers got to the point. "I'll be honest," he began. "I'm curious about the trip you and Steve just made. There've been some new developments while you were gone. I've talked to Steve. I know his clients waived any conflict of interest you may have, so there's no problem with our talking."

Emma quickly sorted out her memories of the trip. It already seemed a long time ago.

"Here's what I know," she began. "Everyone with a motive to kill Gomez has an alibi for the night he died. Everyone except Curt Randall."

Piers nodded. "Steve told me that. Diaz, the cousin whom Gomez was trying to blackmail, was home all night with his wife. Carillo, the jealous husband, was seen working in the onion fields."

"Have you spoken to Cardenas?" Emma asked.

Piers shook his head. "Who?"

"Gomez's friend who dropped out of the lawsuit. We still don't know why."

"Isn't that obvious?" Piers shrugged. "He didn't want to jeopardize his job." Then he raised his hands palms forward. "I know. I know. Legally Randall can't fire an employee for suing him if he's breaking the law. But most workers don't see it that way. Besides, even if they win those cases, all the farmworkers get is a lifetime of appeals."

Emma nodded. "That's exactly what Cardenas said. But there's a rumor someone paid him to sabotage the lawsuit."

"Who?" Piers asked.

"Rob Peters? "Emma suggested. "He had a lot to lose if his uncle lost that lawsuit."

Piers nodded. "The police are already questioning Peters. They found a second set of prints on the murder weapon," Piers explained. "That's the first new development since you left town."

"What exactly is the murder weapon?" Emma asked, remembering Maureen Tompkins' slip about the elk horn handled knife.

Piers shook his head. "A knife," he replied. "A knife that allegedly belonged to Curt. He swears he lost it weeks ago. That's all I'm allowed to say."

"What about Silas Bugbee?" Emma replied.

Piers scoffed. "The Save the Prunes nut? Why would he kill Gomez?"

"To end the lawsuit?" Emma shrugged. "To give him more time to stop the Chinese fire sale." She stared quizzically at her son-in-law. "Speaking of Chinese fire sales. What was Bob Monroe talking about at dinner last night?"

"A client in Sunnyvale," Piers explained. "Chinese buyer. Just like HoCo. Due diligence turned up arsenic in the water. Buyer used it to lower the price." Piers frowned. "Sounded like more than a coincidence, so I poked around. Found three similar sales. All involving Chinese purchasers."

"What will you do?" Emma asked.

"Already done it," Piers answered. "That's the second new development. I've convinced Curt to back off the sale. Till we get more information."

"That will make a lot of people in Blissburg happy," Emma replied. Suddenly she felt very tired. "But it sounds like we've uncovered more mysteries than we've solved."

As she spoke, Emma looked out the window and saw a car pull into the driveway. She rose from the couch and walked into the hall. A few seconds later Harry flew through the front door and into her arms.

"Nonnie! Nonnie!" her little five-year-old grandson cried. "Mom," he looked over his shoulder. "Nonnie's here."

"I told you she was coming," Julie laughed. "Didn't you believe me?"

But Harry had already moved on to his next thought. "Come outside, Nonnie. I'll show you how I shoot baskets. Dad put up the new hoop."

Emma looked over her shoulder at Julie.

"Go. Go," her daughter motioned with her hand. "I'll make dinner."

Five minutes later she and Harry were shooting baskets. Emma watched her grandson grow in confidence every time he shot the ball. His face assuming a determined look that she remembered seeing on Julie's face.

Emma suddenly felt so lucky she feared her heart would burst. Then the image of Curt Randall popped into her head. A man broken by his loss.

"Nonnie, it's your turn," Harry called, waking her from her reverie.

She walked slowly to where he stood. He handed her the ball. She took a deep breath, aimed at the basket and let the ball fly. Swoosh!

"Wow, Non! You made a basket," Harry called.

But Emma had done more than make a basket. She'd understood something with a certainty she could not explain. Curt Randall needed to know what she'd learned about Maria Hidalgo-Muller.

After the family had finished dinner Emma read Harry a story. Then Piers put the little boy to bed.

When he returned to the kitchen where Emma and Julie were still cleaning up, Emma told them everything she'd learned about Maria Hidalgo and Cory.

"Wow!" Piers exclaimed. "Sounds like *West Side Story*,"

"More like *Love Story*," Emma corrected him. "I don't think Tony went to Stanford. And Cory more likely was in a fraternity than the Jets."

Julie rolled her eyes at Piers. "Speaking of fraternities, what came over you and Buck last night?"

Piers shrugged his shoulders. "Just 'cause you never went to prep school."

"Thank goodness!" Julie glanced at Emma. "You did that one right."

"Thanks, Julie," Emma smirked. "But back to Maria."

"Back to what?" Piers asked. "She got over Cory. She improved her life."

"Piers!" Julie cried. "What about Maria's son? As I understand it, Maria Hidalgo has a son who could be Curt Randall's grandson."

Emma nodded. "If the dates work. He's in his forties."

"Curt needs to know about this," Julie exclaimed. "Don't you see, Piers? This could change his life."

Piers didn't agree. "First of all, the chances of this kid being Curt's grandson are slim. And if he's not, it'll be like losing Cory all over again. I say drop it."

"If it *is* Curt's grandson, that might kill him too. Given what a bigot he is," Julie mused.

"I say, let sleeping dogs lie," Piers said.

Emma disagreed. "It's got to be Curt's choice."

In the end, Julie agreed with Emma. "The old man's going to die soon anyway. He should know. And he should know what happened to the only woman his son ever loved."

"What if she doesn't want to talk?" Piers asked.

"I'll find out," Emma answered, "as long as you'll let Curt decide."

24

———

MONDAY MORNING – LOVE GROWS

At 9:15 the next morning, Emma called the number listed on the University of California at Riverside's website for the Department of Biology. When someone answered, she started to say, "May I speak with Professor Hidalgo-Muller," but she choked up. That's when she realized how nervous she was.

"Hello. Hello," the woman on the other end of the line repeated.

Emma tried to clear her throat. Then she got embarrassed and hung up the phone. At 9:30, she tried again hoping the department telephone didn't have caller ID.

This time she cleared her throat before she dialed, and even tested her question a few times out loud.

"Hello," she began. "May I speak with Professor Hidalgo-Muller?"

"Who's calling?" the voice on the line replied.

Emma had also practiced her answer. "An old friend from Coachella. I happened to be in town." Emma hoped this would, at least, peak Maria Hidalgo-Muller's curiosity.

Apparently, it did. After a few seconds, a different voice picked up the call. "Hello," the person said. "Who is this?"

Again, Emma was prepared. "Is this Maria?" she said.

"Yes," the woman replied cautiously.

"Hi," Emma began. "My name is Emma Corsi…"

The woman interrupted her. "Wait. You said…"

"I work for a lawyer in Sonoma," Emma continued, "and I need to ask you some questions that relate to a murder here. The Gomez murder."

Emma heard a sharp intake of breath on the other end of the phone.

"Have you heard of it?"

"Ye-es," the woman said even more cautiously than before.

"I think you once knew one of the suspects," Emma added. "A man named Curt Randall. And I thought you might have some information…"

"Look," Maria answered, "I haven't seen Curt Randall in almost fifty years. Believe me. There's nothing I could tell you about him that could possibly help in your investigation. Now if you will please excuse me, I have other things to do."

Emma could tell that Maria was about to hang up. Without thinking, she blurted out the truth.

"Maria, please wait. This is not about Curt Randall. It's about Cory, his son. You knew him, didn't you?"

There was a long silence on the other end of the phone. "Of course I knew Cory," Maria finally said. "What do you want to talk about? What does this have to do with the murder? Cory died a very long time ago."

"Yes. I know that," Emma answered. "In the war. And I know you have a son who is in his forties," Emma added. "And I wondered…"

"How dare you!" Maria Hidalgo-Muller shouted into the phone. Then she hung up.

A few minutes later, Emma called Piers.

"OK," he answered after she repeated her conversation with Maria. "I agree. She sounds defensive. Maybe…" he paused. "I'll tell Curt. Maybe there's something there."

Half an hour later, he called Emma back.

"I'm warning you, Emma, you may regret this."

"What's up?" Emma asked. "Did you talk to Curt?"

"I talked to Curt," Piers replied. "He's beside himself."

"What?" Emma asked, her mind racing. *Beside himself* could mean a lot of things: angry, hopeful, sad, unhinged.

"He wants to see her," Piers replied. "Today. Now. We leave in an hour from the Sonoma Airport on his private plane."

"We?" Emma asked. "Do I need to call Steve?"

"Fine. Call Steve," Piers answered. "But bet your bottom dollar you are coming. I am not directing this soap opera all by myself."

The news about Maria Hidalgo-Muller left Steve unmoved. At the mention of the private plane, however, he went ballistic.

"That takes the prize," he replied bitterly when Emma asked if she should go. "I spend sixteen hours from hell driving back and forth to Coachella with you eating junk food in a ten year old Subaru; while that murdering…"

"Alleged," Emma cut in, smarting at his choice of words. She hadn't thought their trip together was *that* bad.

"Alleged murdering bigot," Steve continued, "flies there in his private plane. To determine, after almost fifty years, whether some poor Mexican girl whose life he ruined along with his son's, has miraculously provided him with the immortality he does not deserve."

"He hardly ruined Maria Hidalgo-Muller's life," Emma pointed out. "She's head of the Department of Biology at UC Riverside. She's a huge success."

Her comment, Emma realized, only made things worse.

"You mean, unlike Steve Zimmer," he shot back, "working for peanuts in some obscure rural outpost trying, unsuccessfully, to get poor people a fair shake."

"That's not what I meant at all, Steve," Emma interrupted. "Blissburg is hardly a rural outpost; and, furthermore, you're the most admirable…"

"Go!" he yelled. "Thanks to you, I'm taking my wife wine tasting today. By the way, don't forget to enjoy the leather seats on your private jet. And the Terra chips. And the gourmet sandwiches from Pain de Lyon. At least you don't have to worry about poisoning yourself on Micky D's." He hung up the phone.

Half an hour later, Emma was sitting in the lounge of the private plane terminal at the Sonoma Airport sipping a complimentary bottle of San Pellegrino and waiting for Piers.

I could get to like this, she mused. *No security line. No stress. Piped in Vivaldi.*

The stress levels rose considerably, however, a few minutes later when Piers, Curt, his housekeeper, and an armed Sonoma County police officer walked into the waiting room.

Emma glanced questioningly from Piers to the policeman.

"Condition of bail for travel in state," Piers shrugged. Then he introduced everyone.

Of course Emma recognized Curt. He had always reminded her of John Wayne. Tall. Confident. All-American. But his features were more cartoonish. His blue eyes, under a wide forehead and a full head of white hair, were large and set wider apart. His nose more like a ski jump than Roman. His mouth, too, was bigger than Wayne's. So he almost looked goofy when he tried, unsuccessfully, to smile. His flinty eyes too full of hate and hurt.

"Curt, I'd like you to meet Emma Corsi," Piers said. "She's the one who located Maria Hidalgo after all these years."

"Glad to meet you," Curt stuck out his hand mechanically.

After she shook it, he crossed both arms across his chest defensively. Then, as though the effort had been too much, the old man limped to one of the waiting room chairs and sat down with a wheezy gasp.

The housekeeper nodded at Emma. Then she hooked Curt up to a portable oxygen machine.

Soon they were ushered from the waiting room out to the tarmac where they met their pilots and boarded the small plane.

The minute she stepped into the cabin, Emma understood Steve's harangue. She settled back into one of the incredibly comfortable seats. A bottle of water sat on a table in front of her, along with a small bag of Terra chips to munch on during the flight. One of the pilots described their route. The skies were clear. The whole flight was expected to last a little over an hour. Seconds later, they were on their way.

I could get used to this, Emma reminded herself again.

Half way through the flight, the pilot announced there were sandwiches and salads, if anyone wanted lunch. Piers passed them around in a wicker basket along with more drinks. Emma noticed that the sandwich she chose – a prosciutto with Brie and fig on a walnut baguette – was indeed from Pain de Lyon, a chic Sonoma bakery. *How did Steve know?* she couldn't help wondering. *Does he lead a secret life?*

No one spoke, except for Piers who leaned over while passing out lunch to whisper in Emma's ear. The fingerprints on the murder weapon had tested negative for Curt's nephew. They were back at square one.

Everyone was intent on finishing lunch before the airplane began its descent on the relatively short flight to the Ontario, California airport. Before Emma knew it, Piers had collected the trash. The pilot announced that they'd be landing in fifteen minutes.

It was later, seated across from Emma in the limousine driving to UC Riverside, that Curt Randall addressed her again.

"Tell me," he leaned forward in his seat and stated in an even, low voice. "What did she say to you on the phone? What were her exact words?"

Emma closed her eyes for a few seconds. Trying to replay the brief, emotionally charged conversation in her head.

"When I asked her about her son," Emma finally replied, "her only words were, 'How dare you?' Then she hung up the phone."

Curt's face composed itself into a far off expression that, at first, Emma was at a loss to name. Till she realized she'd seen it before. On Julie's face staring at Santa Claus. Or on a batter's the split second he saw his ball arcing towards the outfield.

The expression was hope. Pure, shameless, desperate hope. She wondered if Steve was right after all. Perhaps she should have let sleeping dogs lie.

Curt nodded slowly. "I want to know everything she said," he explained.

Emma told him everything she remembered, except for her own initial lie about the reason for the call. "Finally," she concluded, "I told her I was calling about," she hesitated even mentioning the name, "about Cory, your son."

"Cory," the old man had clasped his hands together under his chin, like he was saying a prayer. "Yes. About Cory. What did she say?"

"She said she knew him," Emma replied. "She asked what I wanted to know." Emma shrugged. "I answered that I was interested in her son. That's when she hung up."

"What did she say when *you* called to set up the interview?" Emma asked turning to Piers.

Piers shook his head. "We *didn't* call her. We figured she wouldn't talk to us, so what was the point? Curt decided to fly down here and confront her instead."

Confront her! Emma thought. *After all these years, with what?*

IT WAS a quarter past 1:00 p.m. when Emma, Piers, Curt, his house-keeper and the Sonoma County police officer finally arrived at the Department of Biology on the campus of UC Riverside. The office was staffed by an administrative assistant. It served as a kind of information clearing house. It was furnished with a few chairs, and tables covered with pamphlets and brochures.

The assistant looked up from her desk, obviously perplexed when the parade of unlikely visitors entered the small room.

"Can I help you?" she asked.

Piers started to take the lead, but before he could say anything Curt Randall replied. "We're here to talk to Maria. Maria Hidalgo," he added.

"Professor Hidalgo-Muller?" the woman answered.

"That's right," Curt nodded. Nobody smiled.

"May I ask who wishes to see her?" the assistant replied.

Curt had folded his arms across his chest again. He was breathing hard. His housekeeper offered him some oxygen, but he waved her away with an irritated swat of his hand.

"Tell her Curt Randall wants to talk to her," Curt said.

Emma glanced around the room and then at Piers, wondering why he didn't intervene. *It's the Department of Biology, for goodness sakes, not Dodge City*, she told herself.

The assistant, she realized, was staring at them. She frowned. "I'm afraid Professor Hidalgo-Muller is still at lunch," she said. "Curt Randall, I think you said. Is that with a 'C' or a 'K'?" she asked.

"With a 'C'," Randall replied.

"I'll tell her you called on her," the assistant said. "If you give me your phone number, she'll get back to you."

Curt shook his head. "We'll wait."

Then he motioned to Emma and to his housekeeper to take two of the three visitors' chairs. He sat down in the other. Piers leaned against one of the tables and pretended to peruse a pamphlet labeled "Careers in Biology." The police officer stood by the door.

In the next few minutes, two or three student types entered the room. Looking around, they quickly beat a retreat out the door. Finally, after half an hour of waiting, the door to the office opened and a woman whom Emma recognized entered the office. It was Maria Hidalgo-Muller. She was even lovelier in person than she was in her picture. With her long face and dark sad eyes, she reminded Emma of a cross between a Latin Virgin Mary and Joan Baez.

She glanced at the assistant. "Sorry I took so long. Have there been any calls?"

The assistant squinted back at her apologetically.

Suddenly Maria Hidalgo glanced around the room. Then her eyes landed on Curt Randall. They hardened and her body went stiff.

She stared at him for almost a full minute before shaking her head. "You sad old man," she finally said between clenched teeth, "OK," she shrugged disdainfully, motioning towards an office behind the assistant's desk. "What do you want?"

With that Curt Randall stood up and moved slowly towards the door, followed by Piers motioning to Emma to come too. The housekeeper remained seated.

The police officer also strode forward from his post. But Maria waved him away. "Please," she said. "What harm do you really think this pathetic old man is going to do that he hasn't already done?"

With that, she followed the three of them into her office. Emma, she dismissed immediately with a wave of her hand. "You must be the one who called. The Corsi woman!"

Emma nodded.

"Who are you?" she turned to Piers. "Oh, of course," she muttered before he could answer. "You're probably the lawyer. There always has to be a lawyer these days."

Piers nodded. "Yes. My name is Larkin, Piers Larkin," he replied.

Maria sat down behind her desk. It was large, Emma noted, and covered with folders. Emma also noticed a couple of photographs on a credenza behind the desk where two computers screens sat side-by-side. One of the photographs was of a smiling man in his sixties. Presumably Mr. Muller. The other of a younger man and a girl. The young man looked exactly like Maria.

She motioned them to sit down on a couch and one of three chairs. Curt and Piers took the couch. From the chair, Emma watched the three other occupants of the room.

"So, Mr. Randall, what do you want?" Maria repeated the questioned she'd asked in the other room.

The old man wasted no time. "I want to know what happened all those years ago. I want to know about your son."

Maria quickly made it clear that she was in no hurry to satisfy the old man's curiosity. She answered the questions in the order they were asked.

"You want to know what happened all those years ago," she repeated. "But your son, Cory, told you, right? Before he left for Viet Nam and broke both our hearts. You know what happened, Mr. Randall. Cory and I were young and we fell in love, working side by side in the onion fields. Probably too young, as you explained. But that wasn't really the problem, was it Mr. Randall? The problem was something else. The problem was who I am."

"Who you were," Curt whispered.

"Who I still am," Maria replied. "Despite all this," she gestured around room. "Despite all I've 'accomplished' as they say, I'm still the same. Maria Hidalgo. The Latina who cut the onions on your farm."

Emma watched Curt squint at her, staring around the room shaking his head.

Still, Maria did not answer the old man's second question. "And since you couldn't stand the thought of your son marrying, procreating with such, such filth – that's the word you used when you visited my parents – you sent him away..."

"He volunteered," Curt cried.

"No. He would not have volunteered if you had let him marry me," Maria stated, shaking her head. "Instead, you threatened to disown him." She continued speaking, seemingly to herself. "He begged me to marry him anyway. After all, by then I was eighteen. But I, thinking myself noble, refused to marry without his father's blessing. I was a fool. He enlisted the next day."

Still, Maria waited to answer the crucial question. The tension in the air got so thick, Emma wanted to scream.

"Then there were the months of waiting," Maria continued. "Worrying. Blaming myself. Finally, after Cory's letters stopped, I got the news. Not from his family. From a member of his platoon. Cory was killed in an ambush, the letter said. One night, he'd poured his heart out in a foxhole about the girl back home. The one he couldn't marry. Most likely, the letter said, I had not heard about his death. The army wouldn't have known to write me. So sad to be the bearer of such bad news."

For a moment, Maria sat lost in thought. Almost as though none of them was there. Then she roused herself, shook away whatever ghost it was that haunted her. And raised her head to stare Curt Randall in the eye.

"But you don't really care about my pain, do you Mr. Randall? All you ever cared about was yourself. You never even cared about Cory. About what *he* wanted. Who he really was."

The cruelty of the challenge startled Emma. She looked at Curt, bracing herself against his fury. To her surprise, the old man cowered in his chair. Like a hound who'd been kicked.

"Now," Maria continued, collecting herself. "About my son. He was born three years after Cory died. I have a daughter, too, born two years later; but of course, you don't care about her. So," she laughed harshly. "No worries, Mr. Randall. I was a good Catholic girl. There is no brown half-breed to lay claims on your estate *if* you ever die."

Emma glanced from Curt to Maria and back again. The old

man's eyes were swimming. Tears big as marbles coursed down his cheeks. "I'm sorry," was all he said trying to wipe the tears away with his hands. "I wanted it. I wanted a grandchild. I wanted it too much." He added, pathetically, "Are you absolutely sure?"

At last, it seemed, Maria Hidalgo was disarmed. Her eyes welled up. She stood, walked around her desk, and stared down at the old man. Her sad eyes winced in pain. "Of course I'm sure. Don't you think there were times I wished I'd carried his child. Then, at least, there'd have been something left of him," she said simply.

Curt hunched forward now, eating the air in what looked like labored gulps, bracing his distended torso with his forearms pressed on his knees. "Tell me," he finally said. "If you wouldn't mind. Tell me about yourself. He loved you. Now you are all that's left."

At first, Maria seemed at a loss for words. "What do you want to know?" she asked.

"How you got here," Curt said, gesturing around the room.

Maria still stood towering over him in front of her desk. After a few seconds she replied. "When I learned of Cory's death," she began, "I was already in school. At first, I wanted to drop out. I blamed myself, you see. Then I realized that the only way I could," she hesitated, "honor him - honor all he stood for, honor all he felt for me – was to go on. To succeed. So I worked even harder. A year later I met a young mathematics professor, Doug Muller. He was a wonderful man. He died last year," her voice caught as she spoke. "I loved him. And I wanted to be his wife, to erase all the guilt and sadness I felt about Cory. We had kids right away, even though I was in school. Eventually, I was happy again. Doug got me through."

She pointed to one of the photographs on the credenza behind the desk. "First, I had Xavier, then Paz. It was having Paz that helped me realize something. Love isn't like money. When you use it, it doesn't disappear. Instead, the more you use it, the more it grows. Till you have so much love," her voice caught again in her throat, "you think your heart will burst."

"Once I realized that," Maria continued. "Once I realized that there's plenty of love to go around, I knew I didn't have to erase Cory from my heart. That I could go on loving him, and love Doug and my children. That realization changed my life."

Maria suddenly stopped talking. She turned and faced her desk, searching it. Finally, her eyes rested on a carved Chinese jade pen holder.

"Ah," she said picking something up. "Here it is." She showed it to Curt. "Do you recognize this?"

Emma let out a gasp.

She looked at Piers. His jaw dropped too.

"Of course I do," Curt smiled. "That was Cory's knife. The one he used to cut onions. My father gave it to him years ago when Cory came down here to work in the fields. I had one like it. Mine was a little bigger. The elk horn on mine has an extra notch." He shook his head. "I always wondered what happened to Cory's knife. He treated it like his prized possession."

"Cory gave it to me," Maria answered. "Before he left for Viet Nam. When he handed it to me, he said, 'Never forget who you are, Maria. Never cut your roots. They give you life.' I've always kept it on my desk to remember. To remember who I am. Who I've always been. So you see, I have not changed despite," she gestured around the room at the photos and the awards, "all this."

Curt stood up. The old man and the professor stared at each other for a few seconds. "Thank you," he said. "I've taken enough of your time."

They awkwardly shook hands.

Curt was about to leave the room, when he stopped. He turned to Maria again and said. "One more thing, could you tell me about your children?"

Maria smiled. This time she was clearly touched. "My son is a doctor. He works in a clinic in the valley. My daughter is a social worker with the Rural Legal Assistance Fund."

Curt smiled and turned to Piers. "I hope they're not the ones trying to sue me."

Then the three of them left.

THEY WERE DRIVING BACK to the airport in their limousine when Curt brought up the knife. "I almost asked her for it," he sighed. "Seeing as mine is lost."

Emma looked at Piers. The minute she saw the elk horn knife, she thought of the murder weapon. It was exactly like the one Chief Tompkins' wife described.

From the look on Piers' face, Emma suspected Piers recognized the elk horn handled knife too. But since Maureen Tompkins had sworn her to secrecy, she decided to play dumb.

"What happened to your elk horn knife?" she asked Curt. "How did it get lost?"

Curt glanced at Piers, sitting across from him in the limo. Then he glanced at the police officer.

"That elk horned knife sure must be important. Danged if the police haven't asked me that question a hundred times," he said. "Like I told them, I lost it. Haven't seen it in weeks."

"Where did you keep it?" Emma asked. "Maybe remembering where you kept it will remind you of where it went."

Curt swatted his hand at her impatiently. "Nah. I've wracked my brain. I kept it on my desk in my study. By the photograph of my dad sitting on the front porch of the ranch. That knife had been there for years. But it's gone. We've looked all over for it." He glanced at his housekeeper. "Haven't we, Teresita?"

She rolled her eyes and nodded. "I've looked everywhere, *Senor*."

"Do you remember the last time you saw it?" Emma ask.

"You're wasting your time," the old man barked. "The police asked me that, too."

The old man settled back in his seat. "After all these years," he muttered. "I've always wondered what happened to Cory's knife. Then, out of the blue, there it is."

He had closed his eyes, as if he wanted to sleep. But all of a sudden, his eyes fluttered open. He stared around, blankly, as though searching his mind.

Suddenly he laughed. "You know what? That Chinese pen holder. The one Maria had on her desk. Danged if it didn't just remind me of something."

"What?" Emma asked.

"The last time I saw the knife," Curt replied. "It was a few days before the murder. When Cheng Bo brought over that new report."

"The one that said there was arsenic in the water?" Piers asked. "I couldn't figure out why Cheng Bo bothered to hand deliver it. He'd already mailed me a copy of the report."

"Said he wanted to drop it by in person," Curt answered. "I invited him into my study for a drink. Seemed like a personable guy. And tall. Almost my height. Not short like they usually are."

Emma winced.

"See, that's the last time I saw the knife," Curt added. "It was sitting on my desk when he handed me the report. I remember it well now. He picked it up and admired it."

A FEW MINUTES LATER, Piers had told the limo driver to turn the car around.

"What's the name of that laborer Yolanda Gomez said was paid off?" he asked Emma.

"Louis Cardenas," Emma replied.

"Lets go talk to him," Piers replied.

25

MONDAY AFTERNOON – NO WAY OUT

An hour later, Emma had helped the limo driver retrace her steps from the Motel 6 outside Coachella to Louis Cardenas' shed.

When the limo pulled to a stop and they got out of the car, the same wall of heat sucked the air out of Emma's lungs like it had two days before.

"Where are we?" Curt asked wheezily.

"On your property," Emma explained.

When they approached, the shed Louis Cardenas called home looked deserted. They went inside. The metal shell had heated up to well over one hundred degrees. Emma swore you could fry an egg on the floor. Of course, the shed was empty except for a filthy mattress, a duffle bag spilling out old clothes, and a table with an empty beer can.

"Who lives there? No one should be in there," Curt said. He was sweating and looked dazed from the effort and the heat. "I wouldn't let one of my dogs live in a place like this."

No one answered. They exited the shed and Piers led them towards the old barracks.

"I remember these," Curt commented as he approached one of

the long, low buildings. "I think I lived here one summer," he added. Then looking through a broken glass window he shook his head. "Can't be. We had bathrooms and outdoor showers. This place is too run down for anyone to live in it."

Nonetheless, a few seconds later, a man ambled out of one of the barracks kicking at the dirt with his boots.

"You seen Louis Cardenas?" Piers called to him.

"Down the road at the cantina." The man motioned with his thumb. "Who's asking?"

"His boss," Piers called over his shoulder as they got into the car.

When they reached the cantina, Piers told the housekeeper to stay in the car with their driver – and to keep the engine running. Then he motioned Curt and Emma to follow him, telling the police officer to stand watch by the door.

Once inside, Emma quickly identified Louis Cardenas. He was sitting alone at the bar drinking a beer. Piers and Curt approached him. Emma held back, but close enough so she could hear.

Piers did not beat around the bush.

"Louis," he said. "My name's Piers Larkin and this is my client Curt Randall, your boss. The defendant in the class action lawsuit you dropped out of a while ago. I'd like to talk to you about that."

Emma watched Louis's eyes get wide and scared. Then he scowled. "I don't have to talk to you," he said, pushing by Piers.

"I think you do," Piers said.

Louis started to run for the door, but at that moment, the police officer stepped sideways blocking the exit.

Louis stopped in his tracks.

Piers approached him again. Emma marveled that he kept his voice very calm. "Talk to me, Louis," he said. "I know someone paid you to drop out of the suit. Paid you something to make it worthwhile."

"I didn't kill him," Louis shouted.

"That's right," Piers repeated, "you didn't kill him. But you *did* poison the water tank on my client's ranch. The same person paid you to do that too. Tell me who it was."

Emma realized with a shiver that Piers was shooting the moon, risking everything on the same hunch she had.

"Tell me who paid you," Piers repeated, "and I promise my client won't prosecute you for poisoning that tank. "

The room suddenly grew very still.

When Louis Cardenas did not answer, Piers tried again.

"I can make this easy for you if you cooperate," he said. "Or you can make it hard on yourself. Who paid you to poison Curt Randall's water tank?"

Louis glanced again at the police officer blocking the door. Then he stared back at Piers. "Bobo," he finally said. "The Chinese. He promised to pay me good to slip something in the old man's water tank." He gestured with his chin towards Curt. "But Gomez saw me. Followed me up the path and figured out what I'd done. Then he tried to blackmail me. I told Bobo. The dirty Chinese rat blamed *me*. Refused to pay me what he'd promised." He glared defiantly at Piers. "But I didn't kill him. I didn't kill Gomez." He pointed to Curt. "That man did."

"ARE you really not going to press charges?" Emma asked after they'd left Cardenas under the charge of the local Riverside County police department and were sitting in the limo headed back towards the airport.

Piers shook his head. "Not if he continues to cooperate."

"Are you thinking what I'm thinking?" Emma asked.

Piers nodded. "We need to find Cheng."

That's when Emma thought of something.

She dialed Maria Hidalgo's number.

"Maria," she said when the woman picked up the phone. "Is

there any way you could mail Cory's elk horn knife to me? Overnight? I just want to borrow it."

"No," Maria replied. "I've had enough. Enough dredging up the past. It took me years, but I'm finally done with it. Done with blaming myself. Curt will have to do the same. Without my help."

"Please," Emma pleaded, hoping to persuade Maria before she hung up. "There's a killer out there. He's already murdered one Mexican worker. He has to be stopped. We only need the knife for a couple of days. Then we'll return it. Please do it. For yourself, not Curt."

Maria took a long time to answer. "You need it to catch the killer?" she repeated uncertainly. Then, after a long pause, she finally said, "OK".

"Just put it in a well padded envelope, then send it here," Emma said.

She gave him Piers' address.

"Thanks." Emma hung up the phone.

26

TUESDAY MORNING – BO SHAMBLES

The package arrived at Piers' office at 9:45. Emma was already there. Then Piers called Cheng Bo.

"You're on your way to the airport?" Piers said, grimacing at Emma over the phone. "What time's your flight?"

Emma's heart sank. This was going to be harder than they thought.

"Look," Piers said. "I'm not saying this will change your mind, but as you know, my client has a noose around his neck. Just between you and me, I'm not so sure he's going to beat this rap. They have him on the murder weapon. They found it in his barn. With his fingerprints on it."

Piers chuckled into the phone. "Right now, he's up to his ears in legal fees. *My* legal fees, Bo. If you get my drift." He cleared his throat. "The point is, we've got him over a barrel. He needs money fast. I've convinced him to offer you a price on the plum ranch that, frankly, I'd be surprised if you could refuse. All cash. That's the deal."

Piers paused for Cheng Bo's reply.

"Sure. Just come out of curiosity. If you are interested in buying at the price we're offering, we can work out the details later. After you return to China."

Apparently Cheng Bo agreed.

"We'll meet at the plum ranch in an hour," Piers said. "See you there."

WHEN EMMA and Piers arrived at the plum ranch, Curt's housekeeper showed them into the study. Curt sat behind a large oak desk in a wood paneled room. It was furnished in what Emma surmised was the original Stickley style sofa, coffee table, and chairs purchased by his father many years before.

Piers handed Curt the package. A large envelope labeled University of California at Riverside

Curt opened it, tore off the wrapping and removed the elk horn handled knife. He set it on his desk on a green leather Victorian blotter.

Then Piers made a quick call on his cell.

"We're here. Everything's set," Emma heard him say.

They stared at each other in silence. Everyone knew what they had to do.

A few minutes later the housekeeper ushered Cheng Bo into the room. The tall handsome man was neatly dressed for travel in Polo jeans, a striped silk polo shirt, and a chocolate brown leather bomber jacket.

He nodded at everyone, cocking his head briefly at Emma, no doubt wondering what she was doing there.

"My assistant," Piers explained. But Emma noted Cheng Bo's eyes squint with suspicion.

Curt spoke next. "I'm sorry to drag you out here on such short notice," he said. "But I wanted to be present when my attorney, here, presented my offer. He's been pressuring me to conclude this sale." He glared ominously at Piers. "He says you're offering cash."

With that, Piers outlined the terms of the highly favorable sale agreement he'd drawn up the night before.

"As I said on the phone," he concluded, offering Cheng Bo the agreement to read, "we'd love to wrap this up before you go. I've included a generous escape clause."

Piers gave Bo a minute to read through the agreement. Then he directed his eyes to Curt's desk, pointing to the penholder. "If you could just sign…"

Cheng Bo looked at the desk. His eyes fell on the elk horn knife and he did a double take.

Then Curt picked up the knife and offered it to Cheng Bo.

"Here," he said. "Take this. You admired it last time you were here. Take it as a token of trust. It belonged to my father, the…"

Before he could finish, Cheng Bo flinched. "What the…what's that doing here?" he cried.

"Nothing," Curt laughed, handing him the knife. "You admired it. Last time you were here. Take it."

Cheng Bo grasped the knife. Then he let it fall back onto the desk. "What's going on?" he said standing up abruptly as though to leave.

"Not so fast," Piers said.

But Cheng Bo had picked up the knife again and was brandishing it at Emma's son-in-law. "You can't prove a thing," Cheng Bo cried starting to back out of the room towards the door.

Old Curt Randall was fast. He was out of his chair and around the desk before Cheng Bo saw him coming. He knocked the knife out of Cheng Bo's hand with a Karate chop. It flew across the floor.

Wow, Emma thought. *We were wrong. Curt wasn't too sick to have murdered Santiago Gomez after all!*

Then two police officers rushed into the room, followed by Chief Tompkins.

"You're under arrest," one of the officers said to Cheng Bo. The other placed the man's wrists in handcuffs.

Cheng Bo's wrist must still have been smarting from Curt's blow. Emma noticed him wince.

"You have no right," he screamed. "Call my lawyer. It was self-defense. The old man tried to kill me." He pointed to the elk horn knife lying on the floor. "With the same knife he used to kill Santiago Gomez."

The Chief cocked his head at Cheng Bo. "Now how would you know that?" he said.

Then the Chief looked back at Piers and smiled. He nodded at Curt.

"Looks like we finally got our man."

"I have a plane to catch. Let me go," Cheng Bo yelled at the Chief. "I didn't murder the Mexican, Randall did."

"We're not arresting you for murder, yet, Mr. Bo," the Chief replied.

"Cheng," the man muttered sullenly.

"You're under arrest for malicious destruction of property. We have a sworn statement from a Louis Cardenas that you offered him money to poison Mr. Randall's water. I'm also arresting you for threatening Mr. Larkin here with bodily harm."

"Call my lawyer," Mr. Cheng repeated through clenched teeth.

"Right away," the Chief laughed. "You're going to need one after we've matched your finger prints," he pointed to the elk horn handled knife lying on the floor, "with the ones on the knife used to murder Santiago Gomez."

With that the two officers led Mr. Cheng away.

～

A FEW MINUTES LATER, Piers dropped Emma at home. Julie was

waiting for them. They all sat down in the kitchen for a cup of tea. Julie made it. Emma's hands were still shaking.

"My son-in-law was a hero today," Emma told Julie. Then she turned and shook her finger at Piers. "But really, my dear, didn't you take it a step too far? When Cheng waved that knife at you, I thought he was going to kill you."

"For a minute, I did too," Piers laughed. "Till old Curt landed that Karate chop. So much for our murder defense. Good thing Curt never went on trial!"

Julie patted her stomach. "Baby and I are glad we missed all that," she sighed.

Piers had stood up to put his arm around his wife. "The real hero today was your mother," he said.

"He's being silly," Emma interrupted. "I didn't do a thing."

"You caught the killer," Piers replied. "If *you* hadn't uncovered that soap opera starring Maria Hidalgo – I should say Professor Hidalgo-Muller – and Cory Randall, Cheng Bo would be on his way to China right now. And Curt would still be facing a murder charge."

"How so?" Julie asked, shaking her head.

"It was seeing that knife on Maria Hidalgo's desk that revived Curt's memory," Piers explained. "That placed the murder weapon on his desk when Cheng Bo visited him two days before Gomez died. Without that, we wouldn't have put the pieces together that linked the poisoned tanks to Gomez's murderer."

"We knew someone had paid off Louis Cardenas," Emma added. "When Cardenas told us that person was Cheng, and that Cheng knew Gomez threatened to tell Curt Randall about their plot to poison his water tank," Emma shrugged, "well, that's when we knew Cheng was the murderer. He had to stop Gomez from exposing them."

"So he stole Curt's knife to frame Curt for the murder," Piers finished the story. "We couldn't have connected the dots without help from Hidalgo-Muller."

Julie gave her mother a big hug. "You must be exhausted, Mom."

Emma had to agree. She *was* exhausted. She'd crisscrossed the state. She'd also learned a lot. Mostly about love. She'd learned there's plenty to go around.

"Let's have lunch tomorrow, sweetie," she said to her daughter. "Let's celebrate that new little baby!"

EMMA HAD a few more things to do before she could relax. She'd mulled them over lying in bed the night before.

As soon as Julie and Piers left, she went to her computer.

"Dan," she wrote. "Sorry I've been off the grid. Can you meet me Friday for lunch? In San Francisco? I'll reserve a booth at Sam's on Bush Street."

It never even crossed Emma's mind that Dan might not show up.

After she'd hit the send button, she picked up the phone.

"Hi. It's me," she said.

"Emma?" Jack asked.

"Yes," she replied. "And before you hang up – which I thoroughly deserve – I want to apologize for Saturday night. I broke the Cowboy Code. I didn't keep my word. I lied. And I was...Oh forget it," she laughed. "Jack, I owe you one fabulous dinner. Can I come over this Saturday night for a rematch. Same guests. New menu."

Emma could almost hear Jack smile over the phone as he spoke. "Without Andy this time?"

"Cowgirl promise."

Before he could say more, she hung up the phone.

27

WEDNESDAY – BACK AT THE RANCH

Emma spent Wednesday trying to focus on Saturday night's dinner. For appetizers she'd already picked *carciofi alla giudia,* crisp fried whole artichokes – the baby ones from Castroville stripped of all their tough outer leaves. That, along with ripe Humbolt Fog cheese and *bagna caoda* anchovy-flavored dip with cooked vegetables, would keep everyone busy while Emma finished cooking the meal. The meal, itself, consisted of *Trapanese* pesto with homemade *tagliatelle* followed by sautéed spinach and pan roasted shoulder of veal. Of course, she'd make Jack's favorite Bavarian cream for dessert.

Early that morning, Emma had called Cara, Julie and the Monroes to invite them to the party. Cara extended to Emma a grudging congratulations on cracking the Gomez murder. Apparently, she still hadn't forgiven Emma for embarrassing her father Saturday night by bringing her ex-husband to dinner. Jack, however, had already alerted Cara to the new invitation.

"Dad says he's sure your ex isn't coming this time. I hope that's right. It *was* awkward and, I'm afraid, embarrassing for my dad – regardless of whatever relationship you two may or may not have."

There was silence on the other end of the line while Cara waited for Emma to reply.

"I'm aware of that," was all she finally said.

Julie's response when Emma reached her daughter a few hours later was more promising.

"I know, Mom. I know. Mike called Piers. They're playing tennis in Calistoga Saturday afternoon. Piers will drop Harry off at Cara and Mike's with their *au pair*. We'll drive back there after dinner, spend the night in the guesthouse, and stay over Sunday to hang by the pool.

The Monroes, on the other hand, were thrilled when Emma called.

"Emma," Jane replied after receiving the invitation, "to think we get to hear first hand how you and Piers brought down that killer! I'm so excited I could wet my pants!"

Organizing her shopping list, however, was harder than Emma expected. News of Cheng Bo's arrest had hit the airwaves late the night before. Emma's phone rang off the hook with friends calling to congratulate her on her latest crime bust, curiosity seekers at the door and journalists from all over the state calling for interviews.

Steve even stopped by in person to thank her, awkwardly, for finding the killer.

He'd dropped onto one of her wooden kitchen stools to watch her chop almonds for the *Trapanese*. "Can you imagine the wreck I'd be if I'd sent the wrong man to jail? That along with Santiago's murder could've ended my career."

"Stop it!" Emma patted his shoulder. "Santiago should have gone to the police right away when he discovered what HoCo was doing. Instead, he tried to blackmail people. Stir up trouble. That's why he was murdered. You had nothing to do with it. As for Curt, plenty of people blamed him for the murder. Including the police."

"But I was wrong," Steve answered. "I couldn't stay objective.

Keep an open mind. It was too easy to blame the murder on the oppressor."

"Forget about it," Emma dismissed him. "The question is, what're you going to do now?"

Steve sighed. "Rethink my life," he answered glumly. "Of course we'll sue HoCo and Cheng Bo for Gomez's wrongful death. That should be a slam-dunk. HoCo has assets in Southern California that we can tap for a judgment in favor of Yolanda and the kids. As for the class action?"

Emma held her breath.

Steve paused and thought for a moment before he continued. "With all the recent publicity painting Curt Randall as the innocent victim of a Chinese plot to frame him for a murder he didn't commit, it will be hard to win a class action against him just now. But I'm not giving up." He shook his head in disgust. Then his eyes followed Emma's hands as she finished mixing together chopped almonds, basil, garlic, pecorino and tomatoes for the *Trapanese*. "By the way, can I try this?" he added. "It's *Trapanese pesto*, right?"

Emma handed him a piece of sour dough that he dipped into the sauce.

"Delicious!" he exclaimed. Then he continued. "As I was saying, here we sit in California's breadbasket, stuffing ourselves on some of the best food this country has to offer, and we still can't pay a living wage to the people we count on to..."

"By the way, how did the wine tasting with your wife go?" Emma cut in, hoping to change the subject before Steve completely poisoned her *Trapanese* sauce with his guilt.

This time, Steve didn't push the question away. "Very well," he nodded biting on his lower lip.

"Which winery did you go to? Was the wine good?"

Steve smiled like a Cheshire cat. "Jordan. The wine was great. The postprandial nap even better. I think we're back on track."

Emma gave him a thumbs up. Then she shook her forefinger at

her boss. "Remember, Steve, one nap doth not a happy marriage make."

Steve ignored her warning. "The clincher, though, was the poem I wrote. A strategic breakthrough, if I do say so myself. Apparently Professor Gluestick – he's the kindergarten art teacher – had made her a macaroni collage for her birthday. She liked my poem cum pearl earrings better."

"Nice move," Emma laughed.

"Whatever it takes," Steve sighed. "Thanks for the advice."

He got up to leave, but as he headed out of the kitchen towards Emma's front door, he turned back as though remembering something.

"I'm not giving up, you know," he said. "I'm glad we found Santiago's killer, but I'm not giving up on justice for seasonal workers just because I was wrong about Curt. I'm telling Piers that at the meeting tomorrow. I just want you to know. In advance. I'm not backing down."

"Meeting?" Emma asked. "What meeting?"

Steve glanced at her quizzically. "The meeting at the plum ranch tomorrow afternoon. I saw your name on the email, so I figured you'd know all about it. You're invited, along with that Hidalgo woman and somebody named Paz. I'm sure Piers and Curt are just trying to butter me up to drop the class action."

As Steve spoke, Emma grabbed her cell phone and checked her mail. She'd been answering calls all morning, but she hadn't checked her email in a couple of hours. She clicked on a message from Piers and, sure enough, there it was. An invitation.

"Maria, Paz, Xavier, Steve, Emma" it began. "Curt has asked me to contact you to invite you to a meeting tomorrow, Thursday, at the Randall Ranch at 10:00 a.m.

"As I mentioned on the phone, it is vitally important that Maria, Xavier and Paz attend. Curt will send his driver for you at 7:00 a.m. to take you to the Ontario Airport where he will fly you here to

Sonoma. Steve, it is equally important that you attend. Curt has business he wants to discuss that will be of interest to you. Please email me that each of you will be there. Sincerely, Piers."

"What do you suppose this is about?" Emma asked as Steve turned to leave.

Steve shook his head. "I don't know. Piers wouldn't say when I called him this morning. Just something about an announcement the old man wants to make. I figure he'll try to twist my arm to drop the lawsuit. Same old sob story about all the trouble he's seen. Trouble he's brought on himself, I might add." Steve glanced at Emma, "Whatever it is, I figured *you* would know."

Emma shook her head. Then she clicked the "attend" button attached to the email.

28

THURSDAY MORNING – A COOPERATIVE EFFORT

Thursday morning Emma made her way east off of Highway 101 to Curt Randall's plum ranch. The 1870's Victorian farmhouse where Curt now lived alone with his housekeeper was sited at the end of a long dirt drive a mile from the main road. Emma noted that the once impressive yellow wood frame house with its white gingerbread trim looked particularly forlorn that day. Like a once festive party dress yellowed with age and careless wear. The paint was peeling. The front porch sagged. A few gangly rosebushes along the front yard fence bore no buds. The hydrangeas were colorless and dry.

Further up the drive, next to a pickup truck parked in front of the old two-story detached garage, Emma recognized Piers' Porsche side by side with Steve's old Subaru. She noted this with dismay. That comparison alone would put Steve in a bad mood.

Emma parked her Prius next to the Subaru. Then slamming her car door, she saw a limo kicking up dust as it careened up the drive. *Maria coming from the airport*, she thought to herself. *How on earth did Piers convince her to attend the mysterious meeting?*

As Emma stood on the porch waiting for someone to answer the door, Maria Hidalgo-Muller climbed the front stairs accompanied by her daughter. She greeted Emma with the same chilly suspicion Emma had noted when they first met.

"Paz," Maria introduced her daughter, "this is Ms. Corsi. The woman who stirred up all this...." The next word seemed to fail her.

Paz smiled back tentatively, apparently embarrassed by her mother's tone. She was a blond, willowy, fair-faced woman who bore little resemblance to her mother.

"The woman who located you on the Internet," Paz finished her mother's thought with the nonchalance of a thirty-something for whom finding someone on the Internet was no big deal.

"And just in case you're wondering why I came, Ms. Corsi," Maria addressed Emma now, answering the question Emma had not asked, "Your son..." She squinted her eyes, "I'm right, aren't I, the lawyer is your son?"

"Son-in-law," Emma corrected her, feeling as though Professor Hidalgo-Muller had somehow accused her of giving birth to a weasel.

"Your son-in-law the lawyer," Maria continued, "told me the meeting was about Cory. I felt I had to come. Paz kindly agreed to accompany me." She glanced at her daughter who nodded. "To close that chapter, so to speak. Certainly not to start a new one," she added. "Paz agrees it is important that I do that. My son refused. Though why Curt Randall wants to involve us in whatever this is, I do not know. We want nothing more to do with *him*."

Professor Hidalgo-Muller added the last statement with a kind of angry resignation. Emma didn't need to respond, however. At that moment Piers opened the door.

"Ah, you're all together," he greeted them. "Curt and Steve are in the study. Come right in." Turning to Maria he added, "We can get started immediately and not take up more of your time, Professor."

Piers escorted them down a wide hall that ran the full length of the house. It functioned almost as a room, the front furnished with hooks and an umbrella stand, the back with a desk and some chairs. A tattered blue Hamadan runner occupied most of the floor.

Rooms opened along each side of the hall. Peeking through the open doors, Emma noted a dining room with a huge oak table, and a formal Victorian living room complete with tufted red velvet upholstered sofa and chairs. A kitchen with a huge Wedgewood stove could be seen through an open door at the far end of the hall.

Piers, however, ushered them through two open French doors into the same study where Cheng Bo's arrest had occurred. As on that day, Curt sat behind his grandfather's massive oak desk. Steve sat in a Windsor chair facing it. Four additional chairs had been pulled up on either side. Piers motioned the three new arrivals to sit down before taking the seat nearest to Curt.

After all the excitement a few days before, Emma couldn't help wondering what new surprise the old man had in store. Everything about the room looked the same except, she noted, an 8 x 10 inch inlaid wooden box sitting in front of Curt on top of the desk. That, Emma knew, had not been there the day Cheng Bo was arrested. Cory's knife lay next to it.

First Curt offered everyone tea or coffee from a silver service set up on a table in the corner of the room. There were pastries, too, Emma noted, from the Plaza Café. Everyone declined.

Then Curt leaned back in his chair. It was obvious from the start that he, not Piers, was running this meeting. Staring directly at Maria, he spoke.

"A lot has happened over the past few days since we last met," he began. "And I've done a lot of thinking. I'm an old man. I know I can't change the past..."

"I'll have to stop you there, Curt," Maria Hidalgo-Muller interrupted him.

Emma particularly noted her use of the man's first name, immediately establishing them on equal footing. No more "Mr. Randall" from now on.

"If you think I need anything," Maria continued, "that I and my family have ever wanted anything from you, then you are mistaken. And I warn you," she emphasized this by pointing her index finger directly at the old man, "if you offer me anything of any kind by way of trying to 'change the past,' all you will do is grossly offend me. So watch what you say!"

As she spoke, Curt gazed at the woman impassively. When she'd finished speaking he continued, undeterred by her warning. As though she'd said nothing at all.

"I'm an old man and I know I can't change the past," he repeated. "Or buy my way into heaven. But perhaps I can change the present and make it a little better for the people who..."

"Hold on, Mr. Randall." This time it was Steve who interrupted him. "I can't speak to what this has to do with Professor Hildalgo," he glanced quickly at Maria.

"Hidalgo-Muller," she cut in.

"Sorry, what this has to do with Professor Hidalgo-Muller," Steve corrected himself. "But I, too, want to make something crystal clear before you begin." He glanced at Piers. "As I have already told your attorney, nothing you do or say today is going to make me drop the lawsuit I intend to file. A lawsuit on behalf of employees whose basic rights you have denied." He pointed at the inlaid box. "You can't just throw money at us and make us go away. The issues are bigger than that. They're not about money. They're about shining a spotlight on inhumane practices going on right now at Randall Enterprises. A spotlight that will be visible all the way to Sacramento. To Washington. A spotlight that will change policies towards seasonal workers."

Emma watched her son-in-law while Steve spoke. His eyes shot sideways to look at Curt. He opened his mouth once to cut in, but seemed to think better of that and closed it. Finally, when Steve finished, he began to speak. "Steve, you're really out of...."

Curt Randall didn't let Piers finish. He didn't exactly interrupt him, Emma noted. He just talked over him, as though Piers wasn't there. Like a bull unconsciously flicking a flea off his ear while standing his ground.

"I can make the present a little bit better for those who work for me," he repeated as though no one had said a word. He stared down at the inlaid box sitting in front of him on the desk. The elk horn handled knife lay next to it. He picked it up and stared at it instead.

"First, before I forget. Here." He extended the knife across the desk towards Maria. "This is yours. Take it. Cory wanted you to have it, so you're not taking anything from me when I return this to you."

Maria rose from her chair. She leaned forward, reached towards Curt, took the knife and sat back down.

Next, Curt stared at the box. He stared at it for a long time and his eyes began to swim with tears. Emma wondered if the man would be able to continue. The room was quiet. Finally he stood up and, with some difficulty, walked to the tea service in the corner of the room. He poured himself a cup and slowly returned to his seat, the teacup jiggling in the saucer held tightly in his shaking hand. Finally, he sat down and took a few sips of the tea which seemed to compose him.

"For a long time," he began, "all I could see was the farm as it used to be. As it was when my father worked there. When I worked there. Sure. It was hard work. The living conditions were primitive. But we loved it. There was a romance to it. A kind of glory, if you will. And it was ours. When the summer was over, we came back north to Sonoma. To school and our comfortable lives..."

"I can't listen to this." Steve rose abruptly from his chair.

"Sit down, young man," Curt ordered with a thrust of his forefinger. "You can listen and you will!"

Steve sat back down and blushed.

"I don't say this to justify anything. I say it to explain. Yes. I was a horse with blinders on. Those were Cory's words when we argued about how I was running the farms. 'History,' I told him. 'This is the history of a family you are attacking. The history of our way of life.'

'Your version of history,' I remember him shouting back. 'Sometimes history blinds you, Dad. Don't you see what's happened? You should be ashamed of how your workers live!'" Curt closed his eyes. As though seeing it all again in his memory. "My own son said that to me. I still blame it on that danged university. A bunch of lefties like Chavez."

Curt glanced at Maria again. "Well, you know what happened. We argued about the farm. We argued about you. In my mind they were one and the same." Curt nodded sadly. "He tried to explain. But I wouldn't listen. So he left."

Curt tapped the inlaid box. "I never talked to him again. But his mother did. And he wrote to us. She read the letters and put them away, here. At first I didn't because I was mad. And stubborn. Later, after Cory died, I *couldn't* read them. All these years they've sat in this box in his mother's closet where Amelia left them."

Curt seemed to run out of breath. He stopped talking and opened the box.

The room had grown very quiet again. Emma studied her companions. Steve's right leg was crossed over his left knee, his right foot jiggling, agitated and impatient. Maria sat with her arms folded across her chest, belligerent. Beside her, her daughter Paz glanced worriedly at her mother. Piers had closed his eyes; his jaw clenched like he was biting his tongue. Even Emma grew annoyed at the old man's self-indulgence. *What*, she wondered, *do Cory's old letters to his mother have to do with us?*

"So what's your point?" Steve finally said.

His words seemed to wake Curt out of a reverie.

"My point is," Curt resumed. Again it was as if Steve had not spoken. "My point is this. Something you said, Professor, something you said about love finally gave me the courage to read my son's letters. Thanks to you I realized it wasn't too late..."

The old man broke off speaking and started to weep. Then he collected himself. "I realized it wasn't too late to admit how much I loved him. I came back home from our visit and I read all of the letters. Every word. And it turns out, what he'd written to me and his mother was a blueprint. A fine, intelligent, honorable, loving blueprint of how to improve the farm. The farm he loved. The farm that, one day, he hoped to run. With you," he nodded at Maria.

"Of course, that could never happen," the old man continued. "But I realized that the blueprint, my son's legacy – the legacy I'd mourned for most of my life – was right here." He tapped the stack of letters. Then the old man nodded at Piers and smiled. "I showed them all to my lawyer over there. And he helped me figure out what to do. That is why you are all here."

Emma looked at Maria. The annoyance in her eyes had dissolved into sorrow.

Steve's expression, too, had shifted. From impatience to mistrust. He opened his mouth to speak but Piers waved him silent with a stroke of his forefinger across his neck.

"With Piers' help and the Monroes," Curt explained, "I've just concluded the sale of the plum ranch. To a nonprofit that will preserve old Luther Burbank's plums. Under the terms of the sale, I will continue to live here, in the house, for the remainder of my life. As far as I understand these things," he nodded again to Piers, "the proceeds will fund some kind of credit union offering low cost loans to all the employees working at Randall Enterprises."

Curt Randall stopped talking. Emma looked around the room. The agitation was gone. The old man now had everyone's complete attention.

"That's not really my point, though. The point is that, thanks to Piers, Randall Enterprises, itself, has been put into a trust. I no longer have anything to do with it. Again, Piers can give you the details. But it is my wish that the Coachella farms be run according to the ideas that my son, Cory, explained here in his letters. As I understand it, the farm will be turned into a cooperative owned and managed by my employees in a way that specifically addresses the needs of all the workers it employs."

Curt continued, nodding at Steve, "I want Randall Enterprises – or whatever the trust is named – to serve as a model of how a farm could be run cooperatively to make a fair profit and to treat its owner/employees fairly. Steve, I want you at the Free Legal Services Clinic to act as legal counsel for the trust. You've been a doggoned pain in my neck all these years, and I respect that. Sometimes you remind me a little bit of myself. Of course, the trust will pay your organization very well for your services, if you choose to take on this job."

The old man sat back in his chair and seemed to gasp for breath. For a few moments he couldn't speak. Maria finally broke the silence.

"Curt," she said. "I still don't understand what this has to do with me."

The old man raised his hand and nodded. "I'm getting to that, Maria," he said. He took another few gulps of breath. "In fact, it has nothing to do with you. But I'd like your daughter, and your son..." Curt added, "I know he refused to come here today. But I'd like both of them to serve as advisors to the trust. I will have nothing to do with it, be assured. Paz as a social worker and Xavier as a doctor can help Steve and Piers make sure that the new Randall Enterprises, or whatever it's named, does everything it can to promote its workers' health and safety, and to provide them with educational opportunities."

For a moment the announcement seemed to have taken everyone's breath away. No one spoke. Then Curt stood up. "Unless anyone wishes to comment further, this meeting is adjourned. Paz and Steve, please get back to Piers regarding your decisions."

The old man had already turned his back on the group and had started to walk towards the door. Then he turned and added, "Now if you'll excuse me, I need to take a nap."

29

———

FRIDAY – PLUM DONE

fter Curt's announcement, the first thing Emma did was call Jack. Much to Emma's surprise he suggested they meet so he could hear first hand everything that had happened since their disastrous dinner the week before. Over lunch at the Trough, Jack devoured every detail about Cheng Bo's capture. He even sounded excited about the trust Curt established. And answered all her questions about co-ops.

"The idea of a cooperative is that everyone participates in the ownership, management and profits," he explained. "Look, it's not my business model," he added, "but it can work. Particularly in agriculture. The Netherlands has successful agricultural cooperatives. Spain has one of the largest worker cooperatives in the world. If a cooperative is well managed and successful, it can help a lot of people."

Is Jack really that interested in cooperatives? Emma asked herself the next morning, pulling a blue and white flowered print tunic over her head and applying a little makeup to her pale blue eyes.

Later, however, sitting in the car on her way to lunch, Emma tried to banish all thoughts of Jack from her mind. To focus on her reunion with Dan instead. A reunion she'd rehearsed a thousand times in her head. For twenty years. Ever since she let him break her heart.

Of course I understand, Dan, she remembered saying the night he announced that Kim was coming back. *We always agreed our children come first. I won't let you break up your family over me.*

She realized she might as well have said, *It's OK, Dan. I'll be the one to get hurt.*

And Dan let her get hurt. Dumped her like a pizza crust once all the good topping was gone. He never even contacted her. Except for a few calls to complain about Denver and the new life he and his wife were forging there. Emma's sacrifice had seemed so noble then. *But what kind of a heroine talks like that?* she wondered now. *How many Oscars for best supporting actress do I need?*

BEFORE SHE KNEW it she'd parked her car in the Sutter/Stockton garage and was headed down Bush Street to Sam's. Just like old times.

Except it wasn't old times. Something was different. In the old days she knew she'd have flown down Bush Street, giddy with anticipation. Today her feet felt like they were made of lead. She found herself wishing that, overnight, Sam's had burned to the ground. Or been closed for remodeling.

What am I afraid of? she asked herself. *That things have changed? That things haven't changed?* Neither answer was right.

She stopped on the sidewalk, took a deep breath, and slowly counted to ten. *Be quiet,* she told her racing brain. *Be quiet, for once, and listen to your heart.*

Then she swung open Sam's old saloon style door, strode past the polished oak bar and into the dining room. The maître d' who greeted her was new.

"You're the first to arrive," he smiled perfunctorily. "You can wait here at the bar, or I can show you to your booth."

"I'll wait in the booth," Emma replied.

She'd just hung her coat on a large brass hook attached to the wall of the cozy cubicle and settled herself in a Thonet chair when someone pulled aside the green velvet curtain separating the tiny booth from the outside world.

Emma involuntarily braced herself. She'd seen Dan's photograph on Facebook. She knew he looked much the same. So why was she steeling herself? Bracing herself the way she would against an unpleasant smell.

Then the next thing she knew, he stood there in front of her. After twenty years. Dan Worthington. Like a famous actor taking center stage.

"I can't believe I did this," he announced, "but I said I'd be here if you gave the word. And here I am."

Emma stood up and reached out her arms to him, trying to stop her pounding heart. Till suddenly she realized it wasn't pounding after all.

Dan leaned forward to gather her into his arms. Emma's arms fell limp to her sides.

"I can't believe it either," she answered. She almost added, "What on earth *are* you doing here?"

Dan hugged her, then placing a hand on each of her shoulders, he inspected her, his keen blue eyes taking in every detail. Her hair, her eyes, her makeup, her clothes, even her shoes. *Just like an architect*, she thought.

"You haven't changed, Emma," he said.

Emma glanced at the man. His perfectly cut grey hair, his riveting blue eyes, his trim six foot figure, the sharp creases in his khakis, the starched collar of his dark blue dress shirt sticking out of his Denver green fleece. "Neither have you," she said and she meant it.

They pecked each other on each cheek and sat down at the table.

"Listen," he began. "I was hoping we could meet in Blissburg. See, what with the divorce and all. Well, I'd been thinking of retiring anyway. And somehow, Blissburg seems like the perfect place. You're there. There's lots of new construction in Santa Rosa if I ever get the hankering to return to the field."

Something in the look on Emma's face made him stop. "Of course, I'm glad to see you here. Anywhere Emma. Anywhere we can catch up. I can fly up on weekends until I'm ready to make a move. You can come to Denver. You'd love it there. Hiking. Golf."

"You golf?" Emma cut in. That was new.

"Yeah. Kim and I took it up. As part of the reconciliation." He laughed. "Obviously that didn't work. But I, at least, ended up loving it. I'm sure you will too. But maybe you play already. I don't remember."

Emma shook her head. "No. I've never played golf." She wanted to add, "And I never will."

"Anyway, you'll love Denver. You might even decide to move there, now that you're not tied to an office anymore. I see on Facebook that you're some kind of food writer. That sounds portable."

"So you checked out my cookbook?" Emma asked.

Dan shook his head. "Yeah. I mean, no. I haven't. What was it called again?"

Emma shrugged. "It doesn't matter." Her stomach had started to grumble. "Shall we order?"

Dan grabbed her hand and squeezed it. "What was it we always ordered? The cracked Dungeness crab, right?"

"The sand dabs," Emma corrected him. "Crab's not really in season."

"Sand dabs it is," Dan answered as the waiter poked his head into the room. He ordered the fish and a glass of house white for each of them.

Over lunch, they caught up on twenty years of each others' lives. Dan told Emma all about his two kids and his grandchildren. She quickly described Julie. Then Dan provided an overview of his career - the office buildings he'd designed all over the Midwest and recently all over China.

They'd each ordered sorbet when Dan leaned back in his chair and sighed. "See, Emma. It all turned out for the best. Right? Our children turned out great. We're both where we want to be."

Both where we want to be? Emma wondered. *How would he know?* In an hour and a half, the man hadn't asked her a thing about herself.

"I don't mean to rush you," he continued, "But I think we've always agreed that we were meant to be together. Better late than never, right?"

He'd grabbed her hand again and pressed it to his lips.

"Look," he whispered. Then he laughed. "I know these walls are thin. You're retired, right? The afternoon, at least *my* afternoon, is wide open. We can go to the new museum and then stop off back at my friend's place. Where I'm staying on Telegraph Hill. He's away for the weekend. It's a great little spot."

Emma did a double take. Like she hadn't properly heard. "What?"

Dan's shoulders relaxed and he dropped his head to his breast, his blue eyes staring up at her from under the long black lashes that had once captivated her so. "You know," he smiled. "Like the old times. I've never lost those feelings for you, Emma."

But it wasn't like old times. And suddenly Emma knew what was different. She had *no* feelings for this man. None. None at all. It wasn't that he was a stranger. In fact, to the contrary, she knew him very well. It was more like he was a once treasured, beautifully bound storybook. But the story inside the book didn't interest her anymore.

"Thank you," she nodded. Then she paused.

"But..." he smiled.

"But my life has changed in twenty years," she replied slowly.

Dan threw up his hands. "Oh my gosh! Of course. I was so wrapped up in telling you about myself, I forgot to ask. The murder. You solved that big murder with the Chinese developers. It was all over Facebook. It was even on the news. Emma, that's terrific." He looked at her sheepishly. "I guess you're kind of a celebrity now."

She shook her head. "It's not that. Dan, it's been twenty years. *I* have changed."

"You mean...there's someone else?" He raised his shoulders in an irritated shrug. "Why didn't you just say so? Why did I even bother coming?"

"In fact," Emma tried to explain, "there isn't anyone else, exactly," she added. "I mean no one in particular, yet. This is about me. I didn't know that till I saw you again. The truth is, *you haven't changed.* But I have. And I can't just go back to the way things were. To old times, as you put it." She stared at him perplexed. "I'm not sure I even understand it, Dan. I know it sounds sappy, but when I came here, I told myself to be quiet so I could listen to my heart. Well, I did that. And my heart just isn't in this. Not now. Maybe not ever. I'm sorry. I'm sorry, too, that you came all this way. For nothing."

Now it was Dan's turn to look perplexed. In fact, from the look he gave her, Emma thought she might as well have been an alien from outer space. "Well," he snorted. "Can't say I saw that coming. I guess I just sort of took it for granted that you and I were meant to be. That we would always be there – for each other."

"Not exactly," Emma corrected him. "I think you always just sort of took it for granted that I would always be there for *you.* I wish it were that simple. But it's not. I'd have loved to visit the museum with you – and by the way, I hear the Goya show's terrific – but under the circumstances, I think I should go now. For what it's worth," she added, "it took a long time for me to get over you, Dan. Now that I have, I guess there's no turning back."

Emma stood up. Grabbed her purse and coat off the hook on the wall, and made for the exit. But before she pulled back the green velvet curtain, she thought of something.

She turned and winced apologetically at her surprised companion. "You don't mind paying for this, do you Dan? Like old times? I gotta run."

Then she swept the green velvet curtain aside, ducked out of the room, and let the curtain drop.

30

SATURDAY – ITCHY FEET

Lying in bed Saturday morning, Emma watched the sun flood her small cozy bedroom. Its rays finding their way through the sturdy branches of the magnolia tree now exploding in pink spring blooms. Reaching, it seemed to her, into the farthest corners of her bedroom, or was it her heart?

She searched there for the too familiar signs of regret. The second thoughts that, in the past had haunted her life. *Did I do the right thing? How had Dan felt on the flight back to Denver? Was he hurt? Was she to blame?*

She had always weighed each decision she made from everyone else's perspective. Until finally her own feelings, apart from theirs, ceased to exist.

How can I be happy when I've caused someone else pain?

That morning, however, after leisurely stretching she sat up in bed and wondered if, perhaps, there was such a thing as too much empathy. *After twenty years Dan Worthington's happiness is not my responsibility,* she assured herself. *Dan's feelings are different. Different from mine. Who knows what he felt on the plane ride home?*

And the truth was, that morning she didn't care. More importantly, she had a dinner to cook for people she loved – or at least, she corrected herself, people she liked a lot.

Downstairs in her cozy fleece muumuu she treated herself to a latte and biscotti in her backyard: a third of an acre of deck, fruit trees, a play area for Harry, and a small vegetable garden. All of it backing onto a wildlife preserve. Surprisingly it was everything she'd ever wanted in a home. Quite an admission from a city girl!

After that, she dressed for the day in blue jeans, a French striped T-shirt and espadrilles bought on her cookbook research trip to Italy before she published *Dining with the Stars*. The trip already seemed like a lifetime ago. So long, in fact, that she swore her feet started to itch as she slipped on her shoes.

Which reminded her, once again, of Mary. Her best friend. The woman who accompanied her on that trip and encouraged her from the moment Emma first mentioned her idea for the cookbook, right up until Mary's death almost two years before. *Who knows how long before I find such a good travel companion?* she asked herself. *Till Harry's a teenager?* She hoped she didn't have to wait that long.

By then it was well past 9:00 a.m. Time for the Farmers' Market held every Saturday morning in Blissburg from May through November. *But I have to get there early before the best produce is gone,* Emma scolded herself.

The market was less than a ten-minute walk from Emma's front door. It filled half of the civic parking lot across the street from The Trough. *And don't bother going,* she reminded herself, *unless you're ready to meet just about everyone you know in Blissburg.*

She glanced critically at herself in her bedroom mirror, applied a little lipstick, and put on her pearl stud earrings. Then she went downstairs, grabbed her lightweight purple parka off the hook by the front door along with an African shopping basket, and dashed off.

Two blocks up Blissburg Avenue, Jeb from the insurance agency poked his head out the door.

"Great going, Emma, the way you and your son-in-law cracked that murder case! You're two for two. Shouldn't Chief Tompkins be thinking of putting you on the payroll?"

Emma swatted the compliment away with her hand. "I'm just glad the Chief was there to handle the arrest," she replied.

A block later, she bumped into Annemarie from the bookstore. "You did it again, Emma!" she exclaimed. "You must have a nose for murderers as well as a nose for food. Before too long, someone's going to write a book about you."

Emma blushed. "A streak of good luck, that's all," she said.

By that time she was at the market. She looked at her watch. She didn't have time for long chats. She still had to stop at Little Pete's Gourmet Grocery for the rest of the dinner. But kudos kept coming. In fact, every few steps brought another well-wisher, another neighbor hoping for the inside scoop on the murder.

By the time Emma got to Lois's Berry Farm stand, most of the ripe early raspberries were gone.

"Any sweet ones?" she asked.

What little was left of Lois's inventory had green caps and looked sickly and pale. "I'm serving them tonight with Bavarian cream," she added, glad that she'd found the energy to make the cream the night before. When she'd checked the refrigerator that morning, it had set, thick and luscious in its mold.

"For the detective?" Lois winked, "I always save a few pints in my truck. For special customers," she added pointing her index finger at Emma. Minutes later, she handed over six baskets of plump, deep red berries bursting with juice.

A few stands away, Allison from Clark's Creamery pulled a runny ripe disc of aged goat cheese out of a cooler stashed under her display case. It was dusted with tree ash and wrapped in leaves.

"You want to serve this one tonight," she whispered, surreptitiously transferring it into Emma's basket like a stash of illegal drugs. "I set a few aside for my best customers."

"Your *Petite Douce*?" Emma exclaimed. "It won the gold at the State Fair."

"But of course," Allison replied. "I was almost sold out, but I saved one for you. As a kind of 'thank you' for solving that murder."

Emma added a soft cow's milk blend and some butter to her purchase. Much to her surprise, Allison wouldn't let her pay.

When she picked up the warm sour dough baguettes at Claud's booth, the beans and lettuce from Tasso, and the Creminis from The Mushroom Man it was the same.

Finally, she stopped for flowers. She'd decided on sunflowers. Dozens of them. The first yellow blooms of the season that had just begun to appear. She grabbed six bunches to fill Jack's barely lived in rooms.

After that it was Little Pete's to pick up the veal, Marcona almonds, sweet San Daniele prosciutto, and a Mexican cantaloupe – the first of the season. Then back home to pack. The fresh pasta dough she'd made the night before was resting. All she needed was her trusty pasta machine and the food. Jack had everything else.

A couple of hours later, when she got to his house, Jack was on his way out the door.

"Off to the club," he waved. "By the way, I tried to reach you yesterday – to see if there was anything I could do to help. Then I ran into Julie who told me you'd rushed down to the City for the day. Everything OK?"

Traitor! Emma grimaced. "Everything's great. Just a few loose ends." She glanced at the duffle bag Jack held in his hand.

"Tennis date," he said following her eyes. "Don't worry. I'll be back in time to serve everyone drinks. Whaddaya say we go with Margaritas tonight? I figure with a couple of them under my belt, I'll be ready for anything you throw at me!"

With that vote confidence Emma entered the kitchen clutching Tupperware containers in her hands. *Let Celina be here to help me,* she prayed. And Celina was. A few minutes later they had everything put away. Jack's precious Bavarian cream stored safely in the over-sized Sub Zero. The raspberries next to it ready to wash just before she served dessert.

Emma was patting the veal roast dry before browning it in a pan. Celina arranged the sunflowers in the colorful faience pitchers Emma had brought for the centerpieces. Suddenly, she stopped, gathered up two of the pitchers and motioned Emma to follow her to the dining room.

There to her relief, Emma discovered the large glass table was already set. With Provencal placemats in pinks and gold along with freshly ironed napkins. Jack's stark white china set off the sunburst of flowers perfectly. The table looked spectacular.

An hour later, the house was filled with the mouth-watering aroma of milk fed veal roasting slowly in garlic, rosemary and dry white wine. The aromatic theme song of her childhood, Emma recalled. The smell that signaled loved ones were near and the world - at least her world – was happy and safe.

Emma poured herself a glass of the Sauvignon Blanc she'd used to cook the veal, pulled up a stool and assembled her trusty pasta machine clamping it to a large wooden cutting board set on the marble counter.

Then she unfolded the French linen dishtowel she'd used to transport the pasta dough she'd made the night before. The texture of the eight inch pale yellow ball was almost shiny with extra egg yolks and tireless kneading. She cut a wedge and kneaded it again, slowly narrowing the space between the pasta machine's two steel rollers so the sheets grew longer and thinner at each turn. Till they felt like lengths of fine yellow silk.

Finally her favorite part. She attached the cutter. As she turned the long handle, sheet after sheet was transformed into narrow, flat, rich yellow noodles that she lightly dusted with flour and spread on the cutting board, ready to cook.

Emma reached, again, for the bottle of Sauvignon Blanc. Then she stopped herself when she looked at the clock. Dinner was only an hour away. The roast veal barely simmered in its roasting pan on top of the stove – its juices thickening with flavor. Emma scraped every speck of *Trapanese* sauce out of its container into a saucepan ready to heat.

By the time Celina had helped Emma slice the deep orange cantaloupe into bite sized wedges, drape them with the prosciutto and arrange them on a platter, there was no time left to go home to change. The guests would arrive in half an hour.

Emma had just lined up thin slices of baguette around the ripe runny cheeses when Jack returned relaxed and happy. Emma guessed he'd stopped at the Chatham Club bar for a drink before coming home.

"Did you win?" she asked as he ducked off to the shower.

"I always win," he smirked.

The doorbell rang promptly at 6:00. The Monroes were first to arrive. Emma heard Jack greet them while she checked the roast. Then she began, slowly, to reheat the sauce. It wasn't a dinner for chatting with guests. *Just as well,* Emma thought to herself.

The next voice she heard was Cara in the hall. *No doorbell,* Emma mused. She'd let herself and her husband in with her key. Then another chime and Piers' loud voice hailed Mike.

Everyone's here.

But it wasn't until the roast was resting, the pasta was cooked – three minutes, not a second more - and steaming plates of *Trapanese* served at each guest's place, that Emma dared make her appearance in the living room.

"Time to eat," she announced motioning everyone to the dining room table.

Emma only got up once from her seat before dessert. To make sure the veal was thin-sliced and the beans quick cooked. Celina took care of everything else. And well it was that Emma stayed seated. Aside from much oohing and aahing over the table and a few stray comments about the "unusual" almond pesto, all anyone at the table wanted to hear was how Emma caught the crook.

"You mean, you were in the *middle* of all that last Saturday night? The same night you were cooking dinner?" Jane Monroe gasped. "How did you do it?"

"I didn't, if you recall," Emma answered, glancing at Jack. "I had help."

"Your assistant, right," Bob added. "Wait," he did a double take to Julie. "That was also your father, right? I never did figure out what was going on. But the food was spectacular. How'd we get so lucky to be invited again?" He glanced at Emma and blushed. "Not that I'm complaining, mind you."

"Actually," Emma noted. "This is kind of a 'thank you'. You and Jane were invaluable helping us nab the killer."

"How so?" Bob asked. "You mean that stuff about the Sunnyvale deal?"

Piers nodded. "Totally tipped us off. Once we suspected that HoCo had sabotaged the plum ranch deal to lower the price, the other pieces fell into place. Emma knew that someone was getting paid off. The question was by whom. And why. You helped us answer that."

Piers cast an amused glance at his mother-in-law. "Then after we'd followed the money, Emma followed the heart. She uncovered the ghosts of Cory and Maria Hidalgo that have haunted Curt Randall ever since his son died."

Emma nodded, "In the end the poison wasn't the arsenic HoCo slipped into Curt's water tank. The real poison was in Curt's heart: hate and bigotry. They'd been poisoning everything around him for years."

"It wasn't until Curt saw his son's cutting knife on Maria Hidalgo's desk that he finally realized who stole the murder weapon,"

Piers explained. "But we couldn't have figured it all out without Emma."

"You mean HoCo stole the knife?" Jane Monroe asked.

Piers shrugged. "Cheng Bo. He'd admired it the day he delivered the due diligence report. The one that allegedly uncovered pollution in Curt Randall's water supply. Curt finally remembered that was the last time he saw his knife."

"The rest was easy," Emma concluded.

"So who was Maria Hidalgo?" Cara asked.

Celina had cleared away the pasta plates and begun serving the veal.

Piers and Emma exchanged knowing looks.

"It's your story," Piers nodded at Emma.

She glanced at Jack. Then she began the age-old story of forbidden love and the deadly fruit it bore.

When Emma finished, everyone at the table sat quietly for a few minutes. Finally Jane Monroe spoke up.

"Wait a minute," she said. "When did you find all this out?"

"I first heard the story of Cory and Maria last Friday. When I was in Coachella with my boss, trying to figure out who murdered Santiago Gomez. But I hadn't located Maria yet. That took a little time…"

"Friday! You were in Coachella! How did you prepare that fabulous meal?" Bob exclaimed.

"I told you. With help," Emma cut in.

"Help, shmelp!" Jane answered. "You caught the murderer Tuesday. How did you do it all?"

Emma glanced sheepishly at Jack. "I didn't, exactly. The truth is, I let a lot of people down. That dinner was a disaster if you recall."

"The dinner was delicious, not disastrous. Frankly, I'm impressed." Cara spoke like someone who was rarely impressed. "You're a super cook, Emma, and a super sleuth. You deserve a toast." She and everyone at the table raised a glass.

"What she deserves is a vacation," Julie added. "You must be exhausted, Mom. I don't know how you pulled this off tonight."

"I wanted to," Emma replied, glancing again at Jack.

"Speaking of vacations..." It was Jack's son-in-law, Mike, who finally changed the subject. "What did you decide Jack? About that month-long Stanford Sicily tour this fall? Sure wish we could go, don't you Cara? Sounds like a once in lifetime trip."

Cara looked at her husband and scoffed. "A month? In October? Are you kidding? Who besides retired millionaires – and Dad – have that much time off?"

"I've been dying to go to Sicily," Piers cut in. "What's the deal?"

Cara snorted. "Hardly a deal. It's typical Stanford. Way over the top. A faculty led tour limited to, what, twelve or fifteen people and six renowned professors sailing on a luxury yacht visiting Greek, Arab and Norman Sicily. From Syracusa to Palermo. All this with evening cooking classes from famous regional chefs flown in from all over Italy. Sounds great, but who has time? Except for my Dad."

She shook her finger at her father. "Didn't you have to reserve by last Tuesday?"

Jack clearly didn't want to reply. Emma watched his face assume that trapped look. Not the caged tiger. More like the cornered hound who'd just chewed up the leather chair. But everyone was staring him. Gasping, "Wow, what a trip!!!"

Jack kept silent for almost a minute. Then, just when Emma thought he wasn't going to reply, he answered softly, "Yeah. I'm all signed up."

"With the Stromboli extension and the East Coast stop over?" Cara asked. "I know you were worried about that."

Jack nodded.

"So you'll be gone, what? Six – eight weeks?" Mike added. "The kids are going to miss you."

Jack nodded again. "I'll miss them too. But it seemed like," he shrugged, "something I shouldn't pass up."

"Well, I think that sounds great," Julie exclaimed glancing around the table at Piers, Mike and Cara. She didn't, Emma noted, try to catch her mother's eye."

"Wow," was all Emma could muster. "Sounds exciting." She rose from the table then added. "Time for dessert."

Emma walked into the kitchen, her heart slowly sinking lower in her chest. *He's going away for almost two months on the trip of a lifetime and he never said a word.*

Then another thought occurred to her. And her heart slipped further, all the way into her stomach. *Maybe he's not going alone. Maybe he's going with somebody else.*

Emma removed the cold Bavarian cream mold from the refrigerator, her ear still trained on the dining room where the conversation lingered on Jack's trip.

Mechanically, she dipped the mold into a bowl of hot water to loosen the cream. Then she quickly flipped it upside down over a serving dish. She'd done it a hundred times before.

"Norman Sicily," she heard Cara say. "You know, the Rogers, Frederick II - Stupor Mundi. I hear the chapel at Monreale is spectacular. Mike, we've got to go there," she added.

"The food'll be great," Mike replied.

Emma gave the mold a gentle shake. For reasons she dared not explain, her heart was breaking. *Why didn't he say anything?* a voice in her head asked. *Why should he?* the same voice answered.

That's when Emma noticed something. It was happening in slow motion. Right before her eyes. The Bavarian cream, her famous and beloved *Bavarese*, was slipping out of the mold all right. But it wasn't slipping onto the platter she'd carefully poised under it. Instead, the round glob of white creamy jelly was slipping past the platter onto the floor. In a split second it would land and shatter.

Emma must have let out a scream. She didn't know exactly what she screamed, but she guessed it was bad. She dropped the mold. It clattered noisily onto the floor. But she managed to catch half the dessert on the platter. She caught the other half in her bare hand.

Outside the kitchen, the dining room grew eerily silent.

Emma looked up to see Celina staring at her, wide eyed in horror.

"Everything OK in there?" Jack called.

"Everything's fine. Just dropped something," Emma answered.

"I hope you didn't burn yourself." That was Piers.

"Need help, Mom?"

Someone in the dining room pulled back their chair. Seconds later, Jack poked his head around the kitchen door and saw what had happened.

"Leave!" Emma shouted at him, not very politely. "Everyone stay put! Everything's fine! Now get out!"

Jack did as he was told.

By then Emma was almost in tears. Bavarian cream seeped through her fingers onto the floor. What had landed in the platter looked more like English trifle than Italian Bavarian cream.

Emma slopped what was left of the cream back onto the platter and washed her hands in the sink. *That's the trouble with tricky desserts,* she reminded herself. *They're tricky. Why didn't Jack request something simple like,* she tried to think, *like brownies!*

The Bavarian cream now looked like large curd cottage cheese. Tears streamed down Emma's cheeks. But she knew she wasn't crying about the dessert. She was crying about herself. She'd given up Dan and now she had nothing. Or more precisely, no one.

"Is OK, *Senora.*" Celina suddenly stood at her elbow comforting her. "I fix. Why doan ju go sit down?"

Emma dried her eyes. Splashed cold water on her face. Took a deep breath and left the kitchen.

"Coffee anyone?" she tried to sound cheerful taking her seat at the end of the table.

The Monroes smiled politely and shook their heads. Julie glanced around the table and shrugged. Mike raised his hand and started to say "espress...", but Cara cut him off with a glare.

Jack stared at his placemat.

"We're stuffed, Mom," Julie finally replied. "I'm not even sure I have room for dessert."

Everyone else at the table nodded their agreement. Except for Jack.

"I always have room," he smiled. Then, barely able to stifle a laugh, he added. "Wait till you see what Emma's prepared for dessert."

As if on cue, Celina appeared in the doorway. She held a serving dish with what looked like a tower of cottage cheese streaked with red jam. She set that in front of Emma. Then she brought out small glass bowls on cut glass dishes garnished with silver spoons.

Emma smiled gratefully at Celina.

"That looks interesting," Cara exclaimed. "What is it?"

Emma shook her head and shrugged. "Just a little something I invented." She bit her lip and glanced apologetically at Celina. "A variation on an old war horse. I call it a Bloody Bavarian."

"Like a Bloody Mary?" Jane Monroe asked.

"Same idea," Emma replied. "Different victim."

Nobody laughed.

At least the Bloody Bavarian tasted delicious. And thanks to Celina, Mike got his espresso after all.

"WE HAVE a long drive back to Calistoga," Mike explained after the last of the Bloody Bavarian had been devoured by the guests.

"And the kids will be up early," Julie added.

A few minutes later, everyone was gone. Celina shooed Jack into the living room. Emma followed her into the kitchen to clean up.

But Celina shook her head when Emma grabbed a dishtowel. "I no need help. Why no you go keep Mr. Jack company in the living room. He so lonely, *Senora*. He miss his wife. He need someone to talk to."

Emma tried to protest, but Celina would have none of it. So Emma walked to the hall and poked her head into the living room.

"Did everything go OK," she asked.

Jack sat on the couch reading the paper.

"Just OK?" he replied. "Emma, your dinner was fantastic. And the kids had a ball. I really think they like each other."

"I think so too," Emma nodded.

There was an awkward pause before Emma continued. "If you don't need anything else, I think I'll go home."

"Yeah. You must be beat," Jack agreed. Then he added, "Look, before you go, I want to apologize for something. Last Saturday..."

"Please," Emma cut in. "What is there to apologize for? Last Saturday was all my fault. I promised I'd..."

Jack didn't let her finish. "No, last Saturday was *my* fault. You were trying to solve a murder. To do your job. Make a difference. Help people. All I could think of was myself and my stupid dinner party."

"You had every right," Emma protested.

"If there's any excuse," Jack continued, "it's that this dinner was a way for me to move on. Get back a life without Fran. But it wasn't more important than what you were trying to do. Anyway, sorry I was a jerk. I'm really proud to know you, Emma. You solved that murder. You helped a lot of people. I'm impressed."

Tears sprang into Emma's eyes. She turned away. *Impressed!* she thought. *That's not what I want. I don't want to impress Jack Russo. I want him to...*She couldn't finish the sentence. Even to herself. "I better go," she said.

"No wait," he walked over to where she stood and placed his

hand on her arm. "There's something else. I want to explain. About the trip. I didn't mean it to come out this way. I didn't want you to hear about it from Cara."

Emma sniffled and blinked. Then she shrugged. "What do you mean?" She knew she sounded defensive. "The trip'll be fun. You're under no obligation to tell me. Do what you want. It's your trip."

Jack shook his head. "No. Of course, I'm under no *obligation*. That's not what I mean. The point is, I didn't want you to hear about it like that."

"Jack, frankly it doesn't matter how I hear..."

"Listen to me," he interrupted her again. "It does. I wanted to make this nice. Happy," he stammered. "I mean, I was hoping to make this a surprise."

Emma shook her head. "Make what a surprise?"

Jack took a deep breath. "Let's start over. Emma, I reserved two places on the Sicily tour. The point is I'm hoping you'll be my guest. I was going to ask you last Saturday. But I never got the chance. Then, with all the excitement about the murder...Anyway, I'm asking you now. Will you come?"

"To Sicily?" Emma exclaimed. "With you!"

Jack nodded. "You'd do me a great honor if you would."

The invitation left Emma speechless.

"No strings attached," Jack rushed to explain. "Just you and me goin' on a trip together. But I gotta warn you, traveling with me may not be fun. I'm an ornery guy. All that pretentious academia stuff will bring out the worst in me. And the trip's in October. I'll be on my computer a lot trying to catch the playoffs and the World Series, and all the NFL games. And I hate shopping and tourist traps. I like museums. That's in my favor. But I'm only good for half an hour, max. Then, honestly, I get sick."

He shrugged fatalistically. "OK, the food part sounds good, but I'm fussy and opinionated. And you already know that my Italian stinks. So if, despite all that, you still want to take the plunge and accompany me on..."

Emma interrupted him before he changed both their minds. "Accompany you, Jack! Yes. I'd LOVE to go!!!"

THE END

ABOUT THE AUTHOR

A.J. Carton grew up in San Francisco eating her grandmother's Bolognese cuisine. She resides with her husband and children in Sonoma County, California where she enjoys writing about food and drinking the local wine. You may contact the author at: ajcarton-books@gmail.com. Other books by AJ Carton include:

Murder by the Mouthful
TakeOut
A Saucy Murder
Veni Vidi Vin

FICTION DISCLAIMER

This book is a work of fiction. Any resemblance to persons, living or dead, is purely accidental. All of the events, organizations and characters used in this story are fictional and/or solely the product of the author's imagination and invention.